Praise for Sharon Ward

Sharon Ward's IN DEEP is a stellar, pulse-pounding debut novel featuring a female underwater photographer. A heady mix of underwater adventure, mystery, and romance.

> — Hallie Ephron, New York Times bestselling author

Pack your SCUBA fins for a wild trip to the Cayman Islands. *In Deep* delivers on twists and turns while introducing a phenomenal new protagonist in underwater photographer Fin Fleming, tough, perceptive and fearless.

> — Edwin Hill, author of *The Secrets We Share*

How much did I love In Deep? Let me count the ways. Fin Fleming, underwater photographer, is a courageous yet vulnerable protagonist I want to sip Margaritas with. The Cayman Islands are exotic and alluring, yet tinged with danger. The underwater scenes and SCUBA diving details are rendered in stunning detail. Wrap that all into a thrilling mystery and you'll be left as breathless as - well, no spoilers here. You must read it to find out!

> — C. Michele Dorsey, Author of the Sabrina Salter Mysteries: No Virgin Island, Permanent Sunset, and Tropical Depression

Breathtaking on two levels, Sharon Ward's debut novel IN DEEP will captivate experienced divers as well as those who've only dreamed of exploring the beauty beneath the sea. The underwater world off the Cayman Islands is stunningly rendered, and the complex mystery involving underwater photographer Fin Fleming, especially the electrifying dive scenes, will have readers holding their breath. Brava!

— Brenda Buchanan Author of the Joe Gale
Mystery Series

In Deep is a smart and original story that sucks you in from page one. Edge-of-your-seat suspense, a hauntingly realistic villain, and a jaw-dropping twist make this pacy read unputdownable until the very last word.

— Stephanie Scott-Snyder, Author of When Women
Offend: Crime and the Female Perpetrator

Sea Stars

Sea Stars

A Fin Fleming Scuba Diving Mystery
Book 6

Sharon Ward

PENSTER PRESS

Covers by Cover2Book.com

ISBN eBook: 978-1-958478-11-0

ISBN Trade Paper: 978-1-958478-14-1

ISBN Hard Cover: 978-1-958478-24-0

Printed in USA

First Edition

For Jack, who continues to be the best husband in the universe, and Molly, who continues to be the best dog in the universe.

Chapter 1
The Beginning of a Bad Day

IT WAS STILL DARK when I anchored the *Tranquility* in the sand at Starfish Point in Grand Cayman's North Sound. I let out a long line, so the stern of my boat was over the deeper water. Which wasn't saying much since at this site the water only hits about ten feet even if you go pretty far out at this site.

I was planning to snorkel instead of scuba dive today, because I wanted to capture some images of the abundant sea stars that spend their lives in the clear tranquil waters of the area. I thought the sea stars would make a nice change of pace for my monthly column in *Ecosphere* magazine, and I hoped to get the shots I needed and get back to RIO—the Madelyn Anderson Russo Institute of Oceanography—before dawn.

I slipped on an old snorkeling vest left over from a previous RIO documentary. My name—Finola Fleming—was on the back in neon green letters. I'm a little bit famous, so I don't normally like to wear gear with my name on it because it draws attention. But since it was still so early in the morning, I figured no one would be around. And nobody calls me Finola anyway. I'm Fin to anyone who knows me.

I grabbed my camera and slipped into the water, pausing on the surface a moment to get a feel for the area. Luckily, a whole slew of red cushion sea stars lay scattered around the sand just a few feet away. These puffy reddish starfish range in size from a few inches in diameter to about twenty inches across. They travel slowly over the sand as they feed, often traveling no more than the length of one arm in a day. The sea stars are intriguing and highly photogenic creatures. Just what I needed.

I dove in the shallows repeatedly, taking closeups of some of the larger and more vibrant individual sea stars. After photographing individual sea stars, I moved on to group shots. I approached each cluster from different angles, looking to create interesting patterns in the resulting photos. When I had enough shots, I headed out over the sea grass to the drop off to see what else I could find.

A trumpetfish lurked below me, almost invisible in the sea grass where he waited for unwary prey to happen by. A tiny green octopus watched me with enigmatic eyes from her hiding spot in a coral crevice. I photographed them both, and then I lucked into seeing a southern stingray glide across the sand in search of breakfast. With that last image, I was sure I had enough interesting shots to fill my column, so I blew out my snorkel and swam on the surface back to my boat.

While I steered the *Tranquility* across the placid waters, I thought about my upcoming day. First, I had a meeting scheduled with the curators of a new exhibition we were hosting at RIO. The exhibition featured recovered sea artifacts, ancient relics, and precious treasures. Some of the items on display were extremely valuable, and the curators and committee members had expressed concern about RIO's notoriously leaky security.

But I had a plan for that.

First off, my friend Chaun would be installing security cameras in the pool house where the exhibition would take place, and which currently has no security at all. The super-duper high-tech cameras he wanted to use were on backorder, but he assured me they'd arrive any day now. Long delivery times were par for the course when you live on an island, so I knew it wasn't his fault. The cameras would arrive in their own good time.

But in addition to the CCTV cameras, I had even more additional security planned. A genuine Hollywood movie crew was coming to film a flick that everyone expected to be a blockbuster. It would be a series of short vignettes, each segment focused on the recovery story surrounding one of the items in the exhibition, with a through-line that tied them all together. The star of the movie was Rafe Cummings, a Ryan Gosling-lookalike action hero and a major heartthrob. He was currently the hottest actor in show business. Since the Hollywood contingent was bringing their own security team, their arrival would solve my security crisis.

I had a meeting later on today with T-8, the movie's producer. I'd thrown my hat in the ring for the job of underwater videographer, and he told me he'd have an answer for me when he arrived.

I was confident in my experience and abilities, but still a little nervous about his decision. T-8 and Rafe Cummings were Hollywood royalty. Although I'd produced and filmed RIO's annual documentaries for years, this would be my first time working with people of their caliber. My hopes were high.

I tied up in my slip at RIO and hopped over the gunwales to the wooden pier. I rushed over to RIO's rear entrance and let myself in. I'd propped the door open with a rock this morning when I left, and I felt guilty about it. Both DS Dane Scott of the RCIP and my father had warned me repeatedly that it was a dangerous practice. Ruefully, I realized that not only was I a big part of our security problem, but I was also setting a bad example for other employees. I resolved to do better.

I was rifling through my credenza drawers looking for my seldom used employee ID badge when a deep voice with a languid California accent broke into my reverie. "Excuse me. Do you know where I can find Finola Fleming?"

I spun around. The man in front of me was tall. His unruly deep brown hair fell across his forehead, and a trendy man bun with a carefully arranged wisp of hair spiked out of it like a miniature inch-long ponytail. The hair on his nape curled softly over the edges of his collar. He wore a white linen jacket over an ancient gray t-shirt commemorating the farewell tour of a well-known rock band, a straw fedora with a dark blue band, and a pair of perfectly aged jeans. What looked to be handmade Italian leather fisherman sandals encased his feet. His appearance was so artfully designed to look casual that I knew it must have taken hours to put it all together. I couldn't see his eyes behind the enormous Saint Laurent sunglasses he wore, but his tentative smile seemed genuine.

I rose and held out a hand. "You must be T-8. I'm Fin Fleming."

He gave me a fist bump instead of a handshake. "A pleasure to finally meet you, Doctor Fleming. Thanks for letting us use your beautiful facility for our filming."

"It's our pleasure. And please, call me Fin. Everyone does."

He smiled again and lifted his sunglasses to the brim of his hat. "Okay then, Fin. I'll do that. And you can call me T-8." He pronounced it like T-eight. "Everyone does." The story is that his real name is such a deep secret that even his own mother doesn't know what it is.

He slung the expensive-looking Italian leather bag he had over his shoulder to the back of a chair and then sat down, stretching his legs out into the open space of my office. "Any chance of a coffee? It's pretty early for a guy from Cali."

Just then, like clockwork, Noah Gibb, who was working the early shift, brought a pot of coffee, two mugs and a small tray of pastry and muffins without my even asking for them. He set everything on the round table in the corner and then said, "Genevra called it in. Need anything else?"

T-8 was already pouring his coffee. "Nope." He didn't even look up.

Appalled at T-8's rudeness, I smiled apologetically at Noah. "I think we're all set. Thank you."

T-8 took a sip of his coffee. "I saw your reel," he said when he'd swallowed it. "And that documentary you did about the stingray. Impressive work." He didn't look at me, just leaned back in his chair, letting his long legs in their expensive jeans block the door.

His words sounded promising, making my heart leap with excitement. He must be planning to offer me the role of underwater videographer. Holding my breath, I waited a moment for him to continue.

4

He let the silence hang.

When the prolonged quiet grew uncomfortable, I finally spoke. "But?"

"Job went to someone else. Sorry." He didn't look at me, and his words didn't sound sorry at all.

I tried to keep the disappointment out of my voice. "It happens. Who got the job? It's a small community. Maybe I know the person."

"You don't know him. Name is Jeffrie West. Hired by the executive producer. This is his first gig."

I nodded slowly. "You're right. I've never heard of him. If this would be his first gig, why him and not me?"

He shrugged and rose to his feet. "Business. Catch ya later." He picked up his bag, took his coffee, and left.

I took a moment to swallow my disappointment. There'd be other opportunities. Then I grabbed the duffle bag with my clothes and toiletries and hurried out back to the ladies' locker room at the pool house to get ready for my day.

Because I wanted to look professional for the meeting with the exhibition's curators, I blew dry my hair and put on a brand new RIO-branded polo shirt and a pair of cargo shorts I'd had tailored to fit perfectly. My father, Newton Fleming, had been teaching me about the importance of looking professional. Even so, I still wore a bathing suit underneath my clothes. I was in and out of the water so many times in a day that it made no sense not to be prepared.

I gathered up my things and took the shortcut through the pool house to get back to my office. The pool house is a vast space. Because of the size of our pool, which Maddy and Ray had custom designed to be ideal for teaching diving, it has to be immense.

RIO's pool is 164 feet long and twenty-five feet wide. For most of its length, it's level at about four feet deep, but twenty-five feet before the end, there's a row of red tiles that let's swimmers know that the depth is dropping off abruptly to twenty-five feet deep.

The level shallow parts are exactly what's needed for practicing basic scuba skills like mask clearing. The deep end is perfect for practicing advanced scuba and breath hold skills, and the overall length is great for swimming laps.

As I walked by the deep end of the pool, I noticed what looked like a bundle of clothing on the bottom of the twenty-five foot deep end. There were several shiny objects nearby on the pool floor.

Peering over the edge, I realized the bundle of clothing was actually a person. I didn't hesitate. I dropped my bag and jumped in. Within seconds, I'd brought the person to the surface and towed him to the ladder. I used a fireman's carry to exit the pool, with the man slung across my shoulders. He was very heavy, and he must have been quite tall because his arms and legs dangled over my back, nearly brushing the floor. I lowered him gently to the tiles and a loud clang startled me. One of the shiny objects I'd seen in the pool had snagged on his clothes, and the ringing sound it made against the hard surface echoed through the cavernous pool house.

I ignored the shiny object and rolled him onto his left side into the recovery position. After I made sure his airway was clear and checked for obvious broken bones, I rolled him onto his back and began chest compressions. I was screaming as loud as I could. "Help. I need help. Somebody help me."

In less than a minute, Christophe Poisson came rushing in from the men's locker room. He instantly recognized the problem and called 911. Then in rapid succession, he called Doc, RIO's in house medical officer, DS Dane Scott of the RCIP, and then my father— Newton Fleming—who was RIO's lawyer as well as Christophe's friend.

As soon as he finished his hurried calls, Christophe took over the resuscitation efforts. Very quickly, Doc rushed in from RIO's infirmary, and the EMT team followed right behind her. Even with all those skilled hands working together to revive the victim, our efforts proved fruitless. It was soon apparent the unknown man was gone.

Chapter 2
An Investigation Begins

ONE OF THE EMTs had pushed aside the shiny object that had come to the surface during the rescue, so it was on the floor, but quite far away from the body. I walked over and crouched down to see what it was. I knew better than to touch it—Dane would have my head if he thought I'd messed with what I was already sure would turn out to be a crime scene.

My eyes widened. The object was about five inches in length and width, and a perfect replica of a cushion sea star, except for the clear but brilliant stones embedded in its surface in the pattern that represented the zodiac sign for Aries. I recognized it because it's the sign for my mother's birthday of April 18. From the volume of the noise it made when it hit the tiles, I assumed it was metal, and from the weight and appearance, I guessed the metal might be solid gold. If it actually was real gold, the clear gemstones embedded in it were probably diamonds, the birthstone for April. And given its size, it would be heavy, probably weighing around thirty pounds.

"Don't touch that," said Roland Kerwin, Dane's second in command. "And please back away from the crime scene."

I stood up and stepped back. "I'm the one that pulled him out of the pool and started compressions. I'm afraid you're going to find my DNA and a whole lot of pool water all over your crime scene."

"It's never easy with you, is it?" he said, but he smiled when he said it. Dane, Roland, and I had worked together on several cases in the past, so we were pretty good friends.

I pointed at the shining golden ornament at my feet. "What do you make of this? I bet there's eleven similar ones in the bottom of the pool. One for each sign of the Zodiac."

He looked puzzled. "How do you know that?"

His boss, Dane Scott joined us. "She knows it because those gold sea stars are supposed to be part of the upcoming exhibition, am I right?"

I nodded. "You're right. Any ID on the guy yet?"

Dane shook his head. "Who owns the sea stars? We'll have to notify them right away that we're taking them as evidence. And I'm sorry. I know that'll put a crimp in your exhibition and filming the movie." Dane was very familiar with RIO's business because he and my mother had been seeing each other for quite a while now.

I shrugged. "I guess I should know who owns them, but I don't. Sorry."

Dane and Roland both rolled their eyes.

"Can you find out?" Dane asked. "And also get a hold of Chaun and ask him to find out what happened to the security system. Quickly, please. In fact, now would be good."

"There's still no security in here yet. The cameras are still on back order. I'll check out who owns these and let you know. Meanwhile, I'll be in my office if you need me." I picked up my bag and left the pool house. I knew better than to ask Dane if his question could wait while I took another shower.

I'd barely sat down when a tinny voice came from the speaker in my desk phone. "Hi, Dr. Fleming. It's Fred in security. Mrs. Anderson is here to see you."

I opened the calendar app on my computer. "Hi, Fred. I know who you are. And please, call me Fin." I frowned. "I don't see anything on my schedule. Does she have an appointment?"

Fred's response came through the phone's speaker. "She said she doesn't need an appointment." I could tell by his voice Fred knew this reply wasn't going to go over well with me.

Fred's job is to stop people from entering the non-public areas of the RIO building, not to manage my calendar, but I asked anyway. "Did she say what she wanted to see me about?"

"No," he replied. "She said you'll want to see her though."

I highly doubted that, but since she could probably hear both sides of the conversation through the intercom speaker, I tried to be tactful. "I'm sure I will, but I'm too busy right now to meet with her today. Please ask her to check with Genevra to set up an appointment for later this week."

There was a loud clatter, the sound of something heavy falling to the floor, and then a prolonged silence from Fred.

A few seconds later, sensing a presence in front of me, I looked up from my computer screen where I'd been checking the ownership of all the objects in the exhibition. An older woman stood in the doorway to my office. She was petite, although it was hard to realize how tiny she was, because she stood ramrod straight. She carried a polished teakwood walking stick with a gold dolphin handle. Her cream-colored linen pantsuit was completely wrinkle-free, and I took a nano-second to admire the fact that she must be one of the few people in the world who could actually wear linen without immediately looking like a Shar Pei.

Rather than knot the collar ties of her white silk blouse in the usual fussy bow, she'd styled them like an ascot and secured them with a gold pin with an amethyst and a pearl on the end. She wore tiny pearl studs in her ears, an understated Cartier watch with a purple face, and an enormous set of diamond rings on her left hand. I raised my eyes to her face and realized she looked familiar.

She spoke first, and although she pitched her voice low, she sounded stern. "Really? You're too busy to meet with your own grandmother?"

That was startling.

It took a moment for me to respond. "I don't have a grandmother."

She gave a small, sad smile. "News to me. I've been in the role of your grandmother since before you were born. Where's Madelyn? She can clear up your confusion."

She must mean my mother. Maddy Russo, who was born Madelyn Anderson. Anderson is a common surname. I hadn't made the connection when Fred had announced my visitor.

Not once in my life had Maddy ever given any indication that either of her parents were still around. She'd occasionally referred to an inheritance, so I thought her parents had passed away before my birth or while I was still too young to retain any memories of them. I stared at the stranger in wonder, as though she was a rare and exotic sea creature. It was then I realized this woman looked just like Maddy, right down to the unusual turquoise eyes and icy blonde hair. No wonder her face seemed familiar.

A grandparent. I had a grandparent. I couldn't hold back a huge smile. "Welcome to RIO. Would you like a tour, Mrs. Anderson?"

She laughed, and I heard echoes of Maddy's distinctive laughter in the sound.

"Please call me Mimi. And maybe we can take the tour later," she said. "First, I could use a cup of coffee and a few minutes with my granddaughter. We have a lot to catch up on, and I have something serious I want to talk to you about."

"Coffee? Sure. Let's go to the café," I said.

She looked at me like I was crazy. "Can't you get someone to deliver it to your office? You are in charge here, aren't you?"

That was a surprising response. "I am the COO, but technically, my mother is in charge. And I don't like to put the staff out when I'm perfectly capable of getting my own coffee."

Genevra walked into my office, clearly using that sixth sense she had that always lets her know when I need something without my having to ask. "I'm headed to the café. Can I bring you some coffee?"

Mimi smiled, obviously pleased by Genevra's offer. "Yes, thank you, my dear."

A few minutes later, Genevra came back carrying a tray with coffee and pastries for two. She winked at me as she set the items down on the table.

"Thank you, Genevra. I appreciate it," I said.

Mimi watched Genevra leave the office and then smiled at me.

"See? That wasn't so hard, was it?" She paused a moment. "You realize you're soaking wet?"

I wasn't sure I was going to like my newfound grandmother. She seemed pushy and entitled. "Yes, I know. It's been a busy morning all ready, and I expect it will stay that way. What was it you wanted to talk to me about?"

She held up a hand in the universal stop gesture. "Not yet. I believe I said coffee first."

Now I knew for sure I wouldn't like her much. It was hard to believe this autocratic, rude person had raised my perfectly lovely mother who was thoughtful, kind, and impeccably well-mannered.

My grandmother sat with her hands folded in her lap, staring at me expectantly. I finally figured out she was waiting for me to pour her coffee.

I gritted my teeth. "Help yourself." A burst of sympathy for Maddy flooded through me. No wonder she'd left home and never looked back.

Mimi sighed and reached for the coffee pot. "Just like your mother," she said softly, barely loud enough for me to hear her.

She poured coffee into her mug and added a dollop of cream and a few grains of sugar. Then she used the tongs to help herself to a blueberry muffin. When she'd finished serving herself, I poured coffee in my mug and put a muffin on my own plate. We each sipped from our mugs at the same time, and we gave identical sighs as the hot liquid jumpstarted our engines. I gave a start when I realized we had some of the same mannerisms.

We ate and drank in silence, although my grandmother watched me carefully. After nibbling three small crumbs of her muffin and taking another sip of coffee, she dabbed her lips with a napkin. Impressively, the dabbing didn't disturb her lipstick in any way.

"If you're finished, I'd like to talk now," she said.

I looked longingly at the half-eaten muffin on my plate and the wisp of steam escaping from my mug, but my curiosity got the better of me. I couldn't help but wonder what had brought this woman here after all these years of neglect. I could finish my breakfast later in peace. "Sure," I said. "What's up?"

"Quite some time ago I heard about the exhibition of sea artifacts RIO is putting on, and I wanted to contribute. I lent them the Silas Anderson Sea Stars. He was your great-great-great-grandfather, and he recovered them more than a hundred years ago. They've been in the family ever since. They are very valuable, and I believed they would be a welcome addition to the show."

"I've haven't heard of them," I said.

She pursed her lips. "There are twelve sea stars. All solid gold. Each is about the size of a man's hand, and they're all encrusted with a different sign of the zodiac created with precious jewels. I thought it was time the world had a chance to admire them."

"I agree. Thank you." I smiled, wondering if she knew yet that someone had stolen the stars and that they were now at the bottom of RIO's pool.

She held up the imperious hand again. "There was one condition. I wanted you to be the lead videographer for the show."

"I am the lead photographer for the exhibition," I said slowly. "But I don't have any role for the movie."

She looked at me like I was daft. "I meant for the movie, sweetie. You'd obviously be the one to do the photography for the exhibition."

"They already have a lead videographer. I'm sure we'll work very closely together, and they tell me he's stellar..."

"Not as stellar as you, my dear. It's time the world knew that as well."

"Sorry. Not gonna happen. I submitted a reel in a bid for the lead videographer role, and they turned me down. I guess they didn't want to trust such an important task to a novice..."

"You're not a novice. You know that as the co-producer of the film, you should have the right to hire yourself as the lead videographer."

I shook my head. "I'm a producer in name only. My title doesn't come with any rights or responsibilities. Just a screen credit and a hefty upfront fee to RIO for the use of our facilities."

"A chance like this doesn't come along every day. You should seize the opportunity," she said through pursed lips.

I nodded. "But I won't. If they didn't think I was good enough to begin with, I don't want to force myself into the role."

She frowned. "Well then, since you won't take any of my suggestions, I guess the Silas Anderson Sea Stars will go back into my vault. After this, they won't be part of either the exhibition or the movie."

"That would be a shame, but it's your choice, Mimi." I stood up to show her out.

She looked me over for a long moment, and her expression clearly said she found my appearance inadequate. I was wearing my daily uniform of cargo shorts and a RIO-branded t-shirt over a bathing suit. My flip-flops showed my toenails were bare of polish and in desperate need of a pedicure. I was still soaking wet from my rescue attempt, and I was pretty sure my hair was standing straight up. I resisted the urge to smooth it down.

Her eyes seemed to linger over the vestiges of the scar on my face.

I'd had the scar for years, and I rarely thought about it anymore. I knew my father's friend the plastic surgeon had done an amazing job after my accident. The scar was barely visible except in direct sunlight when it showed at the corner of my eye, and even then, only if you already knew it was there. But as she examined my face, I felt like I wore a neon advertisement.

A few seconds later, she nodded and smiled. "I'd have known you anywhere. You look just like Newton."

I'd been wrong that she was staring at my scar. She must have been looking for some vestige of my Anderson family genes.

I nodded. "I know."

"You're lucky. He's a very handsome man," she said.

My father is indeed a very good-looking man. He's continuously depicted in business and celebrity magazines as a "silver fox," and he's been on lists of hottest or most eligible bachelors too many times to count. I had only known Newton Fleming for a few years, and I adored him for his kindness, intelligence, humbleness, and bravery. And his goofiness.

But other than awe at his ability to look like he'd just stepped off the pages of *GQ* under any and all circumstances, I never think about how attractive he is. I knew we looked a lot alike, but I wasn't sure how to discuss my father's good looks with my grandmother. I did know I didn't want to.

And I was in a hurry to check on how things were going in the pool house. "I'm sorry I can't spend a lot of time with you today, Mimi. There was an accident here this morning, and I need to be there. Maybe we can have lunch or dinner while you're on the island."

She didn't stand. "I know about the accident," she said. "Such a pity."

"You've already heard? Did you know the patient?" I asked. In medic first aid classes, they trained us to always refer to someone in trouble as 'the patient,' rather than as 'the victim.' The slight difference in semantics helps keep bystanders, relatives and even the patients themselves calm.

My grandmother nodded. "Oh yes, I knew him. Maybe you do too. He was the chief videographer hired by the movie's executive producer. And he was a very bad man."

I bit my lip. "I hadn't met him yet. Why do you say he was a bad man, Mimi?"

She took a pair of Chanel sunglasses out of her purse and slipped them on before answering. "He seemed nice, but he wasn't. A few days ago, I caught him trying to steal the Silas Anderson Sea Stars." Her lips were tight. "Not only are the Anderson Sea Stars valuable, but they also mean a lot to me. I couldn't believe he would attempt such a thing."

I gaped at her. "Tell me why you think he was stealing your Sea Stars," I said. "And how did you know he was the person in the pool?"

Dane Scott must have been eavesdropping from the hall because I hadn't seen or heard him until he spoke. "I'd like to know the answer to that question myself, Mrs. Anderson."

My grandmother looked at him over the top of her expensive designer sunglasses. "And you are?" she said. Her voice was so cold it could have kept the ice machine at Ray's Place going for a week.

He pulled out his badge. "Dane Scott, RCIP." He didn't mention his rank, but he didn't have to. He was never overbearing or obnoxious about it, but he had a subtle air of authority that always let people know he was the one in charge, even if he never said a word.

She bit her lip. "I see." Mimi looked down her nose at him. "My granddaughter and I were having a private discussion."

He smiled back at her, his eyes not involved. "Now I'm part of your private discussion." He looked at me. "Or if you like, I can ask Fin to leave us alone and make our discussion even more private."

She pursed her lips again, looking like she'd sucked on a lemon. Very daintily, of course. "I'm just getting to know my granddaughter. I would hate for you to chase her off. Why don't you come back later." She did not smile.

I could see this duel was not going to end well, so I jumped in. "Mimi, why don't I call Newton and ask him to come over and sit with you while you talk to Dane? I know Dane, and I trust him completely, but I realize you don't know him yet. I bet you'd feel more comfortable if you had Newton with you."

Dane nodded. "Good idea. I have no reason to suspect your grandmother of any wrongdoing, but I want her to be completely comfortable and candid. So go ahead. I can wait. I won't ask any more questions until Newton arrives."

I looked at my grandmother, who was still tight lipped, but eventually she nodded too.

"Fine."

I picked up my phone. Newton answered on the first ring. "Where are you?"

"My office. Dane wants to talk to my grandmother, but she won't do it unless you're here. Can you come?"

"She's here? That's a surprise. Unfortunately, she may not talk to Dane even if I'm with her. She can be stubborn, but I'll be right there to see what I can do." The phone clicked, ending the call.

I went around the door to poke my head into Genevra's office. She laughed when she saw me. "I'm on it."

"Add some cookies this time, please. And lemonade for Newton." She was already halfway down the hall, but she nodded. Everybody knows food helps tense conversations flow better, and Dane was a sucker for RIO's chocolate chip cookies.

For that matter, so was I. Nobody who's ever had one ever says no to one of RIO's legendary cookies.

Noah Gibb was on duty, and he popped into my office within two minutes carrying a tray. "Hi, Fin. DS Scott. Ma'am," he said with a cheerful smile for my grandmother. He placed the icy pitcher of lemonade, the fresh pot of coffee, and the cookies on the table and passed out plates and napkins.

"Fin, it's nice to see you taking a break for a change." He winked at me, knowing full well this was the third time this morning I'd had coffee delivered, and it wasn't even 8:30 yet. He held the now empty tray at his side. "Anything else?"

"No thanks, Noah. We'll be fine," I said.

My grandmother poured coffee into the stainless steel RIO mug in front of her. Dane chose lemonade, and when he put the pitcher down, I poured lemonade into a clean mug for me and a fourth to be ready for Newton's arrival. He came in and sat down just as I put the pitcher back on the table.

"Finola," he said. "Long time, no see."

Since I'd just seen Newton in the pool house a few minutes ago, I thought this was a strange thing to say. Then I realized he was looking at my grandmother. Although I'd never known which one, I always knew my parents had named me after one of my grandmothers. I just hadn't realized I shared my first name with my new acquaintance.

Mimi smiled at him. "It's good to see you, Newton. How have you been?"

Newton smiled at her. "I've been fine, but let's catch up later. Dane's a busy man, so how about if we let him ask his questions and then he can be on his way, okay?"

She patted his hand. "Whatever you say."

"Ready now, Mrs. Anderson?" said Dane. "Did you know the man in the pool?"

She nodded. "He said the committee hired him to work on the exhibition brochure, so he came to my home in Philadelphia to photograph the Silas Anderson Sea Stars. He was also one of the movie production people. His name was Jeffrie West. I think he was supposed to be the lead videographer on the film crew. And he was a liar and a thief. I know that much for a fact."

Chapter 3
Thievery

DANE AND NEWTON EXCHANGED GLANCES, then Dane said, "What makes you say he was a thief?"

She looked at him like he was slow. "He tried to steal the Silas Anderson Sea Stars. I couldn't let him get away with that."

"What are the Silas Anderson Sea Stars?" Dane asked.

She reached into her Prada leather handbag and handed him a bogus brochure for the upcoming exhibition. This was not the brochure we'd approved. A picture of several golden stars like the one I'd seen in the pool house was on the cover. There were twelve, each one showing a different Zodiac sign. Even the photograph was breathtaking.

She pointed toward the brochure's cover with a perfectly manicured finger. "Those are the famous Silas Anderson Sea Stars. Recovered from the ocean depths at great risk by my great-great-grandfather. Extremely valuable and held in trust until now. Someday they'll belong to Fin. There's no way I'd let the likes of Jeffrie West have them. I'd kill him first."

Had she just confessed to killing the man in the pool? Newton and I sucked in a breath, but Dane never missed a beat.

"And did you kill Jeffrie West to make sure he didn't get away with taking your Sea Stars?" he asked gently.

Mimi snorted delicately. "Certainly not. Do I look like I could have overpowered a large man like Mr. West?"

Dane smiled, a reassuring, almost merry smile. "Nope. You don't. So then did you ask someone else to kill him for you?"

She smiled coldly back at him. "I assure you I did not. You'll find out soon enough that I have the financial resources to have done so—I might as well tell you that up front. But I would never do such a thing. Besides, somebody beat me to it."

Newton put a hand on her shoulder. "That's enough, Finola. Let's you and I go to the conference room, and you can tell me everything. Then we can come back and talk to Dane again."

They rose and left my office. Dane groaned when he heard the conference room door shut. "Maddy's mother. That's Maddy's mother. What am I gonna tell her?"

Dane 's relationship with my mother had been going on for quite some time now, but they'd had their ups and downs. One of the worst downs was when my mother remarried my father to expedite the adoption of my brother Oliver. Maddy and Newton's second divorce had been a high point for them, but I had a feeling the current situation might be another low. A very low point indeed.

Dane and I sat in uncomfortable silence while we waited for Newton and Mimi to come back. Finally, Dane's phone rang, a welcome break in the thick atmosphere. "What's up, Roland?" A pause. "Uhhuh…Uhhuh…Okay. Thanks for letting me know."

He turned to me. "You didn't tell me you lost out on a big job to Jeffrie West. What was that about?"

I gave a little start. "Surely you don't suspect…"

He held up a hand and said, "Just tell me. No need to get defensive."

I shrugged. "I submitted a reel to the producers for the lead videographer's job. I found out this morning I didn't get it. This guy Jeffrie West got it instead. Apparently, he has…had…an in with one of the executive producers. T-8 stopped by to let me know this morning."

"You just found out this morning? Before or after you found the body?" Dane's voice was casual.

But his innocent tone didn't fool me. I knew he loved me like a daughter, but he'd arrest me in a heartbeat if he truly thought I'd done it.

"Before. But no more than ten or fifteen minutes earlier. Not enough time to track the guy down and drown him. I didn't know where he was or anything about him. And sure, I was upset about not getting the gig. But not enough to kill someone over it. There'll be other opportunities."

Dane nodded. "And who is T-8? What's his full name?"

I ran my hand through my still damp hair. Now I was sure it was sticking straight up, but I was too upset to do anything about it anyway. "The producer. No idea what his full name is. Apparently, he goes by T-8, and his real name is a big secret. Nobody knows it."

Dane nodded again, lost in thought. "The sea stars we found in the pool with him are not the ones your grandmother described. These stars are just a cheap alloy and fake gems. Good reproductions, but not worth more than a couple of thousand dollars, if that. So then where are the real Sea Stars?"

Mimi's voice came from the doorway. "They're in my safe where they belong. I wasn't about to trust them to anyone outside the family. And I've heard that the security here is rather...poor," she said.

She looked at me and tilted her head. "Sorry, my dear. But facts are facts."

I shrugged. I couldn't argue with the truth.

Mimi continued. "I had some duplicates made up for the exhibition to keep Fin's birthright safe. They must have been pretty good fakes since they fooled an experienced thief like West."

Dane smiled at her. "They were very good fakes indeed, but they couldn't fool the lab guys. So, the good news is that your duplicate sea stars are safe, but the bad news is we've impounded them as evidence. They may not be available in time for the exhibition."

Mimi drew herself up to her full five-foot height and opened her mouth. I could see by her expression that she was about to give Dane a tongue lashing, but Newton put his hand on her arm.

"That won't be a problem, Dane. And Mrs. Anderson is ready to talk to you now."

"Excellent," Dane said. "Fin, can we continue to use your office, or would you prefer we move to the conference room?" He moved his head slightly toward the door, so I knew he wanted me to leave.

"You can stay here," I said. "I have a meeting with the exhibition committee soon. I'll be using the conference room for that, so you should be fine here for the next few hours. Feel free to ask Genevra if you need anything else. She's usually right next door."

I rose and walked out to head for the locker room. When I arrived at the inside entrance Roland made me go around the long way to use the outside entrance rather than cross the pool area itself, since the entire pool space was now a crime scene.

When I'd finished my shower and the blow drying ritual, I opened the door to the pool, earning a glare from the crime scene team. "Other way, Fin. Use the other way," Roland grumped at me.

I sighed and walked outside and around to the front entrance, since I didn't have my keycard to open the rear door with me. I gritted my teeth when one of the new security guards the movie crew had hired stopped me from entering. Although his nametag was half-way to falling off his shirt pocket, I could still see it read, "Sammy."

He was short and stubby, with a broken nose and lumpy features like an ex-boxer. His ears were twisted awry, the cartilage broken. His nose bent in two different directions, and his eyes were nearly hidden behind all the scar tissue. His multiple tattoos were very distracting, and there were surgical scars on his cheeks and forehead, as well as across his neck. He'd either been in a terrible accident or had the worst plastic surgeon in the world—possibly both. It was hard to look this man in the face.

He held up a hand to stop me. "I need to see some ID, please." The tone of his voice was unpleasant, as though he were taking great delight in hassling me.

I sighed with exasperation. "I don't have my ID card with me. But I'm Fin Fleming. I'm the COO of RIO."

He smiled a nasty smile, showing several gaps among the remains of his yellowed and broken teeth. "That may be true. But rules are rules. Come back with your ID and I'll let you in."

I assumed that Fred, RIO's long-time security guard, who was at his usual post nearby, still held some sway. I hated pulling rank, but I had to get to my meeting. "Fred, tell him who I am please."

Fred gulped. "Fin, you know I'm not supposed to let anyone in without an ID."

"And you also know I'm the person who made that rule. My ID is in my office."

Fred bit his lip, then he turned to the man preventing me from passing. "This is Doctor Finola Fleming. She runs the place." He pointed to my portrait hanging on the lobby wall and the brass plate below it engraved with my name and business title. "See, that's her. And that's her there, too." This time he pointed to a poster of me displayed in the nearby giftshop window. "See, her name's even on the poster."

The outside security guard grumbled. "Just this once, I can give you a temporary pass based on Fred's word. But next time, bring an ID." He handed me a hastily scribbled name tag and stood aside to let me go by.

I bared my teeth at him and hoped it would pass for a smile.

Chapter 4
In the Hot Seat

I JUST HAD time to rush to my office to grab my notes for the exhibition committee meeting and to take my seat before the clock ticked over to one minute past the hour, when both the committee and I would have considered me officially late. Luckily Dane, Newton, and Mimi had left my office, so I hadn't had to interrupt them to gather what I needed.

I flashed a smile around the room as I took my seat in the center of the long side of the table, which I knew was always the power position in any meeting. I was surprised nobody had taken it before my arrival, but maybe they didn't realize the power seat was the one I was in, not the one at the head of the table as people usually assume. Or maybe these nice, extremely rich people didn't need to worry about where they sat.

I placed my folder in front of my seat but remained standing to shake everyone's hand. A few people did elbow or fist bumps, but by and large we did traditional handshakes. When we'd finished the ritual, I sat down. "I believe we're here today to talk about security arrangements and ticket sales for the exhibition, correct?" I said.

From behind me, I heard Mimi's voice.

"That's correct." She pulled an empty chair from against the

25

conference room wall and wedged it in to the middle spot on the long side of the table across from me. She clearly understood the power position. "Sorry I'm late everyone."

The woman at the head of the table, whom I'd assumed was the committee chair, gave a little sniff. "Rank has its privileges, I guess." She sounded irate, and she squeezed out a small smile that never reached her eyes.

Then she stood. "Ladies and gentlemen of the committee, I regret to announce that I am resigning as your chairperson and as a member of this committee. Effective immediately." She held up a hand to silence the shocked murmurs. "But don't worry. I'd also like to introduce the newest member of the committee, and your new chairperson, Mrs. Finola Anderson. Please give her a warm welcome, and the same level of support and dedication you've shown to me as we planned this event." She clapped her hands together soundlessly, as though she were applauding wearing kid gloves. The rest of the people in the room clapped politely along with her.

Mimi stood up. "Thank you. And thank you all for the warm welcome. I've studied the minutes of all your prior meetings, so I believe I'm up to speed on where we stand. I'll arrange to meet with each of you privately so we can get to know each other and catch up on any last minute details. So given that, let's turn our attention to the original agenda topic for today. Security for the exhibition. Fin, you're up. Do you have handouts?"

I hadn't really been listening because I was watching the former chairperson gather her things and slink out while Mimi was talking, so her words caught me by surprise. Yikes. I hadn't been planning on a full-blown presentation.

But I'm quick on my feet, so I was able to catch the ball she'd thrown my way without flubbing. "Thanks, Mimi. I'll pass out handouts later. I prefer to have the audience's full attention while I'm speaking." I smiled at her. "Let me get the café staff to refresh the food."

I picked up my phone, but instead of calling the café, I texted Genevra Blackthorne, my assistant, begging her to join the meeting to take notes and then turn her notes into a coherent presentation for handouts at the end of the meeting. And to have Noah bring more coffee and cookies.

Genevra was exceptionally competent, so I knew my last minute request wouldn't bother her in the least. By the end of the meeting, she'd have a printed presentation available for everyone to take with them.

While I was texting, several people rose and helped themselves to coffee or tea, and before they'd finished, Noah arrived with a heaping tray of cookies. Our chocolate chip cookies are justifiably famous, so everyone had to get at least one cookie. That gave me another few minutes to gather my thoughts.

Genevra slipped in just as everyone settled back down, and I introduced her. She sat in the former chairperson's vacant seat and opened her laptop. "I'll take notes, if that's okay with everyone," she said.

She winked at me, and I grinned back. She was a treasure, a close friend, and my brother Oliver's significant other. I'd have been lost without her. I rose and stood in the front of the room to fill the committee in about our heightened security measures.

"I'm sure you're all aware that there's a movie being filmed about the treasures in our exhibit, and the production company wants to ensure that your valuables are safe. They also want to ensure the safety and privacy of the actors and crew, so they've agreed to foot the bill for additional security from today until the exhibition and filming end. You probably noticed the additional security procedures when you entered RIO today, and I assure you, we'll have live guards at every entrance twenty-four by seven. We'll have additional guards inside the exhibition area itself, and the film company is paying to have CCTV plus a beefed up alarm system with infrared and heat sensing controls put in place. Chaunsey is doing the install as soon as the cameras arrive, and I believe he plans to have it done in the next few days." I droned on about guards and alarms for a while, then ended with, "We'll also have strict limits on the number of people who can be in the exhibition area at any one time, so the guards won't be overwhelmed."

I paused for a deep breath. "Any questions?"

A tall woman at the far end of the table raised her hand. "I just have one question. Will we be able to meet Rafe Cummings?"

From the avid attention everyone was now paying, it seemed as though this question had been topmost on everyone's mind. I had been negotiating by email with T-8 about this very topic, and I still hadn't gotten anywhere with him. "That remains to be seen. Mr. Cummings is a private individual, and his role in the movie is very taxing. We are hoping he will be kind enough to meet with us at least once, but it's entirely possible he may not feel up to it. As soon as I have an official word from the producers or Mr. Cummings himself, I promise I'll let you know."

The crowd was obviously disappointed, but they seemed to understand. There were no further questions, so since the meeting was over, they started gathering their things. Genevra had slipped out for a few minutes, and when she reentered, she had a small stack of nicely bound presentations to hand out. She was a genius, and worth twice what RIO could afford to pay her.

When everyone was gone except Genevra, Mimi, and me, I went to the sideboard to check out the cookie tray. Nothing left but crumbs, but it did put me close enough to overhear my grandmother offer Genevra a job as her personal assistant. I held my breath until I heard Genevra's answer.

"That's flattering, Mrs. Anderson, but I'm extremely happy here, and paid well enough."

I sighed with relief before heading to see Joely Wentworth, RIO's CFO and another close friend. I needed to find a way to give Genevra a raise. A big one. I couldn't lose her.

Chapter 5
Rafe

WHEN I ROUNDED the corner to her office, Joely and Newton were leaning against the wall next to the window, standing with their heads very close together. Joely jumped back guiltily when she noticed me, but Newton straightened up with his usual poise.

"How'd the meeting go?" he said. "Your grandmother's a force to be reckoned with, isn't she?"

"You never mentioned I had a grandmother," I said. "You might have told me. Or warned me."

He shrugged. "She's not my mother, so it wasn't my place. And as you might have surmised, she and Maddy don't get along very well."

I nodded. "I can see how that would be the case. They are two very strong-willed women, and I can already tell Mimi likes to get her own way."

Newton smiled. "Don't let her push you around."

I groaned. "She already tried to hire Genevra away from me." Turning to Joely, I said, "I need to give her a raise. She's sorely underpaid. What can we move around to free up the funds?"

Joely smiled. "No problem. I put a substantial increase in for her when I revised the budgets last month. You can tell her anytime." She walked to her desk and grabbed a pen and a yellow sticky note.

She scribbled on the top sheet and handed me the tiny slip of paper. "You have this much to work with. Let me know what you settle on and I'll get it processed."

"Give her the whole thing. Whatever we've got," I said without even looking at the number. "I can't afford to lose her, and Mimi's not the first to try to lure her away."

Joely shrugged. "You're the boss."

Newton chimed in. "And you're right. She's much too valuable to lose."

His comment surprised me, and I could tell by the expression on her face that Joely was surprised too. As far as I knew, Newton and Genevra rarely interacted except as family. She was, after all, his son's girlfriend.

"Thanks, Joely," I said. "Let me know when everything is set up so I can tell her." I turned to leave, almost bumping into Rafe Cummings, who was smiling the smile that had melted a million hearts.

I stared, for the first time in my life understanding what they meant when they called someone a star. I couldn't take my eyes off him. Behind me, I heard Joely gasp, and even Newton sucked in his breath.

Apparently, Rafe had become inured to this reaction because he just stood there patiently waiting for us to regain our wits. When he saw that we had recovered sufficiently, he said, "Hi, I'm Rafe Cummings. I'm looking for Doctor Finola Fleming. They gave me directions to her office, but I think I took a wrong turn." He dimmed the wattage on his next smile a tad, otherwise we'd have all gone back into our trances.

"You found me," I said. "It's a pleasure to meet you, Mr. Cummings."

"Rafe," he said. "Call me Rafe." He reached out to shake my hand.

"And you can call me Fin." I was impressed that I could actually speak coherently. I waved my arm behind me where the others were standing. "And this is Joely Wentworth, CFO of RIO, and my father, Newton Fleming, CEO of Fleming Environmental Investments."

He shook hands with them both before turning back to me. "I understand we'll be working together on the exhibition's publicity and the film. I thought maybe we could take a minute to get to know each other and discuss how we like to work. Do you have time now? Can we go to your office maybe?"

"Sure. This way." I willed my feet to move past him into the hall.

We sat at the round table in the corner of my office, and Rafe helped himself to a coffee and a cookie leftover from the earlier meeting. He sighed with his first bite, chewing slowly and obviously savoring the flavor. After he swallowed, he said, "Amazing."

Then he put the cookie down.

His willpower was stunning.

He sipped his black coffee. "You're the one who found Jeffrie's body," he said.

I nodded. "I'm sorry for your loss. Was he a good friend?"

He shook his head. "No. Thank you, but no. He was not a friend. I barely knew him." He paused a moment. "Tell me about yourself."

I gave him a quick recap. Raised by Maddy and Ray Russo, my late stepfather. Mostly aboard the *Omega*, RIO's research vessel. Private education, early college, a master's, and a doctorate. Working at RIO. My column at *Ecosphere*. Liam. Best friends Theresa, Joely, and Genevra. Newton. Oliver. I covered my life story in a few sentences.

"And you?" I asked.

"Nothing to tell," he said enigmatically, "At least, nothing that hasn't already appeared in the rags." He looked pensive for a moment, then he smiled that blazing smile again.

"I've seen your columns in *Ecosphere*. You're very good." He glanced over my shoulder at the massive photograph that hung behind my desk, the shot of Maddy fearlessly facing down a great white. "That one's stunning. Can you do that again?"

"I'll have to talk to the shark's agent. He may be busy," I said, and we both burst out laughing.

When we'd stopped our laughter, I said, "Yes, I can do that again, when and if the opportunity presents itself. Do you dive?"

"Not well," he said. "I just have some basic education, and I haven't been in the water for a few years. But I want to do my own stunts in the film, and that means I'll need to be much better at diving. I'd like to hire you as my private dive instructor, and of course, you'll be with me during the filming. Making me look good." The sun rose in his smile.

I was confused. "I'll be happy to give you private dive lessons," I said. "But T-8 told me I didn't get the videographer's job. I won't be with you while you're diving."

"If I say you have the job, believe me, you'll have the job." He rose, looking regretfully at the remains of his cookie. "I have to go now. I'll see you here at six AM. Is there a back way out of here?"

I'd seen film clips of Rafe mobbed by fans wherever he went. Even with a squadron of personal security guards, it always looked like he was in real danger. I didn't want to be responsible for putting him through that. He was so recognizable that a mob scene was sure to ensue if he went anywhere near people.

I couldn't take him out the back way because that would put him near the crowds at Ray's Place and any divers in the dive shop. The front entrance was out too because of the proximity of the public aquarium, gift shop, and café. The only other exit was through the pool house. I glanced at my watch. Surely Roland had cleared the scene by now, and we could pass through the pool area and out through the locker rooms. In fact, that door would be the best way for him to come and go whenever he needed to be here because we'd allowed the movie company to park their trailers on the empty land out beyond the pool house. But he'd need an employee ID card to use that entrance.

I was just about to call Genevra to ask her to get him some security credentials when she walked in carrying two brand new ID badges, both marked with blue VIP letters. Each hung from a lanyard with a blue strap printed with the logos of both RIO and the movie company.

She handed us each the one with our name and likeness and smiled. "I figured you two would be needing these soon, so I moved you to the top of the queue. They work with RIO's traditional security system as well as the new procedures the film producers have put in place to protect the exhibits and their crew. Don't lose them. Getting a duplicate will be extremely difficult, even for you."

Rafe snorted. He knew nothing was difficult when you were Rafe Cummings.

I didn't say anything, because I knew Genevra's warning had really only been meant for me, not him. I grinned at her. Yes, she was invaluable.

I thanked her verbally and Rafe thanked her with one of those smiles. She seemed impervious to his charm, but I wasn't surprised. I'd only ever seen her react to two men, my brother Oliver and Christophe Poisson, the world-famous freediver who now worked at RIO. So far, her relationship with Oliver was rock steady, but not for lack of trying on Christophe's part.

Rafe and I took off down the hall to the pool area. I sent him through the door to the men's locker room and told him I'd meet him by the pool to show him the outside entry and where he could park his car so it would be unlikely that anyone who wasn't with the film crew would see him.

"I already know where crew parking is. Are you going to show me the door that opens into that area?" he asked.

"That's right. You'll be able to come and go through the pool house through the locker room. You can also access the gym from the locker room if you feel like working out in private. Just remember you'll need that badge to open the outside door and the door from the pool house or the locker room that opens to the path to the RIO offices."

"Got it," he said. "I came in this way earlier, so I'm all set from here. I'll see you tomorrow. Thanks for everything." He smiled his mega-watt smile, and it was a full five minutes before I realized I had no idea what he'd thanked me for.

Chapter 6
Dive Class

I slept on the *Tranquility* that night to be sure I'd be there on time for my session with Rafe. I needn't have worried. He'd been the one to set the time for six AM, but he didn't show up until 7:15.

"You ready?" he asked from the door to my office when he finally arrived.

"Been ready," I said. "Since six."

His smile made it clear he didn't much care if he'd inconvenienced me.

Before speaking, I thought it must be nice to be a star. "You ready to dive? May I see your C-card, please?"

He looked puzzled. "My what?"

I narrowed my eyes at him. "Your diver certification card. I need to see it before I can take you diving."

"Oh that.' He made a no big deal gesture. "I don't have one. I learned to dive on set. Just a couple of guys showed me what to do. It's not that hard."

"Well, you need to be properly certified if you're going to dive with me. Let's start your lessons right now. I'll meet you in the pool." I checked to make sure I had my ID lanyard and stood up.

He gave a deep sigh, almost a moan. "I hate classes," he said. "Too much like school."

I slammed my desk drawer. "It's exactly like school, except unlike algebra, diving can kill you if you're doing it wrong. And you may hate school, but I hate whiners. Either get a grip or find another instructor."

He looked at me in amazement, then he started to laugh. "Got it." He swept an arm toward the door. "After you."

I grabbed a basic open water manual out of my bookcase and my tablet, then led the way to the locker rooms. "You have to shower before you can go in the pool, so you can do it now or after we finish the classroom section. Your choice. Either way, I'll meet you by the pool."

I went into the ladies' locker room and showered before joining him on the pool deck. He was sitting on an overturned bucket, wearing a bathing suit, but dry as a bone. I led him up to the second row of the bleachers and offered him the book or the tablet to complete the lessons. "You need to read the first two chapters, pass the exam, and then we'll spend some time in the pool. How quickly do you need your certification?"

"I don't need to be certified." He was whining. Apparently, Rafe's beauty was only skin deep.

"That's true. You don't need a certification unless you want to dive with me, or if you want to dive using any of RIO's facilities." I was annoyed by his attitude.

His lips twitched. "Man, you're tough. I'll use the tablet." He took the tablet and began reading the first chapter.

While I waited for him to finish, I set up a couple of tanks with rental regulators, so we'd be ready when he completed the reading. I had just finished the second setup when he called out, "Ready."

I was surprised at how quickly he claimed he'd finished, but I'd have to see how he'd done on the exams before I'd believe it. To my surprise, when I checked, every answer was correct.

His eyes twinkled when he spoke. "Pretty neat trick, huh? I have a photographic memory. Always do well on exams."

"That is a neat trick, but it just means I'll need you to explain the key concepts to me in your own words, so I know you understand them." We spent the next fifteen minutes with me

36

peppering him with questions and him explaining what every-thing meant.

"Good. Now do the next two chapters. I'll ask Stewie, the dive operations manager here, to bring you a selection of masks, fins, and other equipment to choose from, unless you want to go out there and take a chance that someone might recognize you in the dive shop or the recreation area."

He shuddered. "A selection will be fine. Just high end stuff, though. I don't do the economy models."

"I never doubted that for a minute," I said. I conveyed his requirements to Stewie, and by the time I was done, Rafe had finished two more chapters.

After I'd quizzed him—his exam scores were once again perfect —we broke to get his equipment fitted. Stewie had brought in several dive suits—two full length and a shorty—several high end regulators, an assortment of mouthpieces, four computers, six masks, and three pairs of dive fins, including a pair of free diving fins.

Rafe looked at it with disinterest. "I'll take it all. He flipped a black AMEX card toward Stewie. "Have whatever I won't need today delivered to my hotel," he said.

"Say please," I added with a stern look at Rafe. "Be polite to my staff."

He looked chagrinned and added a reluctant, "Please."

"At least try on the masks," I said. "You'll want a perfect fit."

He grinned. "I need the one that shows my face to best advantage."

I rolled my eyes but handed him a mask to try. I showed him how to hold it to his face without using the strap. He sniffed just a little, as instructed, and the mask stayed perfectly in place. "That's how you know you've got a good fit."

"But can you see my face?" he said with a grin. "I need to be visible on film."

"Yes. That's the same model Maddy is wearing in the photo you admired. You could see her face, right?'

He made an 'I guess so' gesture, so I set him to polishing both sides of the lens to remove the manufacturing coatings and to prevent fogging. Meanwhile, Stewie and I packed up the rest of his new gear for delivery to his trailer.

Once Rafe finished his task, I told him to shower and then come out and swim a few lengths of the pool so I could assess his abilities.

After he returned from the locker room. he stood on the tile coping. "Big pool," he said.

"Yep," I said. "Two laps. A lap means up and back. Any stroke you like."

He was a good swimmer and finished the laps quickly. He was barely breathing hard when he'd climbed up the ladder. Then I had him put on his mask, and we practiced clearing the mask and clearing his ears. He already knew these skills from whoever had trained him on the movie sets, so the drills went quickly. We progressed to using the snorkel, and again, he completed his laps with ease. In fact, we finished all the lessons and all the pool skills by noon.

"Tomorrow we'll go into open water. What time can you be here?"

"Six AM," he said.

I put my hands on my hips. "I'm not falling for that again. If you're not here by 6:15, the lessons are off. Got it?"

He looked startled. I guess being a star means nobody tells you what to do and when to do it. But he grinned and said, "Aye, Aye, Mon Capitaine." He looked away. "Can I take you to lunch to thank you for your patience—and maybe to make up for being late this morning?"

"Sure. Thank you. I'm starved. Where would you like to eat?"

"Your office. Or a conference room. Somewhere away from crowds.

"I know the perfect place." I called Theresa at Ray's Place and put in an order for delivery to my boat. "Meet me back here when you're ready," I said to Rafe.

When he emerged from the locker room, I led him out the back door. We walked along the grass behind the dive shop, cutting across the ironshore ledge to reach the dock. We scurried down its length until we reached the *Tranquility* and hopped aboard.

In a few minutes, Noah headed our way, laden with bags of food and trays of drinks. "Wait below. I see our lunch is about to arrive," I said.

After tipping Noah, I brought the food below and then started the engines. I backed out of my slip and putted slowly over to Training Site One, just a short hop from RIO's shore. "Do you want to eat below or on the bow in the sun?" I asked Rafe.

He looked chagrinned. "I'm not allowed to get tanned or sunburned before the filming is over, so I guess we'll have to eat below." He looked around. "Whose boat is this anyway?"

"The *Tranquility* is mine," I said proudly. "She's a great boat."

"Nice." He helped himself to a cheeseburger from one of the packages on the table. He didn't touch the fries, and he only ate half the cheeseburger. Once again, he ate only a single bite of his cookie.

"You'll be starving soon, "I told him. "Diving uses a lot of calories."

"I'll be fine." He looked away.

"Since we're already here, do you have time for a couple of training dives this afternoon?" I asked.

"Sure do," he said.

I had him set up his gear. Then, after a briefing on the undersea terrain and the skills I'd ask him to perform, we stepped off the rear transom and followed the mooring line to the bottom. I put Rafe through the required drills, including mask clearing and recovering his regulator with an arm sweep.

He performed the required skills flawlessly, although I noticed his eyes grew huge when he didn't have his regulator in his mouth. When we'd finished the drills, we went on a brief tour around the site. We saw huge brain corals, orange tube sponges, and several blennies. A turtle swam past, and a small nurse shark slept under an overhang. It was a good dive.

We surfaced, and I gave him water and fruit before watching him while he switched over his regulator—the breathing apparatus that goes in a diver's mouth—to a fresh tank. Setting up the gear was the only time I'd seen him fumble on a skill, and I assumed it was because he'd always had someone else to set up the gear when he'd filmed underwater scenes in the past.

When all was in readiness, we still had some time to kill to finish out our surface interval, so I gave him one of Liam's rash guards and a hat with a visor and a neck flap to keep him protected from the sun. Then we sat on the bow and chatted.

"Whose stuff is this anyway? Your boyfriend's?" he asked after I'd handed him a towel to cover his legs and feet to keep the scorching sun from burning them.

I nodded. "Liam Lawton. My fiancé. He's away on business right now."

"Lucky man," he said.

I started laughing. "Lucky he's away?"

He got serious quickly. "No. Lucky to have you. A woman like you…well, they're not easy to find where I come from."

I blushed and looked at my wrist worn dive computer. "Interval's over. Let's go." We dove the same site, and once again, he performed his skills flawlessly. Whoever had trained him had done a good job. Either that or he had some kind of total physical recall, like his eidetic memory.

On this dive, we saw an Atlantic trumpetfish lurking in the sea grass, a flamingo tongue out for a walk across the sand, several banded coral shrimp, a trio of squid, a porcupine fish, a couple of vibrant rock beauties, and a peacock flounder.

After the second dive, I brought the *Tranquility* back to RIO's dock. Before we disembarked, I said, "Keep the hat on until we get inside. People will be less likely to recognize you." We took the same route along the ironshore and behind the dive shop to get to the pool house entrance.

"See you tomorrow," he said when we reached the door. "Six AM sharp."

Chapter 7
An Unexpected Offer

I WAS WAITING for Rafe to arrive, sitting on the edge of the pool at ten minutes of six the next morning when T-8 walked in. He wore a white rock-band T-shirt with an untucked, brightly printed Hawaiian shirt open over it, with khaki cargo shorts and leather flip-flops. He kicked the shoes off and sat down beside me, dangling his feet in the cool water.

"You're the new videographer for the film. I put the contract on your desk. If you can get it back to me by noon that would be great."

"I thought the executive producer didn't think I was talented enough," I said.

"That was the old executive producer. He was Jeffries's dad. But when Jeffrie died, he quit and pulled all his money out. I thought we were going to have to scrub the project, but a new investor stepped in. One of the conditions of the investment was that you be an executive producer and chief videographer. You're in." He sounded aggrieved.

That was a surprise. "Who's the new investor?"

He made a face. "You're kidding. You must know."

I shook my head.

"Your grandmother. Mrs. Anderson," he said. "She stepped

right up. Old man West had barely told me he was pulling out when she called. No flies on her."

"Wow! That's a surprise. I had no idea," I said. "Are you okay with the situation?"

He had a disgusted look on his face. "Sure, why not? It's not the first time I've had to work with a producer's relative. Nepotism is rampant in Hollywood, so it probably won't be the last time either."

I reared back. "I had nothing to do with Mimi's decision to invest in your film."

"Au contraire. You had everything to do with it. You may not have asked her to put in the money, but believe me, she didn't do it because of a late-in-life desire to enter the film industry." He shrugged. "But it's fine. You were actually my first choice anyway. I just hate it when I'm forced into a corner, even if the end result is to make me do what I really want to do anyway."

Rafe, fresh from a shower, had quietly entered from the locker room. "I'm glad you approve, Bro. Fin is my first choice too. I never liked Jeffrie, and Fin is a thousand times more talented. I'd have forced the issue if Mrs. Anderson hadn't beat me to it." He grinned. "Besides, Jeffrie West is dead, and she's right here. I like her. You like her. We know she's got talent. Everything worked out perfectly."

"Not so perfectly for Jeffrie West," T-8 said. "And don't call me Bro."

Rafe just laughed. "Sure thing, T-8."

I was embarrassed by the direction of the conversation, so I looked at my watch. "Right on time, Rafe. Shall we get started?"

Rafe nodded and crossed the pool house to where I had a few tanks waiting for our session. Without being told to, he pulled his regulator from the gear bag over his shoulder and set up his rig. I watched, and he performed flawlessly and without hesitation. Impressive.

T-8 stood. "Contracts later today, right?"

I nodded. "As long as my lawyer agrees to the terms."

He grinned. "He will. Your grandmother stipulated pretty much everything. It's a good deal, especially for a novice."

"But I'm not a novice," I said. "I have more than thirty documentaries under my belt."

He shrugged but didn't say anything, just walked out of the pool house, his hands in the pockets of his cargo shorts.

Rafe was sitting on the edge of the pool waiting for me. "Don't mind him. He likes to think he's in charge."

Don't we all." I walked over to join Rafe. "Let's start by reviewing the skills you learned…"

He interrupted me. "You mean relearned."

"Okay, let me put it this way. Let's start with you demonstrating the skills we covered yesterday."

He plopped into the pool and quickly cleared his mask, doffed then donned his gear, found his displaced regulator, and cleared it. He rose to the surface, spit out his regulator, and swam two lengths of the pool using only his snorkel.

When he climbed the ladder to exit the pool, he was wearing a broad smile. "How'd I do, Chief?" he asked.

"Excellent," I said. I gave him a high five. "You up for some ocean diving?"

"Ready when you are," he said. "If we can get something to eat first. I'm starving."

"Deal," I said. I called Theresa at Ray's Place and asked her to have some food brought to the *Tranquility*. Then Rafe and I exited the pool house, strolled casually behind the dive shop, and then sprinted along the ironshore and the pier until we reached my boat.

We had just finished stowing our gear and getting our first tanks set up when Austin Gibb, Noah's younger brother, brought our food. I was below deck checking the fuel level when he arrived, so Rafe handed him a fifty as a tip. I came out of the cabin just in time to see Austin's eyes widen. I knew it wasn't the fifty that had him excited. He'd recognized Rafe.

I didn't have time to ask Austin to keep Rafe's presence a secret before he tore back to Ray's Place to spread the news. The crowd of people around the bar and at the tables peered at my boat. Then, as though they'd heard the starting bell in a race, they all hurried down the pier toward us.

"You're about to be mobbed," I said. "Hang on tight. We're making a fast getaway."

I quickly climbed the ladder to the flying bridge and started the engines. People were jumping into the water trying to catch a closeup glimpse of Rafe, but I sped away before they could reach us.

He stood in the stern and waved to them. Those who had boats in the marina ran to them to see if they could follow us. This situation could be dangerous for them as well as for Rafe, so I took off as quickly as I could, speeding through the 'no wake' zone and around the point. I kept going, until I reached Gus and Theresa's small dock. I tied up next to their boat, *Sunshine Girl*, and gave Gus a quick call. "May I borrow the *Sunshine Girl*?" I asked. "It's kind of an emergency."

Nothing fazed Gus. "Sure," he said. "Just fill her up before you return her."

"Yes, Dad," I said with a laugh. "And thanks."

"You're welcome," he chuckled. "But you better get Rafe Cummings' autograph for Theresa, or she'll never forgive you."

Rafe quickly transferred our gear to the *Sunshine Girl* while I fished the key out from under the dock where I knew Gus hid his spare. I leaped aboard the *Sunshine Girl*, scrambled up the ladder to the flying bridge, and was away from the dock before anyone else had made it around the point.

Once we were underway, I called Stewie and asked him to pick up my boat.

"Sure thing," he said. "You certainly set off a mob scene here. I'll bring the *Tranquility* to the Barcadere Marina in Georgetown instead of back to RIO, because I think this crowd would tear her to shreds looking for any sign of that movie star."

"Good idea. Thanks, Stewie."

"No problem," he said. "Just be sure to get an autograph for Doc, or both our names will be mud."

I tore several pages out of my dive logbook and sent Rafe below with a pen to sign all the autographs I'd need to keep friends and family happy. I headed back the way we'd come to throw off our followers and set a course for Merin's Playground.

Rafe and I geared up quickly and stepped off the stern. We navigated to one of the shallow sandy areas so Rafe could complete the required skills demonstrations. The current at this site is much stronger than in RIO's sheltered cove, but Rafe took it in stride and completed all the requirements without an issue.

When he'd finished, we took a short tour of the site, meandering through the spur and groove formations and peering into all the cracks and crevices. We saw several spiny lobsters and a juvenile spotted drum, as well as a small group of banded coral shrimp, a nurse shark hiding under a crevice, a black durgon, a queen triggerfish, and a sharpnose puffer. The coral and sponges here were large and healthy, so it was an extremely pleasant dive.

I moved the boat over to the next mooring at a site known as Japanese Gardens. Rafe surprised me during our surface interval by asking me to have dinner with him that night. I bit my lip, wondering how this would look to Liam and our friends.

Rafe must have noticed my hesitation because he said, "Just as a thank you. You've been so terrific, and I feel like I owe you for keeping me safe from the mob."

I hesitated for another minute, and he quickly added, "Of course Liam is welcome to join us too if you'd like."

I smiled. "Liam's out of town. He runs an environmental remediation and advancement company. There's always some corner of the world that needs his expertise."

"Well then, it's settled. You can't sit home alone. Have dinner with me."

"Okay, "I said. "But before you commit, I've got to warn you I'll want to eat dinner very early."

Rafe looked appalled when I told him what time I usually ate my evening meal. I have to eat early. To get enough sleep I have to go to bed early most nights because I get up well before dawn every day. Late nights are a rarity in my life.

But once he understood my reasons, he agreed to my timetable.

"Besides, if we're there early there's less chance that anyone will recognize me. It's a good plan."

Our surface interval was over, so we geared up and did backward rolls off the gunwales. Rafe had performed all his required skills, so on this dive, we just concentrated on seeing what we could see. The site is replete with giant corals, including tube and staghorn corals, as well as fire coral. We spotted several yellowtail damsel fish, some bluehead wrasse, and a Caribbean spiny lobster lurking under an overhang with just his antenna sticking out. Several species of jacks and grunts followed us throughout the dive. We enjoyed watching a group of garden eels ducking for cover into their holes in the sand as we approached, and a large green turtle spent a big part of the dive following us around. As always, time underwater passed quickly, and soon it was time to head back to the *Sunshine Girl*.

I brought the *Sunshine Girl* back to RIO and put her in the slip we reserved for Gus to use. I gave Rafe a RIO ball cap and a pink sun protection shirt that belonged to Theresa. Normally I wouldn't have borrowed her things without asking, but I knew she'd be thrilled when she learned that Rafe Cummings had worn her shirt.

"Get out of here quickly," I told him. "If you hang out, someone is bound to recognize you. I'll text you my address or we can meet at the restaurant. Your choice."

"I'm a gentleman," he said, sounding affronted. "I'll pick you up." Then he hunched his shoulders, affected a limp, and hobbled across the lawn to the parking lot. I swear he shrank himself a good six inches. Nobody would ever expect this tiny, shriveled man was actually hunky action hero Rafe Cummings. He was that good an actor.

Chapter 8
Dane

As soon as I got back to my office, I called Genevra and asked her to stick close to Mimi. I wanted to be sure Mimi wasn't getting into mischief or annoying my staff.

I reviewed the contracts T-8 had given me. I never sign anything I haven't read and understood. Although I'd been negotiating contracts since I turned eighteen—more than ten years now—these were pretty complicated, and there was a lot of fine print and a few unfamiliar showbiz terms. I called and left a voice mail for Newton to ask if he'd review them for me to make sure I hadn't missed anything. I mentioned that I needed them back quickly since I'd promised them to T-8 yesterday, and I didn't want to annoy him by delaying their return any longer than necessary.

I had just finished emailing them to Newton for review when Dane Scott walked in. He looked exhausted and utterly frazzled.

"How's the investigation going?" I asked him. "And did Mimi tell you how she knew Jeffrie West was dead?"

He placed an icy cold cup of lemonade in front of me and took a sip from his own cup before he answered. "She did. She snuck into the pool house before Roland and Morey had finished setting up the perimeter. They finally caught her standing behind one of the display cases that hadn't been set up yet, listening to their analysis

47

of the crime scene. They escorted her out of the pool house, and I guess that's when she tracked you down. But she'd already seen West's body and the sea stars in their evidence bags. She's a wily one, your grandmother."

He sighed with exasperation. "Every time there's a crime at RIO, I think it can't possibly get any crazier or more complicated than the last one, but somehow, it always does."

I nodded sympathetically. "What's the complication this time?"

"Jeffrie West didn't slip, fall in the pool, and drown by accident. It looks like somebody whacked him in the head and then threw him in."

"How do you know he didn't slip and bang his head on the edge of the pool when he fell in?" I asked. "That seems more logical than anybody here deciding to do him in. We hardly knew him."

Dane shrugged. "That's what I thought, but the forensics show somebody hit him with a cylindrical object capped with an oddly shaped attachment on the end. I can't imagine what it could have been, but we're looking for it."

"Did you check all the pool equipment? There's a lot of poles and odd devices for pool maintenance…"

"Did that. Nothing matches." He scratched his chin. "Would you have a few minutes to look through everything there with me? See if anything's missing?"

I put my reading glasses down on my desk. "Sure. Do you want to go with me? We could do that now." At his nod, I slipped my feet into the flip-flops I'd kicked under my desk and walked around to the office door. "Let's go."

Fifteen minutes later, I'd gone through all the pool maintenance equipment twice, and even checked it against our written proce-dures to see if they mentioned a tool that wasn't here. There was nothing missing, and nothing we found matched the wound on Jeffrie's head.

"See, I told you. He must have banged his head on the ladder or something. Besides, no one here would want to kill him. We didn't even know him."

Dane looked at the ceiling and sighed. "I can think of at least two people connected to RIO who might have wanted him gone."

I was incredulous. "And who might those people be?"

"Sorry," he said. "One of them is you. The producers hired Jeffrie West for a job with the film crew that you really wanted."

"I didn't want it enough to kill someone over it. You know me better than that."

He nodded. "Just following the evidence," he said.

"Okay. I get that. Who is the other person of interest."

"Your grandmother. I understand you call her Mimi."

I drew in a sharp breath. Mimi was my mother's mother. And Dane was in a serious relationship with my mother. And he'd often said I was like a daughter to him. No wonder he looked so weary. His two chief suspects were related to the love of his life.

"Surely you don't suspect my grandmother. She must be near ninety. And she's a tiny little thing. I don't know exactly how tall Jeffrie West is—was—but I'm pretty tall and I know his arms and legs were hanging down well below my knees when I carried him up the ladder. And I know how heavy he was for the same reason. He was a big man. Above average height, at least. I don't think Mimi could have taken him out even if she'd tried."

"Exactly," he said sadly. "Now you see my dilemma."

We stared at each other, both of us worried about what would come next.

"You have to keep investigating," I said. "There must be someone besides me with motive and opportunity. Keep looking."

"No need," came a soft voice from the door. "I did it. I killed Jeffrie West." Mimi held out her hands as though she expected Dane to cuff her right then and there.

"How tall are you, Mrs. Anderson?" asked Dane.

She looked grim. "Five foot one-and-a-half."

Dane held back a smile. "From the angle of the blow, we believe the killer was at least five-foot-ten. That lets you off the hook."

"No, it doesn't," she said. "I stood on the bench."

"Good to know. I'll add your confession to my case notes," he replied. He picked up a pen and wrote in his notebook. From where I stood, I could see he was just scribbling.

"You'll do no such thing," said Maddy, who stood in the doorway with Newton behind her. "This is my mother you're talking to. You know she couldn't have killed that man."

"I could too," said Mimi.

Newton burst out laughing, and both Mimi and Maddy gave him withering looks. He stopped laughing quickly. "Help me out here, Dane. What I think you're saying is that you are taking Finola's confession seriously, but you have several other persons of interest to talk to before you're ready to make an arrest. Is that right?" He winked at Dane, who looked relieved at the lifeline Newton had thrown him.

"Exactly. Newton, thanks for helping me clarify that. Mrs. Anderson, you'll be hearing from me soon." I could see he was trying to look stern, but his usual cop-face seemed to have failed him.

Newton put his arms around Maddy and Mimi. "May I buy you ladies a cup of coffee?" He steered them down the hall toward the café.

Dane's face looked grim. "How tall are you, Fin?"

I shrugged. "Five-ten. But you already knew that."

"I'll keep investigating," he said. "See what you can uncover while you're mingling with the film crew. He must have had some other enemies besides you and your grandmother." Dane walked out of my office like the weight of the world was on his shoulders.

Chapter 9
A Surprising Encounter

THE REST of the day flew by, and before I knew it, it was time to get ready for my dinner with Rafe. I texted him Newton's address before driving away in my new KIA Niro EV. My beloved old Prius had finally bit the dust, but I was loving this new car just as much.

I let myself into Newton's condo and went to the bedroom suite he kept for me. I checked out the huge walk in closet stocked full of expensive designer clothes chosen by the stylist he'd hired a few years ago.

I'd told him it was a waste of his money. The only time I ever wore these clothes was when I had a special occasion or event, and I hadn't opened this closet in nearly a year. I flipped through the selection until I finally chose a floaty blue and white midi-length dress with a V-neck and cut-in shoulders. I added a pair of low-heeled blue sandals that matched the dress perfectly, and a single gold bangle. My short hair was spiky and a little bit wild.

I finished dressing just as the chime on the main entry sounded. I hurried across Newton's massive penthouse to open the door. Rafe nearly took my breath away. In his movies, he always looks great in his action hero attire—usually torn and dirty military garb, at least by the ends of his movies—but he looked fantastic in his dress up clothes.

He wore a pair of pleated linen pants and an untucked blue linen button front shirt that exactly matched the color of his eyes. His hair was also a little spiky, and he wore a pair of large tortoise-shell glasses.

I laughed when I saw him. "If you think those glasses will work as a disguise, Clark Kent, I have to warn you your fans will see right through it."

He laughed. "I brought a ball cap too." He pulled a blue cap out of his back pocket, put it on, and pulled the brim low over his face. "See? No one will ever guess it's me."

"Uhhuh. I hope you wore your running shoes. You're gonna need them."

"We'll see," he said smugly. "You ready?"

We rode down the elevator to the ground floor. A limo waited out front, and the driver opened the door for us as we approached. I slid into the backseat, and Rafe climbed in beside me. He handed me a bottle of spring water and took one for himself from the ice bucket on the floor beside us. "Where are we going?" I asked.

"Grand Old House," he said. "It's a big night for me."

"It is? I didn't realize. What's the occasion?" I was glad I'd chosen to dress up a little since this was an important occasion for him.

He laughed, or more like giggled—but the sound was quite charming. "It isn't every day that the world's favorite action hero finally gets his open water scuba certification, even though I've had to dive in nearly half my movies. But now I'm legal, and it's all thanks to you." He clinked his water bottle against mine.

Now it was my turn to laugh. "Well, congratulations then. That's definitely something to celebrate."

It didn't take long to arrive at The Grand Old House, a beautiful Caymanian mansion set right on the waterfront. I'd eaten there occasionally, usually for important business meetings, and once on a romantic night with Liam, and I loved everything about the restaurant including the architecture, the décor, the ambiance, the gardens, the twinkling fairy lights, and of course, the amazing food.

The limo driver stopped at the entrance, and he got out. He

went inside for a minute. He soon came back to escort Rafe and me to the host, who whisked us quickly to a private table in the gazebo. A privacy screen shielded the table from prying eyes but didn't block the stunning view of the ocean. There was only one other table set in the room, and the staff had shielded it as well.

"I thought we were supposed to have a private room," Rafe said, clearly annoyed.

"I'm sorry, Sir. I didn't realize another party had also reserved a private table in this room. He's one of our most frequent guests, but he's very reasonable. I'm sure he'll agree to sit at a different table when I explain the situation to him."

"Whatever it takes," Rafe said. "Just add it to my bill."

The service here was wonderful, and soon we had wine and lobster bisque in front of us. The bisque was delicious.

The waiter had just cleared the soup bowls away when I heard the host bringing the other party to their table. The host was asking the patron if he would mind sitting in another part of the restaurant, and it didn't sound as though the man liked the idea. He and the host were holding a very quiet discussion, and I knew it ended with the couple sitting at the table they had originally reserved. I didn't say anything to Rafe, since I didn't think their presence was a problem. They could neither see nor hear us, so Rafe's privacy was still intact.

I picked up my small, beaded purse. "I'll be right back," I said. I exited the area behind our screen and went to the ladies' room. On the way back, I caught a glimpse of the couple at the other table. To my surprise, it was Newton and Joely Wentworth, looking very cozy. They were holding hands across the white linen cloth, and the soft glow of the lit candles in the center of their table reflected like love in their eyes. I scurried back to my seat before they could notice me.

After that, I was very distracted. Rafe was still a great conversationalist, full of funny anecdotes about celebrities he knew and silly pranks on various movie sets. I continued to listen, smiling, and nodding as appropriate, but all I could think of was Newton and Joely, having dinner together only a few feet away.

After they cleared our dinner plates, Rafe said, "What has you so preoccupied?"

I leaned across the table and whispered. "My father is at the other table. With one of my very close friends. Looking very intimate, like they've been dating for a while."

He paused a moment. "Your father is single, isn't he? Are you concerned about the age difference?"

"No, not at all. Joely is older than me, and age-appropriate for Newton. I'm just surprised neither one ever mentioned they were seeing each other. Newton has always been very open with me, and Joely and I are extremely close."

Rafe nodded sagely. "Maybe that's exactly why. Let's ask them to join us for coffee and dessert," he said. He didn't wait for me to answer, just stood up and walked across the room.

I heard the soft murmur of voices, then I saw Rafe speak with the waiter before he came back and sat down. In a few minutes the waiter came over and moved our privacy screen back to enlarge our space before he brought two more chairs and place settings to our table.

Rafe nodded at the waiter when he'd finished the setup. "Thank you," he said. Then he said to me, "They're just finishing dinner. They'll join us in a moment for dessert. Would you like a brandy while we wait?"

I don't drink much alcohol, and I almost never drink the night before I have an early morning dive planned, but if ever a time called for a brandy, this was it. Rafe waved the waiter back over and placed the order.

"We'll order dessert when our friends join us. And please, put their meal on my tab."

The waiter nodded.

"That wasn't necessary. You know my father is a multi-billionaire, right?"

He looked surprised. "He is?"

"Yes, he's *the* Newton Fleming. Founder of Fleming Environmental Investments. They're into everything. Solar, batteries, remediation. Tiny houses. Anything and everything that affects the earth and our environment. He's famous for his good works."

Rafe shrugged. "I've heard of him. I didn't realize that guy was your dad though."

Just then Newton and Joely came around the privacy screen. Newton had his arm lightly around Joely's slender waist. The color was high in her cheeks. He shook hands with Rafe, then pulled out the chair next to me for her to sit in. He sat next to Rafe.

The waiter brought the bottle of brandy, a pot of coffee, and at least one of every item on the dessert menu, with several forks and spoons for each of us. He set small plates in front of each place before he departed.

Newton poured a brandy for himself and offered the bottle to Rafe, who refilled his glass and offered to refill mine. I held my hand over the glass and shook my head, so he placed the bottle back on the table between Newton and himself. Joely poured coffee for both of us. We sat and looked at each other for a moment, and then we all spoke at once. We started to laugh.

Newton broke the ice. "Maybe we should draw straws to see who speaks first?"

Rafe answered, "No, I want to go first. I wanted to say how much I've always admired your support for environmental causes, and I'm honored to make your acquaintance. I also want to thank you for raising such an amazing daughter. It's been a delight to get to know her."

Newton said, "Thank you for the kind words. And although I agree that Fin is amazing, I can't take any credit for it. Fin's mother and her second husband Ray Russo raised her, and I thank the universe every day that they did, because she's incredible." He raised his glass to me, and they drank a toast while I blushed.

After that, we all chatted as though we were close friends, and even Joely got over her awe at having dinner with an A-list celebrity like Rafe Cummings. In a short while, despite the delightful company, my eyelids started to droop, and I held back a yawn.

Rafe noticed and immediately signaled for the waiter to bring the check. The waiter whispered in his ear, and Rafe nodded. "Thank you, Newton. Next time it's on me."

We rose to leave, and I kissed Newton's cheek. "I'll be at your place tonight," I whispered, "unless you need some privacy."

He turned scarlet but laughed along with me. "You know you're welcome anytime. That's why I keep that suite for you."

Rafe and I rode home in the limo, and he walked me up to Newton's penthouse door. When I entered the passcode to open the electronic locks, he kissed my cheek. "Goodnight. I'll see you tomorrow." Then he entered the waiting elevator. I watched the doors slowly close.

Chapter 10
The Morning After

As always, I was up before the sun and creeping quietly out the front door of my father's penthouse when Newton snapped on a light. He'd been sitting at his desk, wearing a dark blue silk robe, and sipping coffee from a RIO mug.

"Anything we need to talk about?" he asked.

"Nope. We're good." I smiled at him. "I'm happy for you. Joely's terrific. But I've got to run. I'm late, as usual, and I have to get *Sunshine Girl* back to Gus." I blew him a kiss and walked out the door.

I drove my KIA Niro to RIO and hopped aboard the *Sunshine Girl*, still floating serenely in the slip where I'd left her yesterday. I'd just started the engine when I saw Rafe hurrying down the dock toward me.

"You diving this morning?" he asked. "Can I tag along?"

"Sure. Welcome aboard. But I need to return the *Sunshine Girl*. I don't want to keep Gus's boat too long. And I have a meeting this morning, but our shore dive here is fantastic and we can get wet pretty quickly. Want to try it when we get back?"

He nodded and hopped aboard. After stowing his gear bag under the gunwale, he joined me on the flying bridge. I noticed he was wearing Liam's hat again, with the brim pulled low and the flap hanging down his neck. He wore huge, very dark sunglasses, and although he hadn't shaved, he had put a plastic bandage on his chin. Over his bathing suit, he wore a pair of baggy sweatpants and a gigantic sweatshirt with a picture of Elmo on the chest. He looked like somebody's nerdy father, not at all like a Hollywood heartthrob.

"I love what you're wearing," I said. "Very glamorous."

We both burst out laughing, and he settled back in the captain's chair next to mine.

We arrived at Gus's dock quickly, and I tied the *Sunshine Girl* in her usual place. Then Rafe grabbed his gear bag, and we walked across the ironshore to the street, where Stewie was waiting for me in his old open air SUV. I could tell he was awed by Rafe, because his movements were stiff, and he barely spoke a word on the whole trip.

Stewie parked his vehicle in RIO's lot, and Rafe and I took the long way to the dock, scurrying behind the main building and the dive shop to avoid anyone seeing Rafe as we made our way to the shore dive entry. We zipped into the dive shop through the open Dutch door and put on our skins and all our gear except our fins.

Together, we walked the few paces to the shore dive entry site. I held Rafe steady while he put on his fins, and he did the same for me. Then at the same time, we each took a giant stride and plunged beneath the sea.

The water is about twenty feet deep right next to the shore, and the whole area teems with life, thousands of fish and gorgeous corals. I've seen everything here from sharks and stingrays to squid and octopus—and even a tiny seahorse. I was sure Rafe would enjoy it.

We started off kicking toward the deeper side of the site, where the coral is even more lush and healthy. We wove in and out of the coral fingers, checking in all the crevices for the shyer specimens. After a few minutes, I led Rafe back toward the dock because a lot of sea life congregated there.

As we crossed the open sand bowl, I saw something shiny half-buried in the sand. I dove down to get a closer look at it.

I recognized Mimi's teakwood walking stick by the gold dolphin on its top. I hovered over it for a minute, trying to understand the implications of my find. The walking stick had the characteristics of the murder weapon. It belonged to one of Dane's top two suspects. Someone who didn't realize how frequently divers were on the site had thrown it here. Or maybe someone who wanted it found had carefully disposed of it where it would soon come to light.

I knew my duty was to bring it to the surface and hand it over to Dane, but I didn't want to do anything that might make him think Mimi might actually be guilty. I assumed someone else had thrown it here, in an effort to make Mimi or me look like the murderer. But if someone had taken Mimi's walking stick, why hadn't she reported it missing? And if she was innocent of murder, why would she have tossed her own stick into the ocean? I couldn't answer these questions, but maybe Dane could.

No matter what, I knew I needed to bring the dolphin-headed walking stick to the surface. It might be important evidence. I didn't know whether fingerprints or DNA would survive underwater, but I didn't want to take a chance that I could ruin critical evidence by mishandling the cane.

I pulled a mesh catch bag out of the pocket of my buoyancy control device and clipped it to a D-ring on the BCD. Then I swam very low to the bottom—my belly actually scraping against the sand—and swam up to the stick, scooping it into the bag without touching it with my hands. I picked up a lot of sand along with the stick, but the tiny grains of sand immediately drifted out through the bag's mesh. The cane was a lot longer than the bag, but I'd still be able to get it to the surface without touching it.

Rafe had stayed back watching while I scooped up the stick. As soon as it was in the bag, I signaled to him that we needed to head back. He gave me the okay sign, and we turned toward the iron-shore—the calcified skeletons and shells of long dead sea creatures —that makes up the bulk of the Cayman Islands.

Rafe climbed the ladder first so he could help me maneuver around my awkward burden. As soon as we were both on land, we hurried into the nearby dive shop.

I put the stick and the catch bag into one of the dive shop's largest tote bags for safe keeping and then called Dane.

"I'm on my way," he said.

Chapter 11
Production Meeting

IT WASN'T long before Dane and Roland showed up to take charge of the walking stick. "I doubt we'll find any conclusive DNA or fingerprints at this point, but we can at least see if it matches the shape of the wound. It could still be the murder weapon," Roland said. He carefully placed the stick in an evidence bag and labeled it.

Dane nodded. "Tell me again where you found it, and how you happened to see it."

I told him that Rafe and I were doing an early morning dive so there'd be less chance of anyone recognizing Rafe and causing another mob scene. Dane was familiar with the underwater terrain here from previous investigations, so I quickly explained our trajectory. "We were just lucky our path crossed right over the stick, and that the surge hadn't buried it completely yet," I said.

He frowned. "Maybe it was luck. Or maybe the person who ditched it wanted to be sure someone would find the cane."

I shrugged. I was a strong believer in good luck, but since I was pretty sure this stick belonged to Mimi, finding it felt more like bad luck.

Roland was staring at the stick. "Seems to me I've seen this before, or something just like it," he said.

I might as well get in front of the truth. "It might belong to Mimi. Or at least, she used to have one like it."

Dane and Roland exchanged glances.

Dane was totally in love with my mother, and he had been for years. I knew he didn't want to be responsible for arresting Maddy's mother, but so far, his only alternative suspect was me. And he didn't want to arrest Maddy's daughter either. He was in a very tight spot. He groaned, caught between duty and love.

I felt for him. I really did. But I also knew I'd had nothing to do with Jeffrie West's death. And I knew Dane knew it. "If you're done with questioning us, we have a production meeting for the movie this morning. I promise to make myself available for any additional questions you need answered when we get out. Is that okay?"

He scrubbed his face with his hands. "Okay. You can go. Give me a call when you finish your meeting. Maybe something will have come up by then."

Rafe and I walked slowly across the lawn to the back of the pool house and we each entered one of the locker rooms. I took a quick shower, actually blew dry my hair, and dressed quickly in my usual clothing—a practical two-piece bathing suit under cargo shorts and a RIO t-shirt—except today I wore a collared polo shirt instead of my usual tee.

Rafe exited the men's locker room at the same time I came out of mine, and together, we strolled across the pool area to the RIO offices. I led the way to the conference room, which was already filling up with crew members, actors, wardrobe, and production people. T-8 stood at the head of the table in front of the large white board. He also had the title slide of a presentation projected on the nearby screen.

"Now that everyone is finally here," he said when we walked in, "we can get started."

I stole a guilty look at my dive watch, but it showed we weren't late. In fact, we were a full two minutes early.

"I need coffee," Rafe said, ignoring T-8. He went to the side-board and poured two cups. He handed one to me and grabbed a muffin and some napkins for each of us before he finally settled into a seat. He stretched. "Ready," he said at last.

T-8 didn't say a word to his star. He didn't introduce any of the attendees to each other, just started his presentation, running through the scenes he wanted to film in the next few days and assigning various people to be on set. He'd asked an assistant to keep a running list of questions and concerns on the white board.

He was about an hour into his presentation when the conference room door opened and Mimi walked in, followed by Genevra. Mimi slid a chair between two people seated on the long side of the table facing T-8. Genevra took a seat along the wall and opened her computer. Mimi looked at T-8 and said, "What did I miss? Can you do a quick recap?"

T-8 gritted his teeth. "You're an hour late. We don't have time. Maybe someone will lend you their notes. You'll have to figure it out on your own time."

Mimi smiled politely. "I am the executive producer, am I not? And the chief investor? If I think we have time, then we have time."

T-8 blushed and clenched his jaw even more tightly. "Sure. But we don't need to make everyone else sit through a recap. They have things to do. How about if we let them go. I'll bring you up to speed, and we can reconvene with the full team this afternoon. Say 2:00? Everyone okay with that?"

There were murmurs of assent from the people in the room, so T-8 said, "Great. See you then." He turned to me. "Fin. Rafe. I'd like you to get started on some publicity stills. Fin, do whatever you need to do to make the photos happen."

I nodded.

Rafe said, "Sure thing, Bro." He left the room, ignoring T-8's obvious annoyance.

Chapter 12
Photo Shoot

I WALKED out with the rest of the crew. I called Austin Gibb and asked him to join us as my photographer's assistant. He'd been taking photography lessons from me, and he was getting pretty good. Although I didn't tell him who the subject of the photos would be he agreed to meet us at the pool. Then the three of us went outside to the wardrobe trailer parked behind RIO's main building.

"Let's see," Rafe said. "Who do I want to be today?"

We went inside the trailer, and the wardrobe person agreed to deliver the three costumes Rafe selected for the shoot to the pool house. Then we stopped by the makeup trailer and arranged for someone to be in the pool house in case Rafe needed something to smooth out his complexion, but he was so naturally attractive that I couldn't imagine he ever needed any makeup at all.

The pool house was a good spot for us to work. There was plenty of natural light for the makeup crew if they felt the need to touch up Rafe's flawless face; he'd have the locker room nearby to change in; and there was more than enough space for me to set up lights, backgrounds, and my other paraphernalia.

We went by the marketing storage closet to pick up all the equipment I thought I'd need. While we were piling up all the lights and backdrops I wanted to use, Eugene Kerwin and Stanley Simmons from RIO's maintenance team walked by.

"Where's all this going?" said Eugene. "We'll bring it to you on a cart, so you don't have to make multiple trips. How soon do you need it there?"

"As soon as possible," I said. "And thank you." While I was speaking to Eugene, I noticed Stanley staring at Rafe with his mouth open. It was obvious he was a little bit starstruck. On the other hand, Eugene was all business and didn't even appear to see Rafe.

Rafe and I stopped by the café to grab a coffee while we waited for Stanley and Eugene to deliver the gear. We picked up our RIO branded to-go cups and walked down the hall toward the entrance to the pool house.

Rafe sat in the top row of the spectator seats and watched me as I unfurled various backgrounds screens and a plain white one that I would use to project simulated backgrounds. Next came several spotlights and a few bounce lights. Austin and I selected the cameras and lenses I would use and placed them on a small folding table. I had just finished when the wardrobe person rolled in with a rack of costumes, followed by the makeup team lugging a toolbox that made Roland's forensic kit look tiny. All this, to make a man blessed with astonishing good looks seem even more astonishing.

Rafe jumped down from the bleachers two rows at a time and flipped through the garments on the rack. He pulled out a pure white tunic edged with a gold pattern on the hem. This was his costume for the movie segment set in ancient Greece on the island of Kalymnos. This portion of the film focused on freedivers who brought back sea sponges and pearls for trade. Although these early divers were usually naked, Rafe would be wearing this tunic in the interest of avoiding an X-rating for the movie.

He carried the costume into the locker room to change while I set up a projected background of a beach on the shore of an old Grecian seaside village. I rearranged some of the lights while I waited for Rafe to emerge in his tunic. When he did, he looked spectacular.

He shooed away the makeup crew with their brushes and puffs and strode across the tile to stand in front of the backdrop. He automatically positioned himself so he was perfectly lit. He smiled. I snapped several pictures. He looked pensive; he looked grim; he looked tired, all in quick succession. He turned his back and looked over his shoulder. He twirled quickly, letting the hem of his tunic rise to show a flash of manly thigh. He signaled for one of the costume people to bring over an empty bucket stored near the pool maintenance closet. He turned it over and rested one foot on it. "You know you can photoshop this later, so it looks like a rock, right?"

"Duh, of course I know that. I'm a pro," I said.

He grinned, and I realized he'd just been yanking my chain.

He was a joy to work with. Every shot came together perfectly. I flipped off the background projection and took several more of Rafe against the plain white screen, and then a plain black screen, in case T-8 wanted me to insert Rafe's image later into a setting of his choosing.

Rafe headed back to the locker room, re-emerging a few minutes later dressed in a hard hat diving suit. I quickly flipped my background generator to show an underwater scene, with a sunken shipwreck barely visible in the distance. Rafe positioned himself under the lights, and I adjusted one slightly. Then I was snapping my camera's pushbutton as fast as I could to capture this new round of poses. He was a phenomenal model, and I felt like it would be impossible to take a bad shot of him.

For his third change of outfit, Rafe chose a pirate's costume, complete with a stuffed parrot for his shoulder and a massive white plume on his tricornered hat. The makeup team swiped the real sweat off his face—it was hot in that old-time dive suit—and replaced it with artificial sweat, each bead artfully applied.

After a few minutes of their fussing, Rafe brushed them away. "Enough."

I had only taken a few shots when Mimi entered the pool house. "Good," she said. "I'm just in time." As she walked toward us, she used a solid black walking stick with a small curve at the top. The stick looked like black oak, and I could see faint whorls where the maker had removed branches and twigs. The pattern of the grain, though fine, was visible in spots. It was as magnificent as the teakwood stick she'd lost.

Mimi had enlisted Stanley to roll in a large wooden chest for her, and she directed him to place it near Rafe. Rafe's presence had so awed Stanley that he couldn't even look up at Rafe as he approached the movie star.

Once Stanley had placed the treasure chest to her satisfaction, Mimi flipped it open to reveal the twelve glittering sea stars nestled on a black velvet lining. They were so beautiful they drew every eye in the room.

Mimi smiled and chose one seemingly at random. It was the one embedded with sapphires in the sign for Virgo. She lifted it with some difficulty and handed it to Rafe. "Matches your eyes." Then she walked away to sit on the lowest tier of the spectator benches to keep an eagle eye on her treasures.

Rafe shrugged his shoulders and held the sea star near his slender waist with one hand. The position caused the front of the flowy white shirt he wore to gap open, showing a slice of his chest. Then he went into his poses, turning, smiling, winking, but always keeping the sea star visible. It must have been hard to hold the heavy sea star with one hand since it weighed nearly thirty pounds, but he never showed it. He raised his sword overhead as though he were giving the order to attack, and then he carefully placed his booted foot on the rim of the treasure coffer and looked straight at the camera with the sea star clutched to his chest. His blue eyes were wide, and his lips were slightly parted, with the barest hint of a smile. I knew instantly this was the money shot.

So did he. "That's it for today," he said when he heard the click. "I'm done." He put the heavy star back into the chest and walked into the locker room to shower and change while Austin and I packed up all the photography equipment. Stanley had left the cart he'd used to bring it in, so we loaded it up and then Austin trundled off to put all the cameras and lights away.

68

I called after him. "Austin, can you upload the photos to my image gallery for me please? Right away if you can."

Mimi came over to talk to me. "Nice work handling the photo shoot. I think you probably got some of the best pictures ever taken of that man, and that's saying a lot."

"He's easy to photograph. He knows exactly how to present himself to the camera."

She scoffed. "There's more to it than that. Any fool could see the chemistry between you two." She smiled and started to walk away.

I knew I should leave the investigating to Dane, but I couldn't help myself. "Mimi, what happened to your other walking stick? The teak one with the dolphin? It's so beautiful I was thinking I might use it for a prop if you'd allow it."

She spoke quickly. "I would have, and happily so, but it disappeared. Your grandfather gave me that one so it's very special. I don't usually use it outside the house because I love it and I'm always leaving my canes behind wherever I go. I must have left it somewhere, although I can't imagine where it could be. I'm heartbroken."

Interesting.

I wanted to probe a little deeper. "I'm so sorry you lost it. Let me know if it turns up because now that I know how special it is, I want to use it in a few pictures even more." I acted like I was turning away to follow my cameras, then I quickly turned back to her. "Do you remember where you had it last?"

"Somewhere inside RIO. I should have known not to bring it here. Security in this place is terrible. You or Maddy should do something about that."

I grimaced. We'd had some problems over the last few years, but we'd beefed up the security every time. The trouble was bad guys beefed up their methods as fast as we upgraded our security. But I didn't want to argue with my grandmother. "I'll check the lost and found for you," I said.

"Great," she said. "And find a safe place to store the Anderson Sea Stars until the exhibit opens."

Chapter 13
Mother Daughter Chat

WHEN I WALKED by Maddy's office, I noticed her sitting at her desk. Since she'd been ill, she hadn't come into the office very often. She primarily worked from home, and her assistant June brought her anything she needed to handle personally. More and more of the administrative and executive work was falling on my shoulders.

I hated it. But I'd never tell Maddy. Thank goodness I had Joely and Genevra to handle the details.

But I was happy to see Maddy here today, so I poked my head in. "Got a few minutes to catch up? No business. I just miss you."

She looked up and put her reading glasses down on her desk. Her usually luminous turquoise eyes looked tired. "Always time for my beautiful daughter. Come on in." She pushed a button on her desk phone. "June, would you mind bringing us some tea from the café please?"

"I'm on it," said June's voice from the speaker.

I sat down at the round table in the corner of Maddy's office, and she joined me there. "I imagine you have questions about Mimi," she said.

"I do. How come you never told me about her?" I tried—but failed—to keep the hurt out of my voice.

"She hasn't been here very long, but I'm sure you've noticed she can be a very powerful presence. She takes charge and just ignores or walks over anything in her path." She sighed. "We had a blowout when I was just starting RIO. She didn't want me to start it, but if I was going to do it at all—and I was determined that I would—then she wanted it done her way."

Maddy stopped talking when June brought in the tea. Thank goodness June knew enough to bring lemonade for me. As far as I'm concerned, tea tastes like boiled socks. I smiled gratefully when I saw my mug filled with icy lemonade instead of tea.

She placed a tray with half a dozen chocolate chip and half a dozen lemon cookies on the table between Maddy and me. Each of us reached for one of our favorite cookies before June had taken the three steps required to exit the office door. We both laughed.

She nibbled the edge of her cookie and chewed for a second. "We fought over everything. She really wanted me to give the whole idea up and go back to Philly to be a good wife to Newton. But he and I were already over by that time, and she wouldn't listen to reason. Then I hired Ray. She took one look at him and went ballistic, telling me that hiring him was the worst decision I could possibly make." She sipped and swallowed. "But I knew it was the best decision I had ever made in my entire life. I still think that."

"She was so angry that she cut me off from my trust fund. In retaliation, I banned her from RIO and from my life. She was dead to me. Thank goodness Newton came through with the funding I needed to keep RIO going. He bought *Omega*—it was the *Francie Two* when he found it—and then he leased it to me at a crazy low rate. He supplied operating capital for the startup. He did everything he could to support my dream, going well beyond what anyone could expect of an ex-husband, especially after I married Ray."

"About ten years later, I unexpectedly started getting checks from my trust fund again. My father had recently passed away. My mother never contacted me or tried to see you, never said anything about the money from my trust fund. I was as surprised as you when she showed up here now."

I nodded slowly. "You know she somehow finagled her way into being the executive producer of the film…"

Maddy held up her hand. "It's what she does. Nothing stands in her way. I guess she suddenly decided if you wanted to be an underwater videographer, that she'd do everything she could to make that happen. Just don't let her run your life because she'll take over if you don't stay firm."

I'd always thought that Maddy was very determined and single-minded in going after what she wanted. After all, she'd built RIO from nothing into one of the most respected and well-known oceanographic institutes in the world. She'd had a long and happy marriage with Ray Russo, her second husband. But compared to Mimi, she seemed surprisingly mellow and laid back.

I thought of Mimi's remark implying that there was something between Rafe and me. She'd never met Liam, and she didn't know me or Rafe beyond just a few minutes of acquaintanceship. I hoped she wouldn't try to push us together. After all, I was engaged to Liam. And, I realized, I had been for a few years. Why hadn't we moved forward?

I told myself we simply hadn't had time to plan a wedding. He had been traveling so much with his new environmental remediation company that we'd barely spent more than a few days at a time together over the past year. And despite his promise to call every day when he was away, sometimes weeks went by without a word if he was in a particularly remote part of the world. I was lonely, but I'd grown up lonely. I was used to it.

Sort of.

I tried not to sound like I was criticizing her mother. "She made a comment about seeing chemistry between Rafe Cummings and me…"

Maddy smiled. "I wouldn't worry about it. From what I've seen, everybody has chemistry with Rafe Cummings."

I laughed. "Yes, he's charming. And undeniably good-looking. But I'm with Liam forever."

73

Maddy took another cookie. "Hold fast then, and don't let her bully or confuse you. Now I have to finish this report. I'm glad we had a chance to talk."

Chapter 14
Faint Praise

MADDY HAD ALWAYS BEEN A DRIVEN individual, but since her health scare last year, she'd grown more distant and aloof. After Ray's death she'd withdrawn from socializing a little bit, but then when she started seeing Dane again, she'd bounced back. Lately, she seemed to have lost interest in everything, even her family and the research institute she'd founded. She was always very close-mouthed about her feelings and problems, so I had little hope of finding out what was really going on between her and Mimi. I resolved to keep trying.

Just because I'd told Mimi I would, I stopped by the lost and found on the way to my office to see if there was any chance her walking stick was there and that hers was not the one I'd found. The usual assortment of weird items—odd shoes, sunglasses, hats, sweaters, books—but no walking stick. That was not good news for Mimi.

I continued to my office to pick up my computer and stopped short when I saw Rafe Cummings sitting in one of the guest chairs, admiring the photograph of Maddy facing down the great white.

He turned when he heard me in the doorway. "You still owe me a dive like that."

I made a 'maybe' gesture with my hand. "As soon as you get a few more dives under your belt, we can discuss it further."

He grinned. "When can we dive again?"

"Today, if you want. Right after the meeting. It will be a perfect time. The day creatures will still be out or getting ready to sleep, and the night hawks will be starting to venture forth. It's usually still light enough that you can see everything, making it a nice, easy, fun dive. Deal?"

"Deal," he said flashing his adorable grin.

"But I warn you, I'll be bringing my camera on the dive. I want to stockpile a few shots for next month's *Ecosphere* column." I picked up my computer so I could take notes during the meeting.

His grin was impish. "OK. Let's go. The meeting is resuming in a few minutes. No sense in aggravating T-8. Your grandmother seems to have that task well in hand anyway."

We laughed and headed to the conference room. T-8 was standing in front of the white board, waiting for everyone to take a seat. At two minutes past two, Mimi still wasn't there.

"Fin, where's your grandmother?" he snarled.

I cringed. I didn't like him reminding everyone that the executive producer and chief investor was my grandmother. It made me feel like a poser—like I hadn't earned my job. "Dunno," I said. "I haven't seen her since the photo shoot."

T-8 looked disgusted. "I want you to show us what you got at the photo session. Maybe there'll be something we can use for the film's poster." His expression said he highly doubted it. "Since she was at the photo shoot, she can't claim she missed anything if we start without her."

I was angry that Mimi's interference had seemingly turned T-8 against me, but I was confident that he'd have no quarrel with the photos I'd taken. The work was stellar, and the model—well, he was pretty stellar too.

I grabbed the projection cable and plugged it into my Mac. I hoped Austin had uploaded the images right away as I'd asked. Otherwise, I'd have to go back to my office to get the memory cards and the delay would be likely to annoy to T-8 even more than he was already.

I breathed a sigh of relief when I connected to my image gallery and saw the new folder with today's date and the name of the subject. Like his brother Noah, Austin was so responsible he was always a dream to work with

I opened the folder and clicked on the first image. It was Rafe, in his Grecian tunic, seemingly standing on the beach in an ancient city. I'd lit him so it looked like the sun was rising, and he had a dreamy, faraway look in his eyes.

There were murmurs of approval from the other attendees. "Nice work," said the head of makeup. "It looks so real."

T-8 was unwilling to let a single shot mollify his anger, no matter how stunning the image. "Is that the best you've got?" he asked.

"Nope." I clicked over to the next image. More 'oohs and aahs' from the group. I glanced at Rafe sitting beside me, and he had his head down, staring at his hands. He seemed embarrassed that everyone was commenting on his appearance.

After I'd shown a few more images, T-8 started to scowl. "I thought I told you to shoot against a blank screen. Mind you, the background is nice, but what if it's not what we want."

Someone at the far end of the table said, "Why wouldn't we want it? It's perfect."

T-8 scowled again, but before he could snarl anything more, I held up my hand to forestall him.

"I have a bunch against plain screens. They should be coming right up, but I can move right to them if you want."

He nodded curtly. "Please do."

I had no idea why T-8 was being such a jerk, but I'd bet it had something to do with his interaction with Mimi this morning. In a gesture of support, Rafe nudged my knee with his, and I smiled as I searched for the images taken against the plain backdrops.

The onlookers continued to voice their approval as each file came up, but T-8 just stood in the back of the room with his arms folded.

"Enough with the ancient Greeks. What else you got?" he said just as I brought up the last image in the series.

"Hard hat diving," I said, and there was an image of Rafe, blue eyes wide behind the glass of his helmet seemingly floating through clear water with a sunken ship on the ocean bottom behind him. "I can add some fish or sea creatures later if you want."

T-8 grunted but said nothing.

I clicked through the rest of the images, including the ones taken against the blank backgrounds.

T-8 made a rolling motion with his hand that I knew meant 'move on.'

I clicked on the last sub-folder, the one with Rafe dressed as a pirate. Even I was impressed with how good these looked, although I knew by now it was nearly impossible to take a bad picture of Rafe.

The other people in the room continued to show their appreciation for my work. When the last shot came up, I left it on the screen. Someone actually moaned, it was that beautiful.

T-8 stared at it for a minute, his eyes lingering over every detail. "That's the one." He looked at me. "Good work." His tone was flat and sounded like someone had forced the words from his throat against his will.

I didn't care. I knew the entire shoot was fabulous. Not a clinker in the entire reel.

The meeting adjourned after that, and Rafe and I went out the back way to do the late afternoon dive we'd discussed.

Chapter 15
Tarpon Alley

I SENT Rafe on ahead to board the *Tranquility* so he could go below before any of the divers or the people enjoying sunshine and early cocktails at Ray's Place recognized him. He was wearing Liam's goofy hat again, but he also managed to completely change his body, so he once again looked like a frail little old man. I had no idea how he did that, but in my mind, it proved he wasn't just a pretty face but an extremely good actor as well.

Stewie and I carried tanks down the pier, and nobody looked twice at us. I wasn't surprised when he asked, "Where are you headed?" Stewie knew I was prone to taking risks sometimes, so he liked to keep tabs on where I was diving.

"Tarpon Tunnels, I think. Then the Alley. He wants a shark dive, but I'd like to see how he does with a few tarpon and barracuda before I unleash him around the really big boys." Tarpon are large —sometimes growing to over eight feet long. They're also heavy, and they can weigh nearly 300 pounds. Although their size makes them appear formidable, they are not dangerous to humans. And barracuda always show their teeth, but they don't usually bother people who don't bother them first. Both species can look pretty scary if you don't know them.

Stewie chuckled as he slid the tanks into the racks inside the

Tranquility's gunwales. "I don't think a few tarpon will bother Rafe Cummings."

I grinned back at him. "Me either. But I like tarpon."

We chugged slowly over to Tarpon Tunnels, the deeper of the two sites I planned to dive today. After I'd tied up to the mooring, I handed Rafe a small bag from the RIO dive shop. It contained one of the famous lightweight dive skins we all wore in the annual documentaries to protect bodies from stings or accidental scrapes. The sleek dive skin had the RIO logo on the chest. I hadn't had time to have it personalized for him, and besides, he'd probably prefer to remain anonymous given how people tended to mob him when they knew who he was.

He put it on, and after we finished gearing up, we rolled off the gunwales and followed the mooring line down to the reef top at about sixty feet.

We swam along a sandy extension, cluttered with sea rubble and broken coral, until we reached the edge of the drop off. So far, the current was mild, and the visibility was super. We sank over the edge, enjoying the near-vertical wall and the sensation of floating at ease in mid-water.

We'd only gone a little way when we came to one of the tunnels that are the reason for the site's name. It was very likely the tunnel would be teeming with tarpon. I made an 'after you' gesture to signal Rafe that he could go in first. He nodded and swam slowly forward.

I couldn't see past him because the tunnel was narrow, but I knew when he caught sight of the tarpon because he abruptly stopped swimming. He paused a moment, then looked at me over his shoulder. I flashed him the okay sign and he continued.

The tunnel widened after a few more feet, and we were treated to the sight of a dozen or so tarpon, hanging nearly motionless in the dim water. Their downturned mouths made them look angry or unhappy, but tarpon are generally pretty placid. They glided out of our path in a slow stately manner as we approached, never seeming to move quickly or even be aware of us.

On the other side of the tunnel a couple of barracuda swung

around to face us as we swam by. Their mouths were open, showing their fierce looking teeth, but I knew we were safe as long as we didn't do anything they might perceive as threatening. I took several pictures of Rafe with the barracudas and the tarpon in the background.

During our training, I had impressed on him the absolute requirement never to touch the sea life, and he was obeying that dictum. He clasped his hands loosely in front of his body, and he finned slowly and carefully as he proceeded through the tunnel to another exit that led back to the wall.

When he reached the wall, he turned and hung motionless waiting for me to join him. I raised my camera to take a picture, and I caught sight of his beautiful eyes behind his mask. As soon as I emerged from the tunnel, he turned, and as he turned, a gigantic hammerhead shark swam up to him from out of the blue depths. The shark must have been about twelve feet long and probably weighed in the neighborhood of 1,000 pounds. He was sleek, grace-ful, beautiful, and quite possibly deadly.

Now the shark and Rafe were face to snout. Rafe never moved, never flinched, scarcely even breathed. I snapped a picture from my side-on perspective, then took a single gentle kick to change the camera angle. The hammerhead turned his head and tilted it down, so one of his eyes was right in Rafe's face. Rafe's own eyes were huge and luminous behind his mask. I sensed he was feeling no fear, only great joy. I snapped the picture, using the speed burst setting on my camera so I'd have multiple shots to choose from.

The whirring from the camera must have alarmed the hammer-head because he flicked his tail and then he was gone, smoothly disappearing into the deep. Now Rafe's bubbles were coming fast and heavy. I signaled for him to check his air. He did, then gave me the signal for returning to the boat. I signed okay, and we swam slowly up the wall to the reef top.

We meandered across the reef, peering into all the nooks and crannies. We saw several brightly colored creole wrasse flitting through the coral, a tiny yellowhead jawfish no bigger than my palm, and a pair of French angelfish. As we swam across the sandy parts of the reef, a row of gray garden eels ducked undercover as we approached. It was a nice dive, but the last half felt like a bit of a letdown after the close encounter with the hammerhead.

Rafe climbed the ladder in the *Tranquility*'s stern, then I handed him my camera so I could climb unencumbered. He slotted his tank into the rack behind the bench that lined the gunwales and tucked his fins underneath.

"Wow," he said when I sat down across from him. "That was amazing!"

"I promised I would get a shot of you as good as the one of Maddy and the great white, and I think we might have done it today. You were super calm. Good job."

"My heart was beating a mile a minute. I was afraid to breathe. But I looked at you and you kept me steady." He smiled, and it was like the sunrise.

"Some action hero you are," I said with a laugh. "if you need a girl to keep you calm."

"Not just any girl could do it," he said. "It requires a very special one."

I bit my lip and turned my head away. My heart was beating rapidly, and I felt uncomfortable, my mind at war with itself. I couldn't believe Rafe Cummings was coming on to me, but it sure sounded like it. Or was that just my ego talking? And I was upset about my reaction to his words. What about my loyalty to Liam?

I jumped up and filled two stainless steel mugs with water from the cooler in the galley. After handing one to Rafe, I sat back down and turned away to gaze over my shoulder at the sparkling ocean. I didn't want to meet Rafe's eyes, afraid he'd see what I was thinking and feeling right now. He'd probably think I was another silly woman, fancying he was falling for me when he'd probably meant no such thing.

Rafe was sensitive to my mood. "Can we skip the second dive, if that's okay with you? I really want to see the photos you took of me and the big guy down there. And unless that hammerhead comes back, the second dive will seem pretty tame..."

I laughed. "Sure. A hammerhead does have a way of stealing

the show." I climbed the ladder to the flying bridge and started the engines. Rafe stayed below on the deck. I wondered what he was thinking. Had he realized how his words had sounded and hoped to soften the impact by ignoring me now?

On the way back, I concentrated on piloting the *Tranquility*, and within a short time, I'd pulled the boat into her usual slip at RIO. Stewie happened to be on the pier, so Rafe threw him the line. Stewie quickly tied us off to one of the cleats on the dock. Then he hopped aboard and grabbed the empty tanks to lug back to the dive shop.

"Thank you," I called after him.

Rafe was standing on the dock when I climbed down the ladder. He held out a hand to help me disembark. "I'm sorry," he said. "I didn't mean to make you uncomfortable. I was just so excited about that shark. What a rush!"

"No problem," I said. "Of course you were excited. Something as amazing as that doesn't happen on every dive."

Rafe assumed his hunched over posture and pulled Liam's hat down low over his face. We walked slowly to RIO's back door, carrying our gear bags. "Can I take you to dinner tonight? Just as a thank you for what will probably be one of the most memorable experiences of my life."

"I don't think that's a good idea, Rafe. We've been spending a lot of time together and I wouldn't want people to get the wrong idea, especially with Liam out of town."

"Of course," he said. "I understand." He turned away and headed toward the locker room door instead of coming into the office with me.

"Don't you want to come in and see the pictures?" I called after him.

He raised a hand over his head but didn't turn around. "Nope. That's okay." He kept walking.

Chapter 16
A Disastrous Evening

I WAS uneasy with the way Rafe and I had ended our adventure. I wandered around the building for a time but didn't find him anywhere. Eventually, I gave up and decided to head home. I'd work on the images in my office there. I wanted to email a few to Gary Graydon, publisher of *Ecosphere*. They would make a great cover or banner for the magazine's homepage.

Halfway to my house on Rum Point, I pulled into a convenience store and grabbed a pre-made sandwich for my dinner. I continued on home, leaving my car in the driveway so I could start my evening those few seconds sooner.

When I opened the gate to my backyard, Chico and Henrietta, our free-range rooster and hen, burst through the doggie door Liam had installed in the fence that separated our two properties. They were excited to see me. As they raced over to greet me, Chico crowed and Henrietta murmured, "Tut. Tut."

They stood politely by my sliding glass door, waiting for me to open it up and feed them. They always stayed outside unless I invited them in. I smiled at their excellent manners.

After pouring a scoop of seeds in each of two bowls and filling a larger dish with cool water, I placed all the dishes on the ground outside the door. These free range chickens might have excellent manners, but still, they were sloppy eaters. I turned on some soft music to play through the outdoor speakers. I walked outside, kicked off my flip-flops, and sat on the edge of the pool with my feet in the water. The tension was just leaving my shoulders when my front doorbell chimed.

I couldn't imagine who would be ringing my bell. Most of my friends knew I was rarely at home, and even then, I was almost always working. Then I thought it might be Benjamin or Chaun, two friends who lived nearby. Or Oliver and Genevra. People I'd be happy to see, and who would know enough to come around to the back if I didn't answer the door. I thought about ignoring the bell, but then my curiosity got the better of me.

I didn't want to walk through the house with wet feet, and I hadn't brought a towel outside with me, so I went through the gate and walked around to the front of the house. Rafe Cummings stood at my door, a bouquet of flowers and a shopping bag from Fosters in his hands.

I hesitated, then thought, *He's just being friendly. And since he can't go anywhere on his own, he's probably lonely and bored.* "Hello! Come on around this way. My feet are wet, so I don't want to go through the house."

His face broke out into that glorious smile as he headed my way. He held out the flowers. "These are for you." Then he hoisted the Foster's bag higher. "And I brought dinner. Since you wouldn't let me take you to dinner, I brought dinner to you. I'm cooking."

What woman in her right mind could resist Rafe Cummings offering to cook? I peeked into the bag. Prime steaks, baking potatoes, and salad fixings. Ice cream.

"Yum. Thanks for thinking of this," I said.

He laughed. "It's the least I could do."

When we got to the backyard, he walked through the slider and put the food in the refrigerator. He stood in the kitchen, looking around. "Nice place. It looks like you. It has that same easy, warm, comfortable feeling you give off. I like it." He paused a moment. "Can I see the photos you took today before I start cooking? I'm dying to see them."

I laughed. "Me too. Let's go to my office." I wiped the last traces of dampness off my feet on the way inside. Chico and Henrietta followed us down the hall to my office.

I set up my computer to project on the giant monitor on my desk and opened the folder with today's photos on it. Rafe was polite as I clicked through the images of filefish and sergeant majors. He leaned a little forward when he saw the tarpon and barracuda shots, and he stood up and began pacing as I came closer to the shots of him and the shark.

"You sure you want to see these?" I teased.

He growled. "You know I do."

I clicked over to the following image. It was stunning. So was the next one. And the one after that. In fact, they all were. We spent a few minutes deciding which was the best. "I'm going to have this one blown up and framed to hang in my office, opposite the one of Maddy and the great white," I said.

"Will you make one for me too? I'll pay for it," he said.

"No, you won't. Consider it a trade for dinner. Speaking of which…"

He laughed. "Got a grill?"

I showed him how to work the grill, and while it was heating, he placed the steaks in a marinade he whipped together from the spices, vinegars, and oils he'd brought. He put the potatoes on the grill since they'd take longer to cook, chopped the veggies into a salad, and mashed strawberries to go with the ice cream for dessert. He cleaned everything up as he worked, so by the time he finished his prep, the kitchen was already spotless.

I watched in awe. "Can I help?" I'd asked when he started his performance.

"I doubt it," he said, laughing. "I know you don't cook."

Since this was true, the best I could do would be to set the table, so I took care of that task. When everything was ready, we sat at the round table under the pergola in the backyard. I was amazed at how delicious the simple food was.

I swallowed the last bite of my ice cream. "Thank you so much for doing this. There was no need, but it was wonderful."

He grinned. "No problem. I love to cook, and since it's hard for me to eat in restaurants without getting mobbed, I figured I should learn to do it well."

As far as I could tell, Rafe Cummings did everything well.

Even though we were in the shade, it was still hot. "Mind if I swim?" he asked.

"Be my guest."

He took off his T-shirt, placed his phone and his wallet on the table, and dove in. I took off the outer layer of my clothes, revealing the bathing suit I always wore underneath and dove in after him. We each swam a few lengths, then hoisted ourselves up to sit side by side on the tiled edge of the pool with our feet in the water.

Chico and Henrietta had gone back through the doggie door to sleep in the coop Liam had built for them in his yard next door. The sun set; the moon rose; and the twinkling fairy lights along the fence came on. Soft music played through the hidden outdoor speakers.

Rafe leaned over and kissed me. His lips were soft, and his touch was gentle. I closed my eyes, and the kiss continued.

I jumped back when I heard Liam's voice. "Hey, mate. What are you doing? That's my fiancée you're locking lips with."

Chapter 17
An Awkward Conversation

WITHOUT USING HIS HANDS, Rafe leaped to his feet and landed on the pool deck facing Liam. He stuck out his hand. "You must be Liam. Fin's told me a lot about you. I'm very happy to finally meet you." He didn't seem the least bit surprised or upset about Liam catching him kissing me.

I, on the other hand, was trying not to vomit while at the same time attempting to become invisible. I hadn't heard from Liam in over a month, and then here he shows up, unannounced, and at the worst possible moment. What must he be thinking? And what had I been thinking, kissing Rafe Cummings?

I stood up slowly. Liam was still staring at Rafe's outstretched hand. His jaw was clenched, and his eyes blinked rapidly. When I reached him, I put my hand on his shoulder. "I think we need to talk."

"Ya think?" he said, but instead of staying to talk, he turned away and walked out the gate.

Rafe reached out to take my hand. "I'm so sorry. I don't know what I was thinking," he said. "I hope I haven't screwed things up between you and your fiancé."

I bit my lip. "Liam and I have been through a lot together. We'll work it out." At least I hoped we'd work it out.

"I should go," Rafe said.

I nodded and thanked him for dinner. The evening had been lovely—more fun and relaxing than any recent evening I could remember. I wondered how much of that was due to Rafe himself, and how much was owing to the novelty of spending time with the hottest movie star in the world. I needed to figure that out—and fast.

Rafe touched my face, looking deep into my eyes. He stepped away and pulled his T-shirt back on, stuck his hands in his pockets and walked out the gate. I was shaking, but I had no idea why. Everything would be fine. At least, I hoped so.

I stepped over to the gate between Liam's yard and mine. My hand hesitated at the latch, but I gathered my courage and went through.

Liam was sitting in the gliding loveseat on his back deck, idly tossing seeds to Henrietta. As I did every time I saw him, I noticed how devastatingly good-looking he is. Wherever his travels had taken him this time, the sun had bleached his hair into streaks of gold and near white. He had a day's worth of stubble on his face, and it looked great on him. His blue RIO-branded T-shirt was sweaty and a little grubby from the rigors of travel, but it still emphasized the color of his extraordinary eyes. I'd never seen him look so good, nor so downcast. He didn't glance up as I approached.

I walked over and sat beside him. "Where's Chico?" It was a rare occasion that Henrietta and the rooster were not close together.

"He's tired. Went to bed." He stretched and stood. "I think I will too."

"It didn't mean anything, Liam." There was a tremor in my voice.

Liam paused, his back to me. "What didn't mean anything? Us, or you kissing a movie star." He walked through his sliding glass door, locked it, and pulled the window coverings over the glass, blocking my view. The outside lights went off.

I felt more alone than I had since Ray's death.

Chapter 18
Mimi

I ROLLED out of bed at dawn the next morning. The sea relic exhibition opened today, and I couldn't be late. Aside from my usual duties, I had all that to contend with, including a luncheon with the donors and the planning committee, and the grand opening ceremony this evening. I couldn't imagine smiling at all those people. All I really wanted to do was hide my head under the covers and weep.

The ocean is my happy place, and I desperately needed a dive to sooth my ragged edges, but I had neither the time nor the energy. I dressed in a slightly more formal version of what I wore to work most days. Black pants instead of cargo shorts and a blue RIO polo shirt with a collar instead of a tee. In place of my usual rubber flip-flops, I slid my feet into a pair of leather sandals. I zipped a gray blazer into a garment bag for the luncheon. This evening, I'd change at Newton's into something more formal for the gala. Unless the earth opened and swallowed me first, which I profoundly hoped it would.

I stopped at RIO's café to pick up coffee and a muffin. I broke off a small piece of the muffin, but I couldn't eat it. I ended up throwing most of the muffin away.

My desk phone rang, and I considered ignoring it. I didn't want to talk to anyone, but the whole staff was working hard to make the exhibition a success. It was my responsibility to be there for them.

"What?" I said. There was no warmth in my voice.

I heard Christophe's sexy French accent, but even that couldn't brighten my day. "Can you come to ze pool house, s'il vous plaît? It's important."

"Be right there," I said with a sigh.

I was trudging down the hall when I heard the approaching sirens. "No. Oh no!" I started to run, my sandals slipping on the tiled floors.

I skidded to a halt beside Christophe. At his feet, what looked like a soggy bundle of rags and a widening pool of blood stopped my heart.

"Mimi," I screamed, as I dropped to my feet to roll her over.

Christophe stopped me before I could touch her. "She's breathing on her own and her pulse is steady. Better if you don't move her until we know the extent of her injuries. EMTs are on their way." He pulled me to my feet and put his sinewy arms around me to stop my shivering. I buried my head in his shoulder to block out the sight of all the blood.

The pool house door slammed open, caroming off the tile wall as the EMTs rushed in. I kept my face hidden in Christophe's shoulder until I felt a reassuring hand on my arm.

"I'll take over from here," said Liam. He pulled me into his arms where I sobbed inconsolably. I didn't know whether I was crying for Mimi or crying with relief that Liam still cared enough to comfort me. I only knew I needed him there.

Liam led me over to the nearby bleachers and up to the far corner of the top row. From there, I couldn't see what was going on with Mimi even if I tried to look. Which I wasn't about to do. I kept my head tucked into Liam's shoulder.

After a few minutes I whispered, "I just found her. I never even had a chance to get to know her, and now I'm going to lose her."

He stroked my hair. "Let the medics do what they do. Maybe things will turn out okay." It was comforting enough that I dared to turn my head when I heard Dane Scott's voice.

Dane watched the medics work for a minute, talking to the leader of the team. Roland was beside him, carrying his ubiquitous forensics case. A few minutes later Dane must have noticed us up in the bleachers because he took the bleacher tiers two at a time.

"Any idea what happened?" he asked when he sat down beside me.

I shook my head. "Christophe found her and called me. He called the medics before he called you or me. I don't know anything about what happened."

"She's unconscious, but her heart is still going strong," he said. "There's something on the pool deck I'd like you to take a look at if you feel up to it."

"Is she going to make it?" I asked, my heart full of hope.

He shrugged, but his eyes were warm and full of sympathy. "I'm not the one you should ask about that. I'm a cop, not a doctor." He took my hand. "Can you look at the object we found now?"

"I'll go with you," said Liam. "You're still my fiancé, and you shouldn't have to face this alone."

The three of us walked over to where Roland was making a small pile of bagged and labeled items he'd found at the scene. Dane nodded to him, who pulled a large plastic bag with a long dark colored object in it.

"Recognize this?" he asked.

I nodded. "It was…is…Mimi's. She was using it after her teak walking stick went missing."

"Thought so," Dane said. "Well, it's a sure bet she didn't bash herself over the head with it, so I guess she's off the hook for murdering Jeffrie West. It's too far-fetched to think we have two people running around whacking people with walking sticks in your pool house."

I started to relax, until I remembered I was Dane's only other suspect. "What now?" I asked.

"Now that Liam's back in town, I'd guess you have an alibi for this one, so you're off the hook too. Roland and I will have to keep looking."

"Liam and I weren't together last night. Or this morning," I blurted out. "We had a fight." I could have kicked myself as soon as the words were out of my mouth.

Liam took my hand. "But I can vouch for the fact she was home alone all night because I was awake and watching her house. And I followed her car to work this morning, so I know she had no time to do something like this."

Dane looked surprised. "Everything okay? Was somebody threatening you? Is that why Liam had to watch your house?"

I shook my head. "No threats. Liam and I weren't together because we'd had a fight." Heat suffused my cheeks.

"I was watching to see if that jerk came back. Or if you went out." There was no mistaking the coldness in Liam's voice.

"I assume I'm the jerk you're referring to?" Rafe's mellifluous voice came from the locker room door. "No worries, friend. I admit was out of line. Fin did nothing to encourage me. I get the picture now, and I'll back off."

I could hear Liam's sub-vocal growl, but he didn't say anything to Rafe. He turned back to Dane. "Fin's in the clear, right?"

"It would seem so," Dane was obviously relieved that he wasn't going to have to arrest either the daughter or mother of his significant other, but I could sense his frustration at the lack of progress in the case.

One of the EMTs came over to talk to Dane.

I heard the words "coma" and "hospital.'

"I'm going too," I said. I hadn't known Mimi long, but I realized I already loved her. Sure, she was pushy and a bit of a busybody, but I didn't have many family members. I cherished every single one I had.

Chapter 19
Hospital

"I'LL TAKE YOU," said Liam. "You shouldn't be driving, and you shouldn't be alone."

The set of his lips told me he was still angry about finding me kissing Rafe Cummings, but it was obvious he still cared about me. I could fix this, and I would, once I was sure Mimi was all right.

As soon as we were in Liam's car, I called Maddy to let her know her mother was in a coma at Cayman Islands Hospital. She didn't answer, so I left a message asking her to call me. Then I called my brother Oliver, realizing as I pushed the call button that Oliver didn't even know Mimi existed yet. He didn't answer either, so I recorded another message.

Finally, I called Newton. My brother worked for him, so I knew he'd know where Oliver was, and he'd break the news to him. He'd also be the best one to take care of Maddy if the news upset her, since the investigation would probably consume Dane's time for hours.

"Hey, Fin. What's up?" Newton said when he answered my call.

I told him what had happened to Mimi, and that I couldn't get in touch with Oliver or Maddy. "They need someone to take care of them when they hear the news." My voice was shaking.

"Who is taking care of you?" he asked. "You need someone with you too."

"Liam's with me," I said. "I'm fine."

"I didn't expect Liam back for a few more days," Newton said. The two men worked together closely, since Newton was Liam's primary investor, and they shared a strong interest in environmental protection.

"Well, he's here," I said. "Do you need to talk to him?"

"No need. We'll catch up at the hospital. Oliver is in a meeting right now, but I'll get Gus to sit in for him. We'll leave here as soon as Gus arrives, and then Oliver and I will pick up your mother. I'll see you at the hospital in about a half hour." He disconnected without saying goodbye, as usual. His mind worked so quickly he'd already moved well beyond this phone call to his next steps.

Liam dropped me at the hospital's main entrance and then drove away to park the car. I asked the receptionist where Mimi was, and by the time she'd looked up the record and told me I couldn't see her, Liam was with me.

I blinked back tears when the receptionist said we couldn't go in, but Liam smiled his most glorious smile. "Please ask the doctor to give us an update when he can. This is Mrs. Anderson's granddaughter, Finola Fleming. The rest of the family will be here soon. We're all very worried, and we'd appreciate any news we can get."

Since I'm a little bit famous, the receptionist might have recognized my name, but it was more likely that Liam's good looks and lovely manners had her totally charmed. At any rate, she seemed more sympathetic and directed us to a private waiting room. She promised to ask the doctor to come by when he could.

Liam brought me a glass of water as soon as I sat down. He sat in a chair facing me, obviously still angry about finding me with Rafe.

He knitted his brows. "How could you do that to me? To us?" he said. "Kissing someone else while I was out of town."

I tried to rein in my temper. Yes, Rafe had kissed me, and I hadn't stopped him, but it's not like Liam hadn't made his own missteps. "I'm not the only one with a reason to be distrustful. I forgave you and trusted you after you went back to Australia to divorce the wife you'd conveniently forgotten to mention. Then you ghosted me for a year. Not a word. Not even a text. Just like the last month."

He tightened his lips. "I told you it was hard to track Amelia down. She didn't want me to find her. She was in the Outback, for God's sake. And then I got sidetracked by...well, you know. The other thing that I do."

"The other job you have that you can't or won't tell me about? And when you disappear to who knows where—because you've lied about where you were going in the past—I'm just supposed to be okay with that?"

He looked a little shocked at the anger in my voice. "Fin, you know I'm one of the good guys."

"Really?" I said. "How would I know that? You promised when you started your new company that you'd call everyday while you were away. You just got back from a three month trip. How many calls were there? Let me count." I rolled my eyes. "Oh, yeah. None."

"But I've never kissed anyone except you, not since the first day I met you. I love you. Always have and always will. I'm just unhappy about coming home, hoping to surprise you, and I'm the one who gets surprised. There you are, kissing the biggest movie star in the world like I don't even exist. It'll take me some time to wrap my head around seeing that. I need space to come to grips with what I saw."

I took a sip of water for courage. "You don't have to stay if it makes you uncomfortable. I know you're upset." I prayed he would stay.

But he just said "Okay." Then he walked out of the room without looking back.

I blinked back my tears, but they were still brimming over my lashes when Newton, Maddy, and Oliver walked in. Newton noticed my tears right away and came over to sit beside me on the small loveseat. "You're freezing," he said, chafing my hand. "I know you can't relax completely but try to trust that the doctors are

97

doing everything they can." He looked around. "Liam go for coffee?"

Against my will, my lip quivered. I looked away. Luckily, Doc raced in through the waiting room door just then, so I didn't have to answer. She went directly to her best friend Maddy and gave her a hug. "What have they told you? Anything?"

Maddy shook her head and said, "Nothing yet."

Doc looked at each of us, and one-by-one we each shook our heads.

"Ridiculous," she snorted and stomped out of the room. I knew she'd be back with a full report within minutes.

Nobody moved. The room was so still I didn't think we were even breathing. The door burst open, and Doc returned with a man in a white coat. "This is Doctor Henry," she said. "He's caring for your mother, Maddy."

He cleared his throat and looked down at the iPad in his hands. "Finola Anderson. Eighty-seven year old female is unconscious. She has a large wound on her head caused by a blow with a hard, rounded, or tubular object. It took fifteen stitches to close the wound. She shows no signs that she is in pain or aware of her surroundings…"

Doc held up her hand. "Prognosis?"

"Difficult to predict at this time. We'll know more in twenty-four hours. I recommend we wait and see."

"Thanks," said Doc. "I'll check with you later."

Doctor Henry left the room.

Doc went to her best friend and sat on the arm of her chair. "It'll be fine. Don't you worry," she said.

Maddy was crying. "I was so mean to her. Even now, all these years later I couldn't forgive her…"

Doc stroked Maddy's pale blonde hair. "Hush. She knows you love her. Stay positive. Everything will work out fine."

Oliver rose and gave Doc his seat next to Maddy. He pulled up a chair facing the loveseat where Newton and I sat. "You never even told me she was here. I didn't get a chance to meet her. What if she doesn't make it?" He was angry and sad.

I bit my lip. "I'm sorry, Oliver. You haven't been around much, and it's only been a few days. We're both busy. I figured you'd meet at the gala tonight." I would have been furious if he'd done to me what I'd done to him. Family means everything to both of us.

Oliver glared at me. "Am I a real part of this family, or do you still think of me as an outsider? Because I have to say, when stuff like this happens and you don't clue me in, it feels like I'm an interloper."

I opened my mouth to respond, although I had no idea what I would say. Luckily, I didn't have to say anything because Liam walked through the door, carrying a tray of drinks and a bag of baked goodies. He put them down on the coffee table in the center of the room. "Something for everyone," he said. "I brought every-one's favorites.

He handed a cup of tea to Maddy, along with two delicate lemon cookies on a napkin. He'd brought sodas for Oliver and Newton, and lemonade for me. He passed around the bag of cookies and slices of cake, and everyone took something to munch on.

He sat down and looked at me. I looked at him.

He shrugged. "Sorry I've been a jerk. Don't worry about us. I'll get over it, and we'll be fine."

I thought my heart would burst with joy. It might take time, but we would get through this. Eventually, Liam would understand that Rafe had been the one to instigate the kiss and that I hadn't meant to hurt him.

Newton shrugged and took a bite of his cookie. "That's one problem settled," he said. "Now let's worry about Finola. And you, Oliver." He put his hand on Oliver's shoulder. "Never, never, never think you aren't a real and vital part of this family. We adopted you because we love you, and that will never, ever change."

Oliver bobbed his head a little. "Thanks. I needed to hear that."

He settled back with a sigh just as the door to the waiting room burst open. Genevra and Joely rushed in. I moved to another seat, leaving the spot next to Newton open for Joely.

She smiled her thanks and sat beside Newton. He took her hand

and visibly relaxed. Now that Joely had arrived, it seemed he felt freer to show his concern for his former mother-in-law. He settled back on the loveseat and closed his eyes. His face was somber.

Genevra spoke before she sat down. "I pushed back the exhibition opening and the gala for a few days," she said to me. "Joely helped with the arrangements, so you don't have to do anything but think good thoughts."

I sighed with relief. "Thank you." Genevra was truly a gem. I rarely had to tell her what to do. She always thought ahead and took the initiative on key projects. She'd even saved my life once, although she denies it.

She sat in the empty seat beside Oliver and put her arm around his shoulders. They huddled together for a minute before Oliver sat back and spoke.

"There better not be any more secret family members lurking in the background. It isn't fair not to let us know we have relatives. It should be our choice if we want to get to know them." He shut his mouth with an air of finality and slouched back on the uncomfortable chair.

His words sent terror into my heart. As far as I was aware, I was the only person in the room who knew the truth about Oliver's birth father, who was one of the bad guys. It would kill him when he found out, and I also knew it was only a matter of time until his malevolent twin sister Lily would use the knowledge to twist a knife in her brother's heart.

Should I tell him what I knew? When Lily wanted to hurt him, she'd be sure to let him know that I'd known the truth, just to add an extra little fillip of pain. I bit my lip. There was little hope that Lily would be able to resist hurting him for very long, but I wasn't about to bring his world crashing down on him. Especially now when he was worried about his new-found grandmother.

Someday he would have to deal with the knowledge that his father was Seb Lukin, notorious drug dealer, human trafficker, and all around bad guy, but not today. And not at my hand.

We sat in silence for a while, fiddling with our phones or leafing through ancient magazines on obscure topics. Doctor Henry came in, and stood just inside the door, looking uncomfortable. He cleared his throat.

"You can see her now," he said.

"She's awake?" I smiled with joy until he shook his head.

"No, she's sliding deeper into the coma. I don't know if it will do her any good, but you should all go talk to her. Tell her happy things, or things you need to say that you might never get a chance to. It's possible the sounds of your voices will get through to her..." He shook his head and shrugged. "Possible."

He left the room while Doc glared at his back and put her arm around Maddy to console her. It was obvious she didn't think much of his bedside manner. The only sound to break the silence was Maddy's weeping.

Chapter 20
ICU

Mimi was in the ICU, so even though Doctor Henry had said we could see her, they still only allowed us to go in one at a time. Maddy went first, of course.

Newton was next in line because he'd known Mimi since he was nine years old. Before going in, he told us about the first time he met Mimi. It was at a Christmas party thrown by his parents. It had also been the first time he'd met Maddy, and during the party, he'd told Mimi that he would probably marry Maddy someday.

Oliver and I snuck in together after Newton came out. Since Oliver had never met Mimi, he was shy about barging in, even though she was unconscious.

I was shocked when I saw her. I knew someone had bashed her on the head, putting her in a coma, but her appearance was still scary. The crown of her head was swathed in thick white bandages, and she was so pale that her skin was practically the same color as the dressings.

She had several tubes in her arms, and there were multiple monitors showing her vital signs. I took a quick glance and noticed her blood pressure, oxygen saturation, heart rate and respirations were all low. My spirits plunged. I'd been hoping Doctor Henry had exaggerated the situation, but that didn't seem to be the case.

Even so, I crossed the room and picked up her hand. "I'm here, Mimi. Now that we've met, I can't imagine letting you go so soon. Please come back to us."

I jumped when she unexpectedly squeezed my hand. "She heard me," I whispered to Oliver. "I know she did."

Oliver looked skeptical, but he didn't say anything to dash my hopes. He was too sweet a guy for that. Instead, he came closer, pulling up a chair as he did.

I took his hand and placed it in Mimi's. "I've brought someone you need to meet. It's your grandson, Oliver Fleming-Russo. He is amazing. You're going to love him as much as the rest of us do. You have to wake up. You can't go without having a chance to get to know him."

Oliver sat quietly for a minute before speaking. "Hello, Mimi. Fin's told me all about you. I've really been looking forward to meeting you. Please come back and give me a chance to get to know you."

I was hoping she'd squeeze his hand too, but he shook his head when I looked over at him with the question in my eyes.

Just then the nurse bustled in. "I told you one at a time. You'll overtire her. You both have to leave now anyway since visiting hours are over, but next time, remember the rules. You wouldn't want to make her worse by being selfish, would you?" She put her hands on her hips and narrowed her eyes, practically daring us to defy her, but we left meekly. We definitely didn't want to do anything that could reduce Mimi's chances of recovery.

Our family and friends were waiting for us by the nurse's station when we emerged from Mimi's room. Newton said, "Anyone hungry? I can have something delivered to my place if you are and don't want to cook or go out.

"Thanks, Newton," said Maddy. "But I'm beat. I just want to go home."

"I'll take you," said Doc.

Maddy nodded and gave Oliver and me a hug. Maddy was still a little frail from her recent cancer treatment, so she and Doc decided to take the elevator instead of the stairs.

Genevra and Oliver exchanged glances. Oliver lived in Maddy's condo, and Genevra rented an apartment in a building Liam owned downtown. "We're going to stay in at Genevra's tonight. Promise to call us if you hear anything." They walked to the exit door at the end of the hall and took the stairs down.

"I hope you don't mind, Newton, but I've been away for months, and I just want to spend some quiet time with Fin," Liam said. "I haven't even had a chance to unpack.

A huge smile broke out on my face.

"Just you and me then, Joely. You ready?" She reached for Newton's hand, and we all took the stairs down to the ground floor.

Chapter 21
A Sunset Dive

As soon as he started the engine, Liam said, "Where to? Home or RIO? I could go for a nice, easy, relaxing, recreational dive if you're up for it."

Liam always knew exactly what I needed, and whenever I'm stressed, a dive is always what I need. "RIO. Definitely RIO. I can't wait to get in the water."

"Good," he said. "I have something I want to show you anyway." He wiggled his eyebrows at me.

Laughing, I said "I think I've seen it before."

"Nope," he said smugly. "You have not seen this."

We parked at RIO and stopped by the employee gear lockers outside the dive shop to pick up our wetsuits. I poked my head in the door to let Stewie know we were going diving and would be back in a couple of hours.

"Will you call if you hear anything about my grandmother?" I asked Stewie. Since he and Doc were in a relationship, she would be sure to let him know. "Leave a voicemail if I don't answer."

"Will do," he said. Then he winked at Liam. "She's all ready for you."

"She who?" I asked, puzzled.

Liam laughed. "You'll see."

We picked up our tanks and gear bags and walked toward the pier. There was a striking thirty-six foot Munson dive boat parked in the slip across from mine. Her hull was so white it glowed in the sunlight, and benches and tank racks lined the port side of the gunwales of the open deck, and a small gate in the stern leading to a swim platform. Two ocean kayaks hung on the starboard side, with the paddles stowed beneath them. There was a mini-sized galley.

The boat reminded me of my own *Tranquility*. "What a great boat. It looks so comfortable, and plenty of space for diving. And I love the kayaks. I wonder who owns it."

"I do," said Liam. "I'm really glad you like it."

I noticed the boats name, *Enviroman*. "I should have guessed it was yours." I smiled up at Liam, and for the first time since he'd been home, the lines of stress in his face relaxed.

He smiled back. "I was thinking if we have a large group of divers, we take the *Tranquility*. But if it's just you and me, or we feel like taking out the kayaks, we can use *Enviroman*. Sound good?"

I was excited. "An excellent plan. Can we take her out for this dive? I can't wait to try her out."

He grinned at me. "Yup, let's do that. Stewie said she's ready, but there's really only one way to be sure." Liam stepped onto the boat's deck and slotted his tanks in the rack.

"Permission to come aboard, Captain," I said.

"Permission granted, my lady." He stowed my tanks and gear bag, then offered me a hand to help me aboard. "Where to?"

I thought a minute. "How about Dangerous Dan's Dropoff? You probably don't want to take her too far on the maiden voyage." Dangerous Dan's is a deep wall dive, and the coral is spectacular.

"Sure. It's a great site," he said.

Liam sat in the captain's chair and started the engine. I sat on one of the benches in the stern of the boat, and we took off at a stately pace.

Enviroman was a nice change. I loved my boat, and the *Tranquility* was a lot cushier than *Enviroman* since Newton had retrofitted my boat to make it feel homier after I'd inherited it from Ray.

I often lived in the boat a few days a week, but at heart, it was a serious dive boat.

Enviroman rode the waves easily, and Liam was a good captain. We made our way to the planned dive site quickly. I sat on the bench in the stern, relaxing under the Bimini canopy.

Liam brought *Enviroman* up close to the mooring ball, and I hooked the line with a long handled gaff. Once the boat was secure, I raised my arm so Liam would know it was okay to shut down the engines.

The silence was wonderful. There wasn't another boat anywhere in sight. I started setting up for the dive. Liam pulled his gear bag out from under the bench and began connecting his regulator and his tank to his buoyancy control device, known as a BCD.

We finished our set ups at the same time. Liam smiled. "Do you have a dive plan? Will you be bringing your camera?"

"Nope. No camera. And you're the skipper. I defer to your plan."

He nodded. "Okay. We go down the anchor line. I'll check for current when we reach depth to decide on a direction. Maximum depth is one hundred feet. Turnaround at 1500 PSI. Sound good?"

It was a pretty standard dive plan for us, and we'd been to the site often enough that we didn't need a map. "Sounds good."

I shuffled to the dive platform at the stern and used the gunwale to steady myself while I put on my fins. I put one hand over my mask and regulator to make sure I didn't lose them and did a giant stride entry.

I bobbed up to give Liam the OK sign, then I kicked away a few feet to give him room. His entry was perfect. Barely a splash. He gave the signal to descend, and we started down.

We swam at an angle toward the drop off, descending slowly as we crossed the stunning reef and then dropping a little bit faster when we reached the wall, which started at about eighty-five feet. After we'd cleared the lip of the wall, Liam paused to check for current. He signaled the direction we would take, heading into the current on the way out so it would help propel us home on the way back when our energy might be flagging. We leveled off at one hundred feet, and swam slowly along the spectacular wall, peering into the crevices in the coral.

Every few feet I turned and looked out at the deep blue haze, checking to see if there was anything interesting passing by. The second time I looked out into infinity, I saw a Caribbean reef shark and a shiny great barracuda flying by. They were completely uninterested in us and just continued toward whatever their objective was.

We were hovering near the wall, peering at a large fire coral when a gigantic southern stingray flew off the edge and swooped by us. I smiled at the sight, and Liam took my hand, and we continued swimming slowly along the magnificent wall.

I breathed a sigh of relief through my regulator. The ocean is my happy place, and just being underwater drains all my stress and tension away. Since Liam and I nearly always held hands while cruising a wall, the fact that he'd reached out to me convinced me our relationship would be okay.

We stopped to admire a fat spiny lobster sitting in a crevice, with just his antenna showing to give his position away. As we turned from the lobster, a massive black grouper darted out from behind a nearby fan coral. He headed down the wall, probably to avoid a closer encounter with us since black grouper are normally very shy around divers.

We both reached the turnaround point on our air at the same time, so we swam slowly up the wall to the reef top, where we saw a midnight parrotfish, and dozens of tiny hamlets darting about the coral. A gorgeous queen triggerfish circled back and forth in front of us as we swam toward the mooring line.

Back on *Enviroman*, we both racked our tanks. Liam handed me a mug of water and sat beside me on the bench. "Do you mind if we skip the second dive? I was up all night and I'm beat. Plus, you've had a tough day, and I don't want to wear you out."

"Fine by me," I said. "I want to check in with T-8 and see what my filming schedule is for the next week. And I'm dying to show Gary the pictures I got of a hammerhead yesterday. I think at least one of them might be prizeworthy." I didn't mention that the prize-worthy one included Rafe Cummings.

Liam started the boat, and we motored slowly back to RIO. He slid *Enviroman* expertly into her slip and hopped down from the flying bridge, skipping over the last few rungs of the ladder in his eagerness to join me. He took my hand and we headed for the dock.

Rafe Cummings shouting my name as he ran toward us broke the silence.

"Fin. Fin. Come see the movie poster T-8 put together. It's amazing, and it's all your photos." He pulled up in front of us, wearing Liam's cap along with the rest of his old man disguise. He was totally out of breath from running and shouting, and so excited he'd forgotten about not drawing attention from the usual crowd at Ray's Place.

He inhaled slowly and turned to Liam. "I owe you a big apology. I'm sorry for what I did. Fin didn't encourage me in any way. I was totally out of line. I promise it won't happen again." He stuck out his hand. "Friends?"

I held my breath, unsure how Liam would react.

He hesitated for just a split second before taking Rafe's extended hand. "I trust my fiancée implicitly. I know she didn't do anything to encourage you, and I appreciate your apology." He grinned. "Just don't let me catch you at it again, Mate. It won't be pretty."

Rafe laughed. "Then I'll make sure you don't catch me next time."

Liam did not laugh.

Chapter 22
The Poster

THE THREE OF us strolled down the dock toward shore, where T-8 stood waiting for us. He wore his usual artfully worn jeans and perfectly faded rock star t-shirt. He'd turned his navy blue ball cap backwards on his head, so the bill covered his neck. Heavy dark glasses so dense you couldn't see even a glimpse of his eyes through them covered most of his face.

He smiled when we reached him and held out his hand. "You must be Liam. Glad to meet you," he said.

"Likewise," said Liam. "I'm a big fan."

T-8 smiled. "Yeah, of course. Fin, come see the poster I put together using those photos you took. I think it's pretty awesome as it is, but I'd like your input."

"Sure," I said. "As long as Liam is invited too. Otherwise, it'll have to wait until tomorrow."

T-8 tightened his lips. It looked like he was about to refuse to include Liam, but Rafe piped up.

"He's invited. The more the merrier. Isn't that right, Bro?" He stared at T-8, daring him to contradict his star.

T-8 glared at Rafe, but after a second, he seemed to relax. "Come along then. Can we use your office? It's more private than the conference room."

"Sure thing," I said. I took Liam's hand, and we walked along beside T-8 and Rafe. Rafe was wearing Liam's cap, dressed in his old man disguise as we crossed the lawn to RIO's rear door.

Liam turned his head to observe Rafe. "Nice disguise," he said. "I'd never have recognized..." He paused. "Wait just a minute. Is that my hat?"

Rafe kept limping along as though he hadn't heard Liam's question.

I put my hand on Liam's arm. "I'm sorry. It is your hat. I gave it to him. He needed a disguise to get by the fans when we came back from his open water certification dives. I'll get you another one."

Liam laughed. "No, I want that one back when he's finished with it. And I want it autographed."

Rafe didn't say anything, just continued on his way, looking for all the world like a little old man. But he did raise his arm over his head and flash Liam the OK sign. He tried to hide it, but I saw Liam's grin.

Rafe had used his security badge to unlock the rear door by the time T-8, Liam and I reached it. We trooped down the hall to my office. T-8 had already set his computer up on the round table in the corner, and moved the cable from my Mac to his PC so he could project on my huge high-def monitor. We crowded around to see his creation.

"Tada," he said when the image came up. It was a great looking poster, and showed exactly what the movie was about—a series of interconnected stories of people retrieving treasures from the ocean.

The central image was one of the ones I'd taken of Rafe in the pirate costume. Pictures of Rafe as a hard hat diver and Rafe as an ancient pearl diver formed part of a circle around the central photo. There were multiple blank spaces that T-8 had filled in with stick figure drawings that represented Rafe in the other vignettes. The artist had done a nice job on the poster's background, which was a watery blue green tone, with the lettering of the movie title styled to look as though it were underwater.

It was a good poster. I knew how to make it great. "Um, T-8. I have another image to show you that I think would make the poster even more compelling."

"I hope you haven't been holding out on me. Your contract says you don't have the rights to any images taken on set..."

Rafe's eyes were shining. "I know exactly the one she means, Bro. I assure you there's no way she took the image on set. We were on a private dive, on our own time. Show him, Fin."

I reconnected the cable to my Mac and searched through my files until I found the folder I wanted. I clicked. The image of Rafe eye to eye with the hammerhead came up. There was a moment of stunned silence.

"Wow," said Liam finally. "That's as good as the one you took of Maddy and the great white." He looked at the wall behind my desk where that near life size image hung.

T-8 was staring at my screen. "It's a great photo," he said. "But it doesn't fit in with any of the stories in the movie. I'd like to find a way to use it, but right now it just won't work."

I bit back my disappointment. "That's okay. I actually owe *Ecosphere* right of first refusal anyway."

That statement obviously aroused T-8's competitive instincts because he said, "What will it cost us to buy them out?" He paused. "If I can think of a way to use it, of course."

I knew that even though it would be a huge coup for his magazine to publish it first, Gary Graydon at *Ecosphere* wouldn't have any problem relinquishing his right to purchase the image. He and Liam were best buddies, and Liam actually owned *Ecosphere*, so they would do whatever was best for me. But T-8 didn't have to know all that.

"I'll talk to him. Maybe get my lawyer involved. See what we can work out," I said. I saw Liam trying to bite back his grin.

"How about this," I continued. "Send me a copy of what you designed. I'll see if I can come up with a revised poster that would make good use of this image. I'll talk to them and try to convince them it's in both our best interests to sign a joint advertising deal with *Ecosphere*. Then we can decide how to move forward if you still want to."

"I'll want to," T-8 said. His eyes were hard and glittering.

Chapter 23
Gary Graydon

LIAM and I left RIO as soon as the meeting broke up. I called Gary from the car. "Got time to see me right now?" I asked when he answered.

"I always have time for my star editor," he said with a laugh. "It's been quite a while since you dropped by. I was beginning to think you're really just an email bot."

I laughed. "Nope, I'm real. See you in a few."

Liam dropped me off at the entrance to the building that housed the *Ecosphere* offices—a building he owned. I ran upstairs to Gary's office while Liam parked his car. I couldn't wait to show Gary my pictures of Rafe and the hammerhead and to start brainstorming about how we could use them to boost *Ecosphere*'s profile.

Gary was just putting down his phone when I walked into his office. He stood up to give me a hug. "I've been missing you. I'm going to have to make it a condition of your employment that we have lunch or coffee at least once a week."

"I can always squeeze in a coffee if you'll come to RIO," I said. "I'd love to spend more time on *Ecosphere*, but RIO's my top priority. And with everything going on…"

He interrupted. "I heard about your grandmother. I'm so sorry. Is there any change? And Maddy? How is she holding up?"

I sighed. "Maddy hasn't really bounced back yet after her cancer treatment. She will, although I'm sure this thing with her mother will set her back somewhat."

Liam walked through the door just then. "Maddy will come roaring back, just you wait. And Mimi will be up pushing us all around in a few days too."

I saw the strange look he exchanged with Gary. Seemed like he didn't want Gary to talk about Mimi or Maddy's health. If he knew something he wasn't telling me, I'd have to pry it out of him later.

Gary got the message. "How's the movie going? People are spotting Hollywood stars all over town, and from what I hear, you're always right in the thick of them."

I laughed. "Not really. I've been photographing some of the bigger names for publicity stills—maybe even the main poster. That's what I want to show you. And I want you to think about how we can tie one of our issues in with the movie's release."

While we'd been talking, I had logged into my files at RIO using Gary's computer. He had a giant lightbox on his wall that connected to his PC, so I turned it on and projected my images there. I started with the pictures of Rafe swimming through the tunnels filled with tarpon and barracuda. They were great, but they weren't electrifying. Gary made polite noises as I brought up each shot.

I could see Liam grinning his stunning smile. He knew what was coming. When the first image of Rafe and the hammerhead popped onto the screen, Gary sat up straight and leaned forward.

I clicked to the next picture. His lips parted slightly, and his eyes widened.

With the next image, he gasped. "These are brilliant. They'll be worth a fortune. They're amazing in their own right, but because they have Rafe Cummings..." he turned to Liam. "Were you there?"

Liam shook his head. "Nope. Just Fin and her new buddy, the biggest movie star in the world." He didn't look at me.

Gary sat back. "I'm assuming the movie company owns these.

What do I have to pay to get some of these shots for *Ecosphere*? They'll put the magazine on the map for sure."

"Well, you're in luck," I said. "The movie company doesn't own any of my pictures unless I took them during filming or specifically for the film's publicity. Newton made sure I kept ownership when he reviewed my contracts. I took these when Rafe and I were diving together on our own time." I smiled at him. "They're mine, so let's figure out the best way to use them."

Gary smiled and shook his head. I could see the admiration in his eyes as he spoke. "Liam, you've got a real good one here. Do your best to hold on to her."

Liam looked me straight in the eye. "I try, Gary. I try."

I laughed and clicked over to the concept poster T-8 had come up with. "I want to brainstorm how we can improve this poster and at the same time, figure out how we can tie *Ecosphere* into the wave of publicity this movie is going to generate. You in?"

"I'm in," said Gary. "Let's get to work."

Three hours later, we'd come up with some ideas. I read from my notes. "We create a new segment for the movie that includes hammerheads, possibly the effect global warming is having on their reproduction since hammerheads birth their young in coastal nurseries near the shore. Or maybe about how Silas Anderson recovered them. Or maybe it'll cover the threat from the international trade in shark fins. We three will volunteer to draft the script for this segment."

I continued, "We'll recommend eliminating three or four of the already planned segments to stay within budget and to keep the movie's running time manageable." That will also allow us to simplify the poster design that T-8 came up with. Instead of having to show eleven segments around the central figure, we can cut that back to six or even four, so each image can be larger." "We will also suggest that although the hammerhead poster will be the main one, that we have other designs that feature the pirate, the Greek diver, and the hard hat diver in the center spot, since those are the other most electrifying of the planned segments."

In exchange for granting the movie company the rights to two of the hammerhead images of their choosing, *Ecosphere* will have exclusive rights to publication in any media of all pre-release photography, and we'll devote the magazine's entire issue the month of the movie's release. *Ecosphere* will not have to pay to use any images or video for any of these purposes, since I own the rights to the images and the movie will benefit from the publicity as much as *Ecosphere* will. Did I get it all right?"

"Perfect, as always," Gary said. "Do you need any help writing up the proposal?"

I shook my head. "Don't think so. I'll ask Newton to do it, although you're welcome to have your own lawyers review it before I present it to T-8. While Newton's doing that, I'll mockup a few of the posters."

Liam piped up, "I'll start working on the outline of the new segment."

"Good. Time is of the essence here. Let's touch base at end of day tomorrow. We should have enough to at least start discussions with T-8."

Liam and I stood up. He and Gary did the man hug thing, awkwardly patting each other on the back while bumping chests and shaking hands. When they broke apart, Gary gave me a regular hug. Then Liam and I walked down the stairs to the parking area and drove back to RIO.

Chapter 24
Double Date

I CALLED Newton from the car to ask him if he would draft the agreement with T-8 and the production company.

"I promised Joely dinner this evening," he said, "but I'm sure she won't mind if I put it off for one night. Sure, I can do it."

"I've got a better idea," I said. "Liam and I both have some work to do on the project too. How about if we have a working dinner on the *Tranquility*, and Joely can come along and enjoy the sunset. I can get takeout from Ray's Place, and you know Liam makes a mean margarita."

Newton laughed. "I'll ask. Either way, count me in. She'll understand. She's knows family comes first. I'll be right there."

"Thanks." I swallowed a lump in my throat. "I love you, Dad." I almost never call him Dad, so I knew my use of the honorific would signal how much I appreciate everything about him.

When I disconnected the call, Liam said, "It sounded from your conversation like Joely and Newton are dating. Did I get that right?"

I hadn't yet told Liam about seeing Newton and Joely at the restaurant when I was having dinner with Rafe. Given that we were barely back on an even keel after Liam had seen that kiss, I thought better of mentioning how I had found out that they were an item.

"Yeah. I guess it's been going on for a while. I just found out the other day when I happened to bump into them…"

Yikes. I'd come close to telling where I'd seen them. The Grand Old House is a very romantic restaurant, and Liam would realize that I would never have gone there alone.

"I think I'll call Theresa and give her a heads up that we'll be ordering dinner to go tonight," I said.

Liam gave me the side eye. "Since when does Theresa need a heads up for a party of four? She could handle a formal dinner for 500 with no warning and one hand tied behind her back."

"Yeah, that's true. I'm just nervous about this deal." I bit my lip.

He pulled into his usual parking spot at RIO. "Don't be. T-8 tried to hide it, but anyone could see he wants those images of Rafe and the hammerhead. He'll give you whatever you want—within reason—to make that happen."

I nodded. "You're right."

We walked into the lobby. I rummaged through my canvas tote for my ID badge so we could get through security, and the movie company guard waved me through. He stopped Liam with a raised hand. "ID, Sir."

"Let him through. He's an important part of RIO, and he's with me," I said.

"Can't do that," he replied. "He needs an ID badge."

Fred, the security guard RIO employed directly, shrank down, trying and failing to become invisible while I glared.

I pulled my phone out of my tote and called T-8. No answer. I threw the phone back in my bag in frustration. Yes, I knew RIO needed better security, but this was ridiculous. We had work to do.

Rafe, hands casually stuffed in the pockets of his cargo shorts, strolled out of the entrance to the aquarium. I guess he could see how upset I was because he stopped short. "Hey, Fin. What's the matter?"

"This guy won't let Liam in." I turned to the guard. "He used to be the CFO here. He's an important donor. And you people are making me look bad in my own place of business. This is unacceptable."

Rafe walked over to the guard. "Do you know who I am?"

The guard smiled, and the smile was so bright it nearly eclipsed the ugly scars and mottled protuberances on his ravaged face. "I sure do." He held out his hand.

Rafe ignored the extended hand. "Good. Then you know I'm a big wheel in the production company. That makes me your boss. So, here's a couple of direct orders. Don't be making up your own rules. Let the man in. And get an all-access badge for him delivered to Fin's office in the next five minutes. Got it?"

"Yes, Mr. Cummings," said the guard. "Will do, Sir."

"Thank you," said Rafe. "And in the future, I don't care what T-8 has said, if Dr. Fleming says let someone in, they come in. No questions asked. She runs this place, and we are her guests, not the other way around. Got it?"

Abashed, the guard nodded and held the gate open for Liam to come through. "I'll get that badge right over to you, Mr...?"

Liam smiled. "S'alright, Sammy. You were just doing your job. And the name's Lawton. Liam Lawton."

The guard's eyes widened. "The *Oh! Possum* guy?"

"That's me. And thanks for taking your job so seriously. There's a lot of valuable stuff around here, especially now. A little diligence is good, and no harm done." He smiled at the guard, and then we walked down the hall to my office to gather the things we'd need to complete the tasks we'd set for ourselves.

I grabbed my Mac for me, a spare PC for Liam, and a bunch of notebooks, red pens, and pencils for Newton. I knew he was sure to bring a fancy computer of his own.

Liam searched the bottom shelf of my bookcase and pulled out a couple of paperback copies of Nicholas Harvey novels. "In case Joely gets bored," he said. By the time we'd packed up everything we thought we'd need, the guard had brought Liam an all-access ID badge.

Liam draped the lanyard around his neck. "Thank you, Sammy. I appreciate it."

Then we picked up all the stuff we needed and walked out the back door and across the lawn toward the marina's dock. Halfway there, I said, "I'll meet you aboard. I just want to touch base with the crew at Ray's Place."

Liam had already set up a workspace at the galley table when I boarded, so I set my Mac up next to him. Noah was right behind me, delivering drinks as well as several kinds of snacks and cookies.

No sooner had Noah finished setting everything out when Newton and Joely came aboard. Newton sat on the daybed with his back against the wall, but Joely decided to spend some time in the sunshine. She picked up one of the paperbacks Liam had brought. "Thanks for bringing these," she said. "I've been meaning to read this one." She poured herself a margarita on her way out to the deck.

"Anybody need a refresher on the objectives?" I asked. "I just emailed my notes to you both, but we can do a verbal recap if you think it would help."

Newton was already typing away. He didn't look up from his screen as he waved a hand in the air. "I'm good."

We worked without a break until the sound of Liam's stomach rumbling and the growing darkness alerted me it was time for dinner. I pulled a menu for Ray's Place out of one of the drawers in the galley and brought it out to Joely.

"Thank heavens," she said. "I'm starved, but I didn't want to disturb you guys."

I laughed. "Thank Liam's stomach. He's like a lion—he goes off with a roar if he's late for a meal."

Joely laughed and made her selections. I went back inside so Newton and Liam could choose, then I called Ray's Place to put in the order. Noah agreed to bring out our food as soon as it was ready. He and his brother were hard workers and always took the initiative on all their responsibilities. I was grateful they chose to work at RIO instead of the restaurant owned by their older brother Stefan.

Joely rejoined us when she saw Noah heading our way with the food, and we all broke off what we were doing to devote ourselves to dinner—and margaritas. When we'd finished our dinner, including a scrumptious dessert, I hoisted my mac back onto the table and flipped it around so everyone could see. "Here's the poster's I came up with. As you can see, there are four separate designs, each one highlighting one of the sections of the movie in the center photo, with the images depicting the other sections arrayed around it. I didn't try to put all twelve sections on the poster, because it just looks too crowded, and then you don't feel the excitement."

Liam nodded. "I came up with the same idea as I was reviewing the existing script while I looked for an idea to let us use the hammerhead photo. It struck me that twelve—now thirteen—sections are just too many for a ninety minute film. I highlighted the ones I think we should drop. The new one, the one with the hammerhead, is based on the research I did into Silas Anderson. Your great–great–great–grandfather was quite a character."

He laughed. "It seems after college he balked at joining the family business. "Borrowed" the family's yacht to take a trip around the world. He did some treasure hunting, and he brought up a lot of valuable artifacts from wrecks he discovered, including the Anderson Sea Stars. Unfortunately, he hit a shoal on his way home. The crash destroyed his boat, but he managed to swim to a small island towing the case holding the Sea Stars. He lived off the sea for several months. When the rescuers finally found him, his wandering days were over. He immediately joined the family business and never looked back."

Liam went on to explain his idea in a little more detail, especially how he envisioned creating a scene with Silas confronting a hammerhead while retrieving the sea stars from the wreck where he'd found them. "Because Rafe is wearing modern scuba gear in the photos, we might have to adapt the story a little to bring it up to present times, but the gist of it will be based on facts." We all nodded along with his explanation.

When he finished, I said, "Sounds intriguing. Newton, how are you doing?"

He smiled. "I'm done too. I just completed our proposal and emailed it to all of you for comments. Do you want me to go through the terms and conditions?"

We all groaned.

I hate contracts. "I'm good. You guys agree?" I said.

"Okay, just so you know, I put in a couple of outrageous asks so if T-8 wants to negotiate, he'll start there. We can give him a win without losing anything we really want."

"Smart," said Joely.

He smiled. "Thanks. I'll email this to Gary. See if there's anything he wants to change, but I think we're good to go."

I emptied the last of the margaritas into our cups. There'd been no more than a mouthful for each of us left in the jug. "To a great team," I said.

Everyone smiled and clinked their stainless steel RIO mugs.

"Now get off my boat. I'm exhausted." I said. "It's been a long day."

Newton and Joely laughed and gathered their things. Liam waited until they'd reached the lighted areas of RIO's grounds, then he shut off the *Tranquility*'s lights and we got ready for bed.

Chapter 25
Rafe and the Committee

THE NEXT MORNING, Liam and I were up before dawn. I showered and dressed in the women's locker room and then headed to my office, where a steaming mug of coffee and a warm blueberry muffin awaited me. Next to the mug was a note from Liam.

In red marker, the note read, "Had to get to work. Sorry I freaked out before. I love you." He'd signed it with a heart with a smiley face in the middle. I loved it.

I had called an emergency meeting of the exhibition committee to be sure we had all our responsibilities straight after the abrupt reschedule caused by the attempt on Mimi's life. I ate my breakfast quickly.

I was in my seat a few minutes before the meeting's scheduled start time. The committee members drifted in one-by-one. They greeted me and each other, then helped themselves to coffee before sitting down. Genevra slid into the seat next to me just as I was about to call the meeting to order.

"Cutting it close this morning?" I said with a laugh.

She blushed. "Things to do," she murmured.

"I bet," I said and laughed again when she turned scarlet.

I called the meeting to order and made sure everybody knew about the changes to the schedule and their revised responsibilities.

Genevra had created a timeline of tasks and assignments for each member, and she handed out copies as we covered the tasks.

I was just about to call the meeting to a close when I heard a voice from behind me.

"Mind if I drop in? I'd like to meet the hard working team that made this all possible." It was Rafe, looking devastatingly gorgeous in a blue RIO T-shirt and baggy denim shorts. He went around the table and introduced himself to each person, just as though they wouldn't have recognized the most famous movie star in the world.

"Can you take some pics if anyone wants one?" he asked me when he'd made the rounds. He managed to look surprised at the rush of people who wanted their photo taken with him, and I knew once again he was a truly great actor.

I set him up near the RIO logo that adorned the wall opposite the conference room windows and shut off the overhead lights. The committee members lined up, and I took several shots of each one with Rafe. He put his arm around them. He kissed the ladies. He shook hands with everyone. By the time he finished, I realized he'd made every person in the room feel special.

Genevra slipped out to make prints on the high definition laser printer in my office. A few minutes later, she came back with the photos mounted in small cardboard folder frames.

Rafe remembered everybody's name and put a personal note on each picture when he signed it. It was impressive. When the committee showed no signs of losing interest in hanging around with Rafe, he shot me a look.

I raised my voice. "Sorry to be the bad guy here, but I happen to know that Rafe is due in a production meeting in a few minutes. Please say your goodbyes and don't make him late. The producer is a real bear."

Genevra added, "I emailed each of you the photos Fin took, so you can make more copies if you want." She walked over and took Rafe's arm. "I'll walk you to the set."

He smiled at her and turned to me with a wink. "I'll see you in the meeting. Don't be late."

The entire committee watched him walking down the hall. Once he was out of sight, they crowded around me with questions about what Rafe Cummings was really like, and what he was like to work with.

I answered honestly. Rafe was a genuinely nice guy, and an absolute dream to work with. Real easy on the eyes too. Satisfied by their encounter with a movie star, they finally drifted out, walking on air.

Chapter 26
Benjamin and Chaun

IT WAS NEARING LUNCH TIME, so I went to the café to grab a sandwich to go. I wanted to have a quiet meal on my boat and prepare my mind for the presentation to T-8 later today. I knew our plan was sound, and I knew he wanted those pictures of Rafe and the hammerhead, but you never know. Sometimes negotiations go awry.

I picked up my sandwich and a lemonade, said a quick "hi" to all the staff and to Marianna, the head of RIO's food services. Then I went out the back door, squinting in the bright sunlight as I strolled toward the dock.

As I passed through the scattered picnic tables in the recreation area, I heard a familiar voice calling my name. Two familiar voices, in fact.

It was my friends Benjamin Brooks and Chaunsey, who was known as Chaun. Benjamin had been the CFO of RIO at one time, and we'd had a somewhat tepid romance that only lasted until the moment Liam returned from his mysterious year-long journey.

Benjamin had resigned rather than watch me find happiness with Liam, and he'd recently gone into business with Chaun, his best friend from college. Benjamin had eventually gotten over his infatuation with me, and we were now very good friends.

131

Whenever I had a technical problem, or someone to help me think outside the box, I called on Chaun. He was a tech genius, and an all-around great guy, even though he was slightly eccentric. He stands about four-foot-eight, and he usually wears long baggy shorts and basketball socks with his bright red Chucks. Although he used to wear plain black t-shirts every day, he'd replaced them with a succession of RIO branded shirts in a variety of colors, interspersed occasionally with shirts that bore his own company brand.

The two men were waving madly at me from under one of the flowered pergolas. I changed direction to stop and say hello.

Chaun rubbed the toe of his sneaker in the sand beneath the bench. "I'm sorry about the security breach the other day. Nobody ever notified us to turn the alarm system on when they finished setting up the exhibits. Next time I'll keep checking. I promise it won't happen again."

"Thanks, Chaun. But it's okay. Alarms wouldn't have stopped the murder, and we got the stolen items back. But let's get together in the next day or so to figure out how we can keep it from happening again, okay?"

He nodded. "Good idea." There was a moment of silence, and Benjamin gave Chaun a nudge.

"Having lunch on the *Tranquility*?" Chaun asked, his face and voice projecting perfect innocence.

"I was planning to," I said. "Would you like to join me? I don't have much time because..."

Chaun interrupted. "Will Rafe Cummings be joining you? We've heard through the grapevine that he's had several meals aboard your boat. The news is everywhere."

I laughed. "I can ask him to join us. If he's free, I'm sure he will."

"Great. We'll be right there." Chaun hurried over to the takeout counter at Ray's Place to get their lunches, while Benjamin and I strolled down the pier to my boat.

"How's business?" I asked him. "Still enjoying being your own boss?"

He shrugged. "Don't tell Chaun I said this, and if you do, I'll deny it. I'm thinking of leaving the island. There's nothing for me here, and Chaun doesn't really need me."

My mouth fell open. "Oh, no. Don't say that. I would miss you terribly. And what about your diving? And your freediving? Could you still do that wherever you're thinking of going?"

He shook his head. "No, and that's part of the reason I haven't left yet. I want to be somewhere I can dive, but I need a job. Chaun and I are barely eking out enough in sales to pay ourselves minimum wage. The business could easily support one of us, but not both. Chaun would starve before he'd say anything, but something's gotta give. I'd rather I left before the business collapses under its own weight."

I looked up and saw Chaun hurrying across the lawn, carrying a salad, a cheeseburger, and two drinks on a tray. "Let me think on this before you do anything rash," I said. "I can try to increase the security budget so we can afford more equipment and full time video monitoring..."

Benjamin sighed. "Sure. Except that puts RIO in a hole. Don't forget, I know the economics of this place as well as you do—probably even better since I know how you struggle with spreadsheets and financial statements."

I nodded. "Maybe there's another solution. Give me a few days. I'll let you know if I come up with anything."

He smiled politely, and I could tell he thought I was just going through the motions, but I felt a real loyalty to Benjamin. He'd always come through for me when I needed help, and I vowed to do the same for him.

By now the three of us had reached the *Tranquility* and we climbed aboard. Benjamin and I sat down, but Chaun stood in front of me. "Did you call him yet?"

"I just got here. I'll call him now." I pulled my phone out of one of the capacious pockets in my cargo shorts and pushed the button for Rafe's phone.

Chaun's eyes widened and he nudged Benjamin with his elbow. "Whoa. She has Rafe Cummings on speed dial."

Rafe answered on the first ring. "What's up?"

"First off, thanks for being so nice to the committee members this morning. You made the day for every one of them, and I think you have fans for life."

"There's only one fan I want, and she's taken..."

I hoped Chaun couldn't hear Rafe, but I could tell by his shocked face that he had. "Thanks. Now I have another favor to ask. Three of my very good friends, Chaun, Theresa Simmons, and Benjamin Brooks, are on the *Tranquility* having lunch with me. Any chance you could join us? If not for lunch, at least to say hi? I'll take care of your lunch if you can make it."

"Be there in a flash." He disconnected.

Chaun was already rushing toward Ray's Place to get food for Rafe.

I called after him "Bring Theresa back with you."

Chaun ordered pretty much everything on the menu just to be sure there'd be something Rafe liked to eat. I could have saved him the hassle. I knew Rafe wouldn't eat more than a few bites no matter what we served him.

A little old man limped out of RIO's back door. The only reason I knew it was Rafe was because I'd seen him completely disappear under his little old man disguise before. He hobbled across the lawn, leaning on a cane, with his head down. He'd pulled the visor of Liam's dorky cap low over his face, hiding those luminous blue eyes. He had a two-day growth of patchy gray stubble on his chin, and he wore a shapeless terrycloth beach robe, long baggy pants that came to an abrupt halt just short of his ankles, and a pair of worn-out fuzzy slippers.

As he drew closer, his eyes darted up over the rims of his dark glasses, and he winked at me. I smiled back as both Chaun and my best friend Theresa Simmons raced past him, laden down with bags of food and trays of various drinks. They reached the boat before Rafe, and Chaun started laying out the food on the table in the cabin.

Theresa looked around. "Is he here yet?"

I laughed. "He's on his way. In fact, here he is now."

Rafe climbed aboard and shuffled under the overhang before he shrugged out of his disguise. He looked at the array of food Chaun was busy arranging on the table. "I hope you didn't get all that for me. That's enough food for a party."

Chaun nearly jumped out of his skin. His eyes grew round. "It's you," he gasped.

Theresa looked equally stunned. She whirled around. "Do I look all right?" she whispered to me.

But Rafe heard her. "Miss, I don't know who you are but you're one of the two most beautiful women I've seen today." He winked at me. "Hello, everyone. Yes, it is I. And I'm just a guy like any other, so relax." He held out his hand. "Rafe Cummings. Good to meet you, Chaun. Any friend of Fin's...well, you know the rest."

Then he lifted Theresa's hand to his lips. "Enchanted," he said. "Rafe Cummings at your service."

"Theresa Simmons at yours," she said with a giggle.

He smiled back, then looked at me. "Any chance you could take the boat out a little way so I can ditch the rest of my disguise? These fake whiskers itch like crazy."

"Sure thing." I started the engines and backed out of my slip. There were no scuba training classes this afternoon, so I figured mooring at RIO's Training Site Two would be safe and far enough from shore for Rafe to be able to relax.

Benjamin made his way from the deck to the galley. He introduced himself to Rafe, and they sat in the captain's chairs to chat. Theresa sat beside Rafe, and Chaun sat beside Benjamin. They all stared at the movie star.

I couldn't blame them. Rafe was an eye magnet. It was hard to look away.

Once I'd moored the boat, we all sat on the bow to eat lunch, Rafe wedged between Chaun and Theresa while Benjamin and I sat cross-legged facing them. Rafe smiled good naturedly, while they all continued to stare at him. He endured their scrutiny as he ate three bites of his turkey sandwich and wrapped up the rest.

He chatted amiably with my friends until after a half hour or so, he looked at his Rolex. "I have a meeting to get to. And if I'm not

135

mistaken, so do you, Fin. Shall we head back?" He went below to put his disguise back on while I brought the boat back to port.

When he'd finished dressing, he pulled three autographed pictures of himself from the pocket of his tatty robe. He addressed one photograph to each of them. "Here you go, guys. If there's ever anything I can do for any of you, Fin knows how to contact me."

He kissed Theresa's cheek before he climbed over the *Tranquility*'s gunwales, looking for all the world like he was so decrepit he could barely make it. Then he hobbled down the pier, limping slightly and leaning on his cane.

"He must be the greatest actor in the world," breathed Chaun.

Benjamin nodded as his eyes followed Rafe's progress. Theresa had a rapturous smile on her face and a faraway look in her eyes. Given their reactions, I'd say the meeting between Rafe Cummings and my friends had been a big success.

Chapter 27
A New Proposal

BENJAMIN PACKED up all the extra food. "I'll drop all this at the Cayman Food Bank on our way home. Thanks for orchestrating this meeting. I know it meant a lot to Chaun. You're a good friend."

I shrugged. "No problem. And I meant what I said about finding a way for you to stay on the island. Don't give up yet."

He quirked a smile at me, picked up the bags of food, and trotted down the pier toward the parking lot. Theresa walked slowly behind them, headed back to work at Ray's Place with a dreamy smile on her face.

I leaned against the galley table and sighed. The problem of what to do about Benjamin weighed on my mind, but I put it aside for now. I had to be sharp for the negotiations with T-8.

I was the last one to reach the conference room. Genevra had set up the table with RIO branded notepads and pens at each place. Liam, Newton, Genevra, and Gary had arrayed themselves on one side of the long table. T-8 was sitting at the table's head, and the sunlight streaming in through the windows made it hard to look directly at him. Rafe sat across from Newton, and I slid into the seat beside him directly across from Liam. We'd agreed on this seating arrangement last night so it wouldn't look like the RIO team had lined up against T-8.

"Sorry to keep you all waiting," I said as I flipped open my Mac and connected it to the projector. We'd agreed that I would be the primary spokesperson in the meeting since I was an executive producer of the film as well as the copyright holder on the valuable photographs that T-8 wanted so badly.

I started by explaining our thinking that with twelve segments, the movie was too complicated to hold a viewer's interest, and we recommended cutting it down to four. I went through our reasoning on the three existing segments we'd chosen, and a quick overview of the new segment idea Liam had come up with to enable the film to use the hammerhead shots for publicity. "There's a draft of the script for the new segment in your handout."

I brought up images of the four posters I'd created. Although I'd started with T-8's idea of the main image surrounded by smaller images of the other segments, the new design was cleaner and more compelling. T-8 nodded thoughtfully as he took in the details of each variation.

"We're proposing a joint marketing campaign between your production company and *Ecosphere*. When you're ready to release the film, one of the hammerhead images will be on the magazine's cover, and *Ecosphere* will devote an entire issue to the film. Gary and I are thinking a few pages for each of the four segments, an interview with you, an interview with Rafe, several pages of stills from the shoot, and more of the hammerhead and other publicity shots scattered throughout the magazine. We're also proposing a raffle to give away a large, framed poster of the best shot of Rafe and the shark."

T-8 nodded and made that rolling motion that means hurry up.

I nodded and pointed to Newton. "A quick overview of the terms we require, please."

Two minutes later, without a single question or comment, T-8 said, "Where do I sign? I need to get this movie going before they yank my funding."

That was a puzzling remark. "I don't think that'll happen, T-8. Isn't Mimi your principal investor?"

He nodded. "Yeah. Give me a pen, please. I'll sign right now."

"Don't you want to read it first? Or have a lawyer look it over?" I asked.

"Nope. Pen please," he said. "I'll sign it as is."

We all looked at each other, wondering why T-8 seemed so frantic to execute the contract without a single question or change. Of us all, only Rafe didn't seem puzzled by T-8's haste.

Newton leaned forward. "I'm not going to let you do that, at least until you read it. Please take it to your lawyers for review. If you're still set on signing after you talk to them, terrific. But you can relax. This deal's not going anywhere." He paused. "At least, not right away."

T-8 flushed bright red, and I assumed he was angry because Newton thwarted him.

We all rose and left the conference room. I stopped Genevra as she passed. "Wanna go diving right now? Somehow, I feel the need to get wet before the big event tonight."

"Yeah," she said. "I know what you mean. A dive sounds good."

"I'm thinking Angelfish Reef. That work for you?"

"Perfect. I'll meet you at your boat." She zipped off to gather her gear.

139

Chapter 28
Diving With Genevra

Genevra and I split up before meeting on the boat. She went to see if Joely wanted to come and hang out, while I stopped by Ray's Place to round up Theresa. Neither Joely nor Theresa was a diver, but they always had fun together hanging out on the *Tranquility* while Genevra and I dove.

My three best friends lined up, shoulder-to-shoulder on the pier, laughing and giggling. Genevra was holding her gear bag, and Theresa and Joely were carrying snacks and a cooler of drinks.

"Permission to come aboard," Genevra finally managed to say between laughs.

"Permission granted."

Then another voice, this one a mellow baritone, said, "Does that include me too, Captain?"

I laughed. "Yes, Rafe. That includes you too." He wasn't wearing his disguise.

While they settled down on the benches, I set a course for Angelfish Reef.

Rafe regaled my friends with funny stories while I piloted the boat. I couldn't hear his voice over the engine noise, but I could definitely hear their peals of laughter. When we arrived at the site, I kept the engine running while Genevra pulled up the mooring ball and tied us off.

I hopped down the ladder and started gearing up. Genevra and I had to wait a minute for Rafe to finish fiddling with his gear, but soon enough, we were ready. I went in first, Rafe went second, and Genevra was last. Once we were all in the water, they followed me down the mooring line to the reef below.

Angelfish Reef is a relatively shallow dive, reaching only about thirty-five feet at its deepest points, but nonetheless, it is one of the most spectacular sites in the Caymans. There are three large coral growths and several smaller patches of vivid coral, all separated by wide swaths of sand. Obviously, there are many angelfish in the area, including queen angelfish, gray angelfish, and French angelfish, all swimming slowly and majestically around the vibrant coral.

And the reef itself is spectacular. Black coral, elkhorn coral and staghorn coral swayed in the gentle current, and large barrel sponges and elephant ear sponges provided a home to thousands of tiny reef dwellers. The coral shelters several cleaning stations manned by Pederson cleaner shrimp, rock beauties, fairy basslets, queen triggerfish, assorted parrotfish, and large schools of blue chromis abound.

Genevra and I like to try to join the schools of chromis by moving slowly, barely kicking, and taking shallow breaths so we don't make the fish nervous. If we do it slowly and carefully enough, the fish will make room for us and let us join their group. Rafe watched us as we approached one of the larger schools. When he saw them allow us to join them, he tried it too. Within a few minutes, we were all part of the school, but then, reacting to some unknown stimuli, the entire group darted off leaving us alone over the coral.

We headed across the sandy bottom, laughing as the huge clusters of garden eels ducked into their hideaways as we approached. Rafe swam over a southern stingray without even noticing him, until Genevra tapped his arm and pointed out where the stingray lay buried in the sand.

She ran low on air first, so as soon as she signaled it was time to turn around, I led the way back to the boat. It wasn't very far, because we had been swimming in a large circle around the dive site, so we were already nearly back where we started. That gave us time to watch the colorful fish go about their daily business as we completed our safety stops.

Since we all had to get back to RIO for the exhibition gala, we only did one dive. While Rafe and my friends stayed below on the deck, I piloted the *Tranquility* from the flying bridge and radioed our arrival time to Stewie. He promised to have our transportation ready when we pulled into the slip.

Stewie, Christophe, and Noah took our gear for cleaning as soon as we docked, and Liam, Newton, Gus, and Oliver stood by to greet us. They whisked us into a waiting limousine that drove us to the Ritz Carlton on Seven Mile Beach, where I had reserved several adjoining suites for us to get ready for the exhibition gala this evening.

The suites were luxurious, as is everything at the Ritz. I'd arranged for hair and makeup people to be there, and Newton had coordinated with the other men to bring everybody's outfit for the event to the hotel while we were off diving.

My friends and I went out onto the deck to sit under a huge awning, where makeup, hair, and nail technicians went to work on us. When they'd finished, we went back inside and dressed. We each looked stunning in our own ways when we were finally ready. We were admiring each other when our dates for the evening arrived, also looking pretty darn good in their own right.

Newton, a bona fide silver fox, always looked fabulous, but in a tux and a blue shirt that matched his eyes, he looked amazing. Joely was wearing a black floor length strapless gown with a spray of pink roses near the mermaid-style hem. He handed her a wrist corsage that perfectly matched the roses on her dress. They were so stylish together that they could have adorned the cover of GQ or Vogue.

Genevra wore a soft green silk dress that set off her bright auburn hair and stunning green eyes. My brother Oliver, with his dark eyes and hair, looked terrific as well. Even though I knew my stepfather Ray Russo hadn't been Oliver's biological father, he looked so much like him that it broke my heart.

Genevra's eyes lit up when she saw him, and I was glad they were so happy together. Oliver certainly deserved it, and Genevra was such a sweetheart that you couldn't help but be happy for them both.

Theresa's husband Gus wore a traditional black tuxedo with a white shirt and a red cummerbund that perfectly matched Theresa's red dress. They smiled when they saw each other, and Gus's eyes misted over.

"Looking pretty hot, Mr. Simmons," said Theresa.

"Likewise, my dear," he said, kissing her hand.

My dress was dark blue velvet with long trailing sleeves, a full skirt, and a scoop neck. It made me feel like a medieval princess. I had matching velvet stilettos on my feet, which were less than ideal from the viewpoint of my comfort, but there was no way I could wear flip-flops to the gala.

And then came Liam, looking like my dream come true. His tux was a dark, very deep blue, almost black, and the color made his tanned skin and sun-bleached blond hair glow while bringing out the vibrant blue color of his eyes. He walked over to me, his eyes shining. "You always take my breath away," he said as he took my hand.

Newton broke the spell. "Our limo is waiting, and we can't be late to our own party. Everybody have everything you need? If so, let's get the party started."

144

Chapter 29
The Exhibition Gala

WE STROLLED into RIO's atrium, which the party planners had completely transformed. Large posters highlighting some of the most intriguing exhibits hung on the walls and fluttered in the cool breeze. Sparkling fairy lights hung around the vast space, rivaling the stars twinkling through the glass roof.

The maintenance team had rolled back the sliding café walls to enlarge the space even further, and the catering staff was inside, putting the finishing touches on a sumptuous buffet. A three piece band tuned up in the corner near the hall that led to the offices, which we'd closed off with a velvet rope barricade.

We'd also shut down the aquarium for the evening to avoid traumatizing the marine creatures, Lighted signs pointed the way to the exhibition of sea treasures, which had been set up in the massive pool house.

We were early, as befitted the hosts of the event, but the wait staff rushed over to offer us drinks and hors d'oeuvres. Liam and I each took a flute of champagne. He knew it always took me a while to become accustomed to wearing heels, since I spent most of my time in plastic flip-flops, so he put a hand on my elbow to steady me just in case I needed support. "Let's go see the exhibits before it gets too crowded," he said.

I sipped my champagne. "Okay. Let's do it."

We strolled arm-in-arm down the wide hallway toward the pool house, which was a separate building, a few steps away from the main building. As we walked along the short outdoor path, the scent of the hibiscus that grew on the pergola overhead was intoxicating. I breathed deeply, and relaxed.

The nasty guard who always gave me a hard time was there at the entrance, and my heart sank. I hoped he wasn't going to make it difficult to get into the exhibition, but I needn't have worried.

"Good evening, Dr. Fleming. Mr. Lawton. Go right ahead in."

After we'd passed his podium, I whispered to Liam, "That's a big change."

Liam laughed. "He's a gamer. Ever since he found out who I am —or was—he asks me for tips on how to achieve new levels in *Oh! Possum* every time I walk through the lobby."

"Do you give him tips?" I asked.

Liam shrugged and laughed. "Sure. Why not? Other people have already posted most of them on the internet anyway."

The committee had transformed the pool house. A retractable platform made from a space-age, high-strength plastic covered the pool area and made a stable floor, so there was plenty of room for guests to walk around and see the exhibits without fear of falling in or getting wet.

Dedicated spotlights lit each of the display cases, so it was easy to see the details and read the printed cards that described the items inside and their provenance. Each card also had a QR code printed on it that would bring the item's description to a cellphone, where it could be either read or listened to. We'd set up a rack of headphones near the entry for people to borrow in case they didn't want to use their phones but still wanted to hear the descriptions of the exhibits rather than read them.

Liam took my arm, and we strolled over to the first display, an enormous natural pearl about the size of my fist. It had once been the possession of a Russian Tsar, and its history dated back to the ancient Greeks. It was a stunning, luminous pinkish color.

Next came several displays of items recovered from pirate loot.

Most included the actual objects, with a few photographs and lists of the various other jewels and coins found during the recovery process. I was surprised to see some of the jewels we'd recovered on our expedition to recover the Queen's Tiara, a cursed piece of jewelry if there ever had been one. The tiara itself was now at the very bottom of the ocean, but the other jewels on display were breathtaking in their own right.

A hard hat diver's suit was part of the next tableau, and the diorama showed a diver ambling along the reef with his attached air hose floating down from the surface. I cringed to see how his clunky boots crushed the living coral beneath him. Of course, at the time this would have taken place, no one had realized that coral wasn't rock, but in reality fragile living creatures essential to the health of the ocean.

A framed print of my photograph of Rafe Cummings face-to-face with the hammerhead shark hung on the wall at eye-level. It was stunning, and I smiled that we'd been able to add it to the exhibition at the last minute.

The real Anderson Sea Stars were in a display case near the back of the pool house, lit by a brilliant spotlight that made them sparkle and twinkle like real stars. They were breathtaking.

We finished walking through the remainder of the exhibits just as the first guests arrived. We greeted the people we knew as we made our way back to the atrium, where the party was now in full swing.

Maddy and Dane arrived with Stewie and Doc. Maddy looked stunning but frail in a sleek one-shouldered sky blue gown that showed off the color of her amazing hair. Doc wore a black dress with a high neckline and long bell-shaped lace sleeves. Dane looked very handsome in his tux, and even Stewie had cleaned up nicely in a traditional black tuxedo.

Vincent Polillo, captain of RIO's research vessel the *Omega*, was Maddy's long-time friend and confidante. He looked amazing in his full dress uniform when he entered. He waved to Maddy and Dane before heading to the bar for a soft drink.

T-8 stood alone in a corner, sipping a glass of champagne. He had ignored the black tie dress code—or maybe his outfit passed for formal wear in the circles he usually ran in. Either way, he looked great, just underdressed. His silky black pants were flowing and hung low and loose on his hips. A knitted white t-shirt that might have been silk peeked out from under a tight black leather jacket that looked as soft as a cloud, and his brown hair flopped endearingly over one blue eye. He looked like the quintessential, totally irresistible bad boy. He waved at me as we walked by, but he didn't make a move toward joining us. I resolved to go speak to him later.

Maddy waited until the band finished their next song, then she took the microphone from the lead singer.

"Welcome to RIO, everyone. I hope you all enjoy the amazing exhibition of marine artifacts we've put together. The sea is a wondrous place. If you love the ocean like I do—and you must or you wouldn't be here—please donate to RIO to support the research and the good work we do in keeping the oceans stable and clean. Thank you and enjoy the party." She handed the mic back to the singer and left the stage.

The band began playing again, and the caterers circulated with trays of hot and cold hors d'oeuvres and glasses of champagne, water, and lemonade. Liam and I put our empty glasses down on a nearby tray and took to the dance floor. He is an incredible dancer, his movements smooth and gliding. I am not at all a good—or even competent—dancer, but he never complains.

After a few songs, Rafe came over and cut in. Liam tightened his lips, but he passed my hand over to Rafe without complaint. He even managed a smile. Like me, Rafe was a terrible dancer, and we laughed together about how we'd finally found one thing he isn't good at.

After a while, Rafe and I looked around for T-8, to get him to join the crowd and have some fun, but he seemed to have disappeared. Shrugging, Rafe took my hand and pulled me back out onto the dance floor.

After we'd danced a few more times, Christophe came over and asked if he could cut in. "I need to speak with you," he said to me.

So off we danced, and if anything, Christophe was an even better dancer than Liam. He pulled me close and whispered in my ear. "I am sorry to do this, but I am resigning. I can't stay here and watch the woman I love with another man."

He was referring to Genevra. Although she and Christophe were good friends and spent a lot of time together, her heart belonged only to Oliver. It seemed the sexy Frenchman had finally resolved himself to the situation, but his decision was putting me in a difficult spot professionally.

"What about the freediving school you set up? I put a lot of RIO's very tight marketing budget into promoting it, and if you walk out now, not only is that money all gone to waste, but it may also look like RIO isn't committed to the freediving community. How do you propose that I spin this news?"

Christophe shrugged. "You'll think of something."

We continued moving around the dance floor. I was even more wooden than usual, until I had a brainstorm.

"What happened?" Christophe said. "You just relaxed and found the beat. C'est un miracle."

I ignored his snark. "No miracle. What if you don't resign? What if you're actually just leaving Grand Cayman to start the second in a soon-to-be worldwide chain of freediving schools, bankrolled by RIO? You can set them up in various locations of your choosing, get them up and running, and then leave someone you trust in charge while you go on to start the next one. The schools can use the RIO name as well as your name and they'll pay a percentage of the fees they earn in exchange for using your name and for RIO promoting them. Like a franchise. You can choose a local freediving instructor to run each one. You'll probably have to visit every school periodically, but that shouldn't be a problem. You love to travel."

He thought a moment. "You don't have the time to manage a freediving school in addition to everything else you do, and you don't even like freediving. There's no one here I trust except you."

"Not even Benjamin Brooks?" I asked.

Christophe stopped still in the middle of the dance floor. Then a huge smile broke out on his face. "You're a genius."

"Yup," I said. Now all I had to do was convince Benjamin that this was the right career move for him.

Chapter 30
Opening Day

As HOSTS, Liam and I had stayed until the last guest left the gala. I was so tired I could barely walk down the pier to the *Tranquility*, where we'd planned to spend the night. My feet were killing me, especially where Rafe had repeatedly stepped on them while we were dancing. As soon as we were at my slip, I kicked off my stilettos. I was asleep as soon as I lay down on the daybed.

I awoke to the sun in my eyes and the smell of fresh coffee. "Bless you," I said to Liam as I took the mug from his hands.

He laughed. "Hurry up, Sleepyhead. The exhibition opens for the day soon, and you don't want to look like you slept in your clothes from last night."

I looked down at myself and realized I had indeed slept in the beautiful gown I'd worn to the gala. I had a moment of regret because the creases might never come out of the delicate fabric, but then I realized the more important part of what he'd said.

"Yikes! What time is it?" I scrambled to my feet. "Am I late?"

"Relax. It's just after sunrise. Go take your shower and I'll have breakfast waiting in your office when you get there."

I realized what a gift Liam was. He was always sweet and supportive, and he took loving care of me whenever he was around.

"Let's get married," I said.

He took a step back. "I thought we'd already settled that. We are still engaged, aren't we?" He looked apprehensive.

I nodded. "Yes, but let's actually set a date and do it instead of putting it off to some vague date in the future."

"Fine by me. Is next week good for you?"

'Maybe." I laughed. "Let's talk later." I ran off to take my shower.

Liam was as good as his word. When I entered my office, there was a steaming mug of fresh hot coffee and a warm ham and cheese croissant sitting on my desk. I smiled and took a bite of the buttery pastry.

T-8 walked in, carrying his own mug of coffee. I smiled when I saw the RIO brand on its face. "What's up? And want half my croissant?"

He looked at my food with distaste. "Vegan," he said. He sipped his coffee and dropped a stack of papers on my desk. "Signed, sealed, and delivered. We're in business."

"Great," I said, surprised he hadn't asked for a single change, even the ones Newton had put in on purpose to provide negotiation points. But I wouldn't look this gift horse in the mouth.

"See you at the production meeting. Ten sharp." He turned and left.

Somebody was having a bad day. I hoped he got over it before the meeting. I took another bite of breakfast and then called Benjamin Brooks.

"Fin? Is everything okay? It's pretty early."

"Everything is super. I couldn't wait to tell you about a great opportunity." Then I outlined the idea Christophe and I had discussed at the gala the night before.

There was a moment of silence when I finished. "I don't know what to say." I heard a gulp. "It's perfect. Are you sure Christophe is okay with me running the school?"

"Absolutely. He called me a genius when I suggested your name to run it once he leaves…"

Benjamin interrupted. "He's a really big name in the sport. You

152

didn't fire him to make room for me, did you? Because that would be a big loss for RIO."

"Nope. I didn't fire him. He was going to resign until I proposed that instead of him resigning, we should start a franchise and open more schools and let someone local run each one while he oversees the entire chain. He jumped at the chance to have you take over here when I put forward your name."

"Thank you. Now how will I break the news to Chaun?"

I smiled. "You'll think of something. Just remind him that you'll still be on the island, and you'll still be his best friend. I think he'll see it's a perfect solution for both of you."

After we hung up, I gulped down the rest of my coffee and threw on a lightweight linen blazer I kept hanging on the back of my office door in case I needed to dress up a little for an unexpected meeting. Then I raced down the hall to make sure the exhibition area was ready for the attendees.

Sammy, the grumpy guard was at the door to the pool house where he was supposed to be ensuring that only ticket holders entered. He recognized me, and probably mindful of Rafe's admonishment to him, he waved me through without the usual hard time.

The room was pristine. The clean-up crew had removed all traces of last night's party. The glass cases that enclosed the exhibits were sparkling and appeared fingerprint free under the halogen lighting. The set up team had perfectly aligned the racks of audio tour equipment, each headset hanging neatly on its own hook. All was in readiness.

I walked outside and down the hall to RIO's atrium, where the first people were just arriving to view the exhibition. I stood just inside the velvet ropes we used to block the entrance when the ticket taker was away or when it was closing time for the exhibition.

I greeted the groups as they entered and handed each person a coupon for a free soft drink in the café. Luckily, we'd only extended that promotion to the first hundred people. I was soon free to go back to work, even though only ten minutes or so had elapsed since the exhibition's official opening.

It looked like the exhibition would be a success and bring in a great deal of money to help keep RIO in business. I sent a thank you out to the universe, because scrapping our annual documentary in favor of the exhibition and the Hollywood movie had been a huge gamble. Maddy and Newton had eventually both supported my idea, but sometimes late at night, the vision of Maddy's face when I'd told her what I wanted to do haunted me.

She'd looked me in the eye and spoke of her misgivings. She'd finished with, "Are you sure, Fin? Really sure? Because if this fails it could mean the end of RIO. My life's work."

I'd nodded. "I'm really sure." I'd answered her with assurance, despite my own misgivings.

Thank goodness I'd been right. It would have killed me to disappoint her or to see her lifetime of hard work go down the tubes.

I felt more relaxed than I had since I'd made the decision to open the series of businesses whose revenue would support RIO's research. I was practically walking on air when I went back to my office to hang my emergency blazer back on the hook behind the door. I picked up my Mac and headed off to the daily production meeting.

Chapter 31
Cancelled

THE CONFERENCE ROOM was a mob scene when I walked in. All the members of the movie crew were there, filling every seat. People lined up three deep along the walls once all the chairs were in use. It made me wonder what T-8 had on the agenda for today.

Genevra waved me over to the far side of the room, so I snaked my way through the crowd to stand next to her. "What's up," I whispered.

She shrugged. "Nobody has any idea."

About seven minutes after the scheduled start time, people were started to grumble about leaving and going back to the tasks they had been doing. By ten after, they were edging toward the exit door, hoping to be one of the first ones out the door—as long as nobody could say they were the very first one to leave.

Just as the group as a whole was starting to lean in the direction of the exit, T-8 swept in. He appeared to be very tired, with deep dark circles under his eyes. His skin looked pasty white, and his hair looked dirty. His clothes were always casual, but today they looked rumpled and unwashed.

"Sorry to be late. Thanks for waiting," he said when he stood at the head of the table. "I have some bad news I need to share." His voice broke.

I gasped. Was he going to tell us that Mimi had died without ever coming out of her coma? I bit back a sob before realizing that the doctors would have told Maddy or me long before they got around to telling T-8. He wasn't family, only a business partner. I shook my head and turned my attention to T-8, along with everyone else in the room.

"There's no easy way to say this..." he started in a soft, sad voice.

"Then just say it, man. Rip off the bandage and get the pain out of the way, Bro" came Rafe's voice from somewhere behind me.

T-8 nodded. "Okay. Our funding has fallen through. I'm shutting down production, effective immediately."

I felt every eye in the room turn to me. They all knew my grandmother had put up the funding.

I stepped forward. "Hold on a second, T-8. How is this possible? Mimi made a commitment to funding the project, and she has plenty of money to do it. She's still in a coma, so she hasn't changed her mind. What's really going on?"

There were subdued murmurs from the people around me, and Genevra quietly touched my hand for moral support. I gave her a grim half-smile.

T-8 nodded. "It's true that your grandmother committed to providing the funding for the movie, and after receiving her assurances and checking out her background to be sure she had the wherewithal to follow through, I proceeded on the assumption that she would live up to her word. But she never completed the funds transfer, so we no longer have enough money to stay operational for even another day. I'm sorry. I'm letting you all go."

"Wait a minute." I held up my hand. "Let me talk to Newton. He handled her finances, and he can probably complete the transfer on her behalf."

Newton walked in just then. "I'm sorry, Fin. T-8 is right. Mimi never completed the transfer of funds she promised. Your grandmother trusts me as far as she trusts anyone, but fundamentally she's not a very trusting person, especially when it came to money. There are caps on how much of her wealth I can transfer at any one time or to any single project without her informed consent and cross-validation. I tried every way I could think of to release the money, but it's a no-go." He turned to the room at large. "I'm sorry that we raised your hopes, and I'm sorry that we won't be making the movie. With your help, it would have been incredible."

I knew Newton and I were both thinking the same thing. Without the money to make the movie, RIO wouldn't receive any of the profits I'd been counting on. We wouldn't have the money to stay open more than a few weeks, or a couple of months at best.

I felt sick. I thought of Maddy's face when she'd asked me to be really sure before I did this, and this meant I'd let her down. I could only hope that this fiasco of my making wouldn't kill my beloved mother.

Chapter 32
Stolen Goods

I WAS SITTING at my desk, my head in my hands. I still couldn't believe it. This was a disaster. Genevra sat quietly in the corner, letting me think, but ready to help if I needed her. She knew as well as I did that shutting down the movie would mean shutting down RIO very soon afterwards, since I'd bet the next two years of funding on the movie. She'd be out of a job just like the movie crew, although she'd have a little bit more notice than they did.

And Benjamin. I'd just offered him a job. I hoped he hadn't told Chaun he was quitting yet. Although Chaun would probably eagerly take him back, Benjamin's pride wouldn't allow it.

I thought about everybody employed at RIO. My best friend Theresa, who'd worked so hard to make Ray's Place a success. Eugene Kerwin and Stanley Simmons, who toiled tirelessly to keep the place clean and in good repair. Noah and Austin Gibb, who willingly pitched in wherever and whenever we needed them. Vincent Polillo, the *Omega*'s captain, and the entire crew of RIO's massive research vessel. Our roster of esteemed scientists, and even the aquarium attendants. Stewie and Doc. Mariana in food services would be retiring soon, but this would affect her crew. Fred the security guard, too old to find another job. The list went on and on.

But mostly I thought about Maddy, and how this would break

her heart. This could be the final straw that destroyed her health, and I couldn't bear that.

I moaned softly, convinced that I couldn't possibly have screwed things up worse when the grumpy guard knocked on the wall of my office. "Dr. Fleming, do you have a minute?"

"Time is about all I've got left." I smiled at him, a sad, sick little smile, but at least I'd tried. "And please call me Fin. I have to apologize, but I don't know your name."

"It's Sammy Douglas, ma'am. And I'm sorry to add to your burdens, but there's a problem in the exhibition hall."

"What now," I said. "Don't tell me somebody managed to fall in the pool."

He shook his head. "The pool floor is securely in place, and no one has fallen in, but it's even worse than that. One of the exhibits is missing."

I sat up straight. I knew what he was going to say before I even spoke. "Which exhibit?"

"Your grandmother's Sea Stars. They're gone. Just vanished."

Genevra gasped. I groaned. My grandmother's prized possession. Her memento of her late husband. The thing she'd called her legacy. Even if she never woke up, this would haunt me to my own grave. If she did wake up, I wouldn't be able to bear the hurt and disappointment in her eyes.

I straightened my shoulders. I was in charge here, and I had to act. A leader couldn't hide sniveling in her office. It was my responsibility to fix things, especially since I was the one who'd messed up.

"Have you called the police?" I asked.

Sammy shook his head. "I didn't know if you'd want to get them involved."

"How else are we going to get the Sea Stars back?" I asked.

He shrugged. "I heard you solve crimes all by yourself. I figured you'd want to do it on your own so there wouldn't be any publicity."

"Well, you're right about not wanting publicity, but I most definitely want the police on the case. I'll call them myself. In the mean-

160

time, see if you can keep everybody who's at the exhibit here until the police arrive. If someone insists on leaving, please get their name and contact info." I turned to Genevra. "Will you please see if Marianna can rustle up some free refreshments? That will help to keep people around."

She nodded and left the office, brushing by Sammy, still standing in the door.

I looked at him. What was he waiting for?

He drew in a deep breath and blew it out before speaking. "I'm very sorry this happened. And I'm sorry about giving you a hard time when I first started. I was just having a little bit of fun."

"Right," I said. "But now the fun is over. Please go back to the exhibition and start taking names like I asked."

I picked up my cellphone to call Dane.

"Hey Fin. What's up?" he said when he answered. He sounded happy and relaxed, so I knew he must be with my mother.

I bit my lip. "Don't say anything to Maddy, but I need you and your team to come to RIO right away. It's important."

"Don't tell me there's another dead body at RIO?" he said, sounding apprehensive.

I heard Maddy's startled gasp through the line.

"Nice job playing it cool," I said. "No dead body. Just grand larceny. Mimi's Sea Stars are gone."

Chapter 33
Angel Investor

I WENT to the lobby to see if Sammy was having any success keeping people around, but I saw patrons drifting out in ones and twos. Before I could figure out a way to keep them around until Dane arrived, Marianna and Genevra wheeled a portable freezer out of the café's kitchen. Marianna precariously hoisted a large sign reading "Free Ice Cream" above the freezer. I smiled my thanks at her just before a horde of people hoping to score a frosty treat formed a small mob and swamped her.

As soon as she was sure Marianna was okay, Genevra made her way through the crowded lobby to the aquarium entrance. She spoke to the ticket taker who shook his head. She pointed to me, and I nodded. Whatever she had in mind, I had enough faith in her to know that it would be a good idea.

The ticket taker shrugged and helped Genevra unfurl a huge sign that said "Free Admission*. Today Only." In smaller letters it said "*If you sign up for our mailing list." She was brilliant. We'd have the contact information for anyone who took advantage of the free offer, even if Sammy Douglas was unsuccessful in keeping people in the pool house.

Less than a minute later, Dane walked over with Maddy by his side. She reached out and touched my arm. "This is not your fault.

You couldn't have known this would happen, and it's not the first time RIO's had to worry about money. We'll figure something out and get through this."

I saw the sadness in her eyes and knew she was being brave for my sake. I was so grateful. I hugged her. "Thank you," I whispered.

"Ahem," said Dane. "The faster we get this investigation started the faster we'll recover the Sea Stars."

Maddy slipped out of the hug. "I'll be in my office if anyone needs me." She stopped by the impromptu ice cream stand to say hello to Marianna, who handed her a gigantic cone along with a broad smile. Everybody knew Maddy had a weakness for chocolate ice cream.

Roland went into the pool house to put police tape around the kiosk where we'd had the Sea Stars on display. Shards of glass littered the floor. Eugene from maintenance was standing by to clean up the glass as soon as his twin brother Roland had taken photos and finished his examination. Eugene knew well that we couldn't afford to let any of the glass make its way into the pool.

Roland and Eugene exchanged a few words and clapped each other on the back before Roland left to join Morey at the front entrance to help question the crowds of people who were leaving. They took contact info from anyone who had a legitimate need to leave right away and searched every large bag and parcel, but the Anderson Sea Stars were so heavy that it would actually have taken a wheeled cart or a dolly to remove them.

The police stationed at the front door intercepted people trying to leave and sent all of the exhibition attendees who couldn't come up with a good enough reason to avoid on site questioning back to the pool house to wait for their turn. Theresa was in the pool house presiding over a free make-your-own taco bar. I was impressed that the team had managed to execute my idea so quickly.

I was sticking close to Dane so I could eavesdrop on the process of the investigation. After the third time I accidentally jostled his elbow while trying to overhear someone's response to his question, he sighed in exasperation. "You don't have to hang back. If you're going to be here, just stand beside me. Keep a sharp lookout for anything that seems suspicious, and don't say anything to anyone except me. Okay?"

I nodded and took a step forward so Dane and I were shoulder to shoulder as he questioned the people in line to leave. After he dismissed them, I apologized for the hassle and thanked them for coming. I handed out free passes to the aquarium and coupons for a free drink at Ray's Place.

If the loss of the funding for the movie doesn't drive us into bankruptcy, the cost of all these giveaways might do it, I thought morosely. But I smiled gamely as I continued handing out coupons until the room was empty. Dane and I tried to figure out how someone could have removed the Anderson Sea Stars without anyone seeing them do it.

The Anderson Sea Stars had been in the center of the gigantic room, visible from every corner and lit from all sides. The glass case had physical and electronic locks equipped with an ear piercing alarm. Even though there was no CCTV in the pool house, it seemed impossible that the Sea Stars could just disappear. Dane's frustrated sigh told me he was quickly coming to the same conclusion.

A few minutes later, Roland came in with his forensic case and said with despair. "You never make it easy on me, do you?" He got to work picking up bits of litter and lifting fingerprints off the broken glass of the case where we'd had the Sea Stars on display.

"See anything?" Dane said.

I shook my head. "Nope."

"Okay then, why don't you go on back to work. I'll come get you if we find anything interesting."

I knew I wouldn't be able to work, but I recognized that Dane and his team would be more effective without me in the mix, so I nodded and left the pool house. I made a point of stopping to thank everyone who'd worked so hard to keep the exhibit attendees around until Dane could get to them.

Marianna just waved a hand in the air. "I scooped a few ice cream cones. No big deal." Then she handed me a requisition to replace the ice cream inventory she'd used. I signed it without even looking at the bottom line.

"By the way," she said, biting her lip. "It's time to retire. I'd like to work through next month and then be gone. We can talk again when you have more time, but I wanted to give you a heads up as soon as I'd made the decision."

Inside, I was dying, but I smiled brightly at her. She'd worked at RIO since the first day it opened, and it wouldn't be the same without her. I'd have to give some thought to how we'd replace her. "Congratulations, Mariana. We'll miss you, but I understand. Let's talk when we get the exhibition back on track and we'll work out a plan for your departure."

She agreed and walked away just as my phone rang. Caller ID said Theresa. After we said hello, I thanked her for setting up the taco bar.

She laughed. "Thanks for giving out all those free drink coupons. There are people lined up three deep at Ray's Place, and I'm all alone out here. Can I call in Noah and Austin for a little overtime to help out, please?"

I gave the okay and trudged the last few feet down the hall to my office. With each step, I felt like more of a failure. I slumped behind my desk.

Newton came in and sat down in one of my guest chairs. "What's your game plan?"

"I don't have one yet. I may have to call the network and beg them to renegotiate our old documentary contract." I knew that even if they agreed, I'd be lucky to get terms anywhere near as favorable as our old deal.

I had been so pleased when I'd been able to remove our dependence on the whims of the network. The last few years they'd been paring back on advertising and other benefits, and the cuts had resulted in a drastic drop in our revenue. I'd thought the profits from the movie and the exhibition tie-in would tide us over until the new businesses I'd started—Ray's Place, Christophe's freediving school, and the soon-to-open submarine tours—started

166

turning enough profit to fund our vital research. But now I'd be lucky if my decisions didn't force us into bankruptcy.

"My trust fund?" I asked.

He shook his head. "You can't withdraw enough to make a difference, and even if you tried, as a trustee I wouldn't allow it. I know you don't take a salary from RIO, and if you deplete your trust, it wouldn't leave you anything to live on."

"And before you ask, I've already donated my limit for this year. For tax reasons, if I put in any more money, RIO would lose its non-profit status because it would look like I owned it."

"I can sell the *Tranquility*," I said.

He shook his head. "The *Tranquility* has a lot of sentimental value, but it wouldn't bring in much money. Not even enough to keep the place running for a couple of weeks. I'm sorry, Fin, but you need to start working on a plan to cut back expenses. Maybe even an exit plan. Shut the place down and get out completely."

'I'll never allow that to happen," I said.

"And neither will I," said Liam's voice from the doorway. "I can't donate any more directly to RIO this year either, but I'll happily fund the movie production.

Newton slapped his forehead. "Why didn't I think of that? And I'm supposed to be the brilliant financial guy!"

Liam laughed. "You are indeed a brilliant financial guy, but everybody has blind spots." He turned to me. "Can you get what's-his-name, T-8, in here so we can get moving on this before the crew disperses?"

"I'll give him a call," I said, remembering again how lucky I was to have found Liam. There were grateful tears in my eyes, but I didn't want anyone to see them, so I turned away to rummage for my phone.

Five minutes later, T-8 was in the doorway to my office. "Lucky you caught me. I was on my way to the airport."

I smiled at him. "Well, cancel your flight. We've got an angel investor willing to fund the entire film. Get everyone back. We're ready to roll."

He looked startled. "Who's the investor this time?" he asked. "Your previous money person didn't work out all that well."

Liam said, "It's me, and I assure you, I have access to all the funding you might need. Let's go somewhere quiet and talk terms."

T-8 stared at him mouth agape. "I don't want to waste my time again. You sure you've got enough money?"

Liam nodded. "Billions."

T-8's mouth dropped open. "Oh, wait. Douglas told me you're that *Oh! Possum* guy, right? Is that for real?"

"It's for real. Let's go."

They left with Newton to hash out the terms of the deal in the conference room.

Roland walked in right behind them, rolling a large black case. "Dane decided we don't need to hold on to these—if you think you can manage not to lose them." He lifted the lid of the case to reveal the Anderson Sea Stars, shining brightly enough to dazzle the eye.

"Wow! Thank you. I was afraid we would have to shut the exhibition down since we didn't have the stars of the show on display."

Roland groaned. "That pun was very bad, Fin. Even for you."

We both burst out laughing. When we'd regained control of ourselves, he closed and locked the case. "Eugene and Stanley are making a new display case out of thick plastic with reinforced steel at all the seams, and Chaun is coming by with some new alarms since we still don't have CCTV in the pool house. That should make it harder for any bad guys around to break the case and steal these."

Roland sat in a chair in the corner until his brother came in.

"Case is ready. You want to check it out, Ro?" said Stanley.

Roland smiled. "Nope. I trust your work. But I will help you set up the display." The two men trundled out, and I sighed with relief.

Now at least I wouldn't have to contend with disgruntled exhibition patrons. I sent a text to Genevra asking her to amend the information card of the display case and the audio file connected to the exhibit's QR code to ensure they stated the sea stars we had on display were copies. Then I thanked the universe that had surrounded me with such good and caring people.

Chapter 34
Suzie Q

NEWTON LEFT to tell Maddy and Oliver the good news. I tracked down Genevra to let her know and asked her to tell anyone she saw that RIO was on financially sound footing once again, and that the movie was a go. Then I stopped by Joely's office to ask her to work up some potential short term budget cuts, just in case, before going back to my desk to work on refining the movie posters I'd drafted the other day.

An hour later, Liam came back into my office. "Everything's all set. T-8 is calling everybody back right now. The wire transfer will go through automatically as soon as he returns the signed contract."

I breathed for what felt like the first time all day. "Thank you for doing that. I hope it turns out to be a good investment for you."

He looked at me. "Anything that makes you smile like that is a good investment." He held out his hand. "C'mon. Let's get out of here. Production resumes in the morning, and you'll be pretty busy."

"Don't you have to wait for the signed contracts?"

"Nope. He's going to e-sign, and he'll get the funds automatically. Let's get out of here."

I jumped up. I'd been through so much in the last few days that

I was more than ready to call it a day. "Got time for a dive? I don't think I've seen Suzie Q in more than a week."

"You're right. She'll be wondering what happened to us," he said.

I grabbed my canvas tote bag and my ID badge and together, we walked out RIO's front door. We took Liam's car for the drive to Rum Point.

Once there, I grabbed our gear bags, a couple of tanks, and two solid black dive skins from my breezeway and tossed them into the trunk of Liam's car while I waited for him to feed Chico and Henrietta.

"Hurry up," I called out. It wasn't like me to rush caring for our animals, but I couldn't wait to get wet. I was instantly ashamed of myself. Chico had once saved my life, and at the very least, I owed him the courtesy of an unhurried full bowl of seeds each day.

Liam grinned at me, but he continued with carefully filling the seed bowls and water dishes for the formerly "free range" fowl who'd become pretty domesticated since we'd started feeding them.

It wasn't long before Liam jumped in the car and drove us to our favorite dive site at Rum Point. We geared up, then shuffled into the warm, clear water. Liam held out a steadying arm while I slipped my feet into my fins, and I did the same for him. We both put anti-fogging drops in our masks, rinsed them in sea water, and slipped them on. Then, with our snorkels in our mouths, we kicked our way over to the line that marked out the 'no boats allowed' area.

Once there, we switched over to our regulators and sank into the depths. The bottom here was sandy, with occasional clumps of coral and large sponges that provided a home to hundreds of tiny sea denizens. We followed a major sand chute toward the drop off to the nearby wall, searching the sand for the telltale outline of a stingray.

I raised my head to look out toward the reef and saw a male stingray flying by. I touched Liam's arm and pointed. He broke into a huge grin. More than likely this was one of Suzie Q's sons from a litter we'd watched being born not so long ago. I was happy to see they were thriving.

We stopped to peer into a giant elephant ear sponge, where we were delighted to see a healthy colony of shrimp and a tiny seahorse watching their every move. A nearby tube sponge was home to a group of juvenile glassy sweepers, who were barely visible except that they moved continuously and so drew my eyes toward them. Liam reached out for my hand as we continued toward the wall, and a queen conch traversed the sand below us, leaving a faint trail behind her.

We dropped over the edge of the wall and saw the large green turtle we'd named Norbert. He looked at us with an expression of utter disinterest before continuing on his way. I laughed into my regulator, and I could tell by the pattern of his bubbles that Liam was laughing too.

We swam into the current without seeing anything truly note-worthy, just the usual assortment of grunts, wrasses, and spiny lobsters lurking under the coral crevasses. Liam and I hit the turn-around point on our air at the same time, and we headed back the way we came, rising slightly as we swam to prolong our bottom time.

Back on the flat of the reef, we meandered along the sand trails that wove among the coral heads, looking for Suzie Q, our favorite southern stingray. At this point, she had known us for years, but she still made it clear that there would be no socializing.

Just as we neared the string of buoys that marked the swim area, I looked down and saw her flying across the sand toward a spray of staghorn coral that grew next to a yellow brain coral. She settled onto the bottom and fluttered her wings to cover her body with sand, leaving only her inscrutable eyes uncovered. She watched us warily as we continued to swim away from her toward shore.

I didn't care that she never let us get close. I was always just happy to see her and to know she was doing well.

After we'd swum under the line of buoys, Liam and I surfaced and switched over to our snorkels for the swim back to shore. In waist deep water, we removed our fins and then walked through the gentle wavelets, hand in hand.

We loaded our gear into the back of Liam's car and returned to my house. As we got out of the car in my driveway, Liam asked, "Would you rather cook dinner or rinse the gear?" He could hardly keep a straight face.

"I'll rinse. You cook," I said with a laugh. "I'm starving, so I'd like my dinner to be edible." I opened the garage door and dragged out the large plastic bins we used as rinse tanks. I leaned against the door while I waited for the garden hose to fill the tubs.

I'd just hung our now clean but still soaking wet dive skins in the breezeway when I heard Liam calling me. "Dinner's ready. I'm at my place."

Liam and I own houses next door to each other. Both our yards have fences around them, but we'd put in a gate in them so we could easily go back and forth between his place to mine. I sniffed the fragrant air appreciatively. Whatever he'd prepared, it smelled delicious, even all the way over here.

I loaded our empty tanks into the trunk of his car and hurried through my yard to the adjoining gate. As usual, I laughed at the sight of the tiny doggy door he'd installed next to the people gate so Chico and Henrietta could join us regardless of which yard we were in.

Just like on my property, hundreds of twinkling fairy lights lit Liam's backyard. Although there was no pool on his side of the fence, he did have a water fountain with a mermaid endlessly pouring recirculated water from a jar back into the basin, and the gentle sound of the falling water was always soothing.

We both used the same yard maintenance service, and the beauty of Liam's space showed they took excellent care of us. An abundance of flowers and flowering trees filled the nearby areas, and the fragrant blossoms came in all colors. A flagstone path wound through the flowers to a rear garden, where Liam grew fresh vegetables. He'd given the garden crew permission to take the ripe veggies home with them for their own use so they wouldn't go to waste while he was traveling, but tonight we had fresh peas, ripe red tomatoes, and small ears of sweet corn.

We didn't eat chicken at home, in deference to Chico and Henrietta, and I never eat fish. Liam had marinated bite sized cubes of pork loin and cooked them on the grill, wrapped in aluminum foil with the veggies fresh from his garden. The result was heavenly.

"You're a good cook," I said as I finished my meal.

He laughed, and there was an impish gleam in his deep blue eyes. "If you think I'm a good cook, wait until you see what I've got planned for you next. It's spectacular."

"Bring it on," I said.

And he did.

Chapter 35
Submarine Rides

I WAS STILL SMILING when I arrived at my office at six-thirty the next morning. As usual for Grand Cayman, the day promised to be glorious, sunny, and warm, with enough of a light ocean breeze to keep it pleasant. I'd just taken my first sip of coffee when someone knocked at my door.

"Davy," I said. "You're here early. Welcome to RIO."

Davy Jones limped across the room to sit in one of my visitors' chairs. He and I were friends of a sort. A few years ago, he'd taught me how to pilot RIO's personal submarine, but I'd never truly been comfortable with him because of the company he kept.

He'd recently sworn off associating with the bad guys, so I was willing to give him a chance. Now he was here to help me launch another money-making business to support RIO's never-ending need for funds to support our research. The new business— submarine dives for tourists— was exciting.

Davy had once been a member of a notorious gang, but he'd drawn the line when they descended into the depths of depravity and started dabbling in human trafficking. Tucked away on a ship in the middle of the ocean, he hadn't had the ability to contact the police directly without compromising his own safety, but he'd done his best to help the victims. That help was the reason he'd only had to spend a year in jail, but the fact was probably little consolation to him since everybody else in the gang was still roaming the world, free as the proverbial bird.

While Davy had still been consorting with the traffickers, the gang leader discovered that he'd tried to help the victims, clapped him into leg irons, and shot him during the rescue attempt. The badly infected abrasion from the manacles on his leg had healed but left him with the slight limp. Luckily, the bullet wound they'd given him in his arm was a through and through, but it left a scar.

In retrospect, Davy was lucky to have gotten out of the situation with the traffickers alive. The police had released him a few days ago, and as I'd promised, I had a job waiting for him.

He was holding a cup of coffee from the cafe. He sipped deeply and gave a satisfied sigh. "Best coffee I've had in a year." He put his coffee down. "Before we start, I have to thank you for offering me this job. It isn't easy for an ex-con to get a job at all, especially when people find out what I was in for. Thank you. I promise I'll do my best and I'll work hard."

I stared at him sternly. "Good. And I also need you to stay out of trouble. No more consorting with criminals, no matter how big the payoff. Got it?"

He bit his lip and nodded. "I got it. I don't want any more trouble in my life. What do you have for me to do?"

Joely and I had been working on this venture's business plan for months, so I was ready. I pulled two three-ring binders out of a desk drawer and handed one to Davy. The binders contained my plan for the new business. All the major factors except the detailed budgets were also in a presentation I had cued up on my Mac. I ran through the highlights of the new business, which, in the presentation, I'd called RIO Presents Davy Jones' Locker Submarine Adventures.

I wasn't sure how Davy would feel about linking his actual name with the legendary 18th century pirate, and I wasn't sure how I felt about linking RIO's name with his notoriety.

The Davy Jones legend is that he escorts drowned sailors into the afterlife. And the modern day Davy Jones had an unsavory reputation. But I wanted to give Davy the feeling that he had a hand in creating the business he'd be running.

Davy looked at the title slide for a minute, obviously thinking deeply. "Don't do it, Fin. It's a bad connotation all around. How about just calling it RIO Submarine Rides? Or Submarine Rides With RIO?"

"Hmmm. You're right. Those are much better choices." Submarine Rides With RIO was actually the name I'd wanted, so I smiled with relief. It was simple, straight forward and would provide customers the comfort and security of the famous RIO institute name.

I went through the rest of the presentation, offering Davy the chance to provide input and making notes of his ideas, many of which were quite good. When we'd finished the high-level stuff, I said "How are you at reading financial statements like profit and loss? Budgets? Stuff like that."

He shook his head. "Not so good. Can you explain it to me?"

"Nope, but I know someone who can." I led him down the hall to Joely's office. As RIO's CFO, she was great at explaining financial stuff. In fact, she'd done the statements in the binders for me.

Joely had been a victim of the gang that Davy belonged to, so I'd been concerned that she and Davy wouldn't get along because of his past. We'd talked about it, and she assured me that she was fine working with Davy. She knew he'd done his best to keep her and the other victims safe, and he'd helped her escape at the first opportunity.

She wasn't effusive in her greeting, but she was polite and business-like, so she seemed to have put the bad stuff behind her. I figured that was the best I could hope for, and I was grateful to my friend for what she'd agreed to do to help him.

"Send him back when you're through, please." I gave her a sympathetic look. Even though she seemed to be handling the meeting well, this couldn't be an easy task I'd asked of her.

She nodded. "Will do."

She sat at the table in the corner of her office. I noticed she took the seat with easy access to the exit door, but maybe that was just a coincidence. Either way, Davy would have to get comfortable with the idea of re-earning people's trust.

An hour later, Davy was back in my office. "What now?" he asked.

"Let's go inspect the submarine. I haven't used her much while you've been away, so it probably needs a lot of maintenance. I'll show you where it is, and you can make a list of what you think it'll need, okay?'

He nodded, and we walked out of the RIO building and across the back lawn to the boathouse where we stored the submarine.

I pushed the sliding doors apart and smiled when the sunlight hit the iridescent blue-green sub. It could hold six passengers plus the pilot, and the sub could descend to 1600 feet and stay down for up to ten hours. It had a top speed of three knots, but that was fine for sightseeing. We'd painted over the previous owner's logo, and it now bore the RIO brand.

Unlike some unsafe subs used for tourist rides that were seemingly made from chewing gum and old tin cans, this one was a beauty, commercially made and purpose-built at a cost of more than thirty-five million dollars. Luckily, RIO hadn't had to buy it, or we wouldn't have it at all.

Stewie must have seen us walking toward the boat house because he put the "back in fifteen minutes" sign on the door and headed our way. I'd talked to him before I'd offered Davy the job at RIO, because Stewie was the head of diving operations. Nominally, although Davy would be running a separate business, he'd report to Stewie, who was a straight shooter. He wouldn't easily forgive what Davy had done.

But like Joely, Stewie was business-like and blandly pleasant when he re-introduced himself to Davy. He didn't offer to shake hands, but a lot of people had learned to avoid handshakes after the last few years, so maybe he was just being careful.

"I can take over from here if you need to get back to work, Fin," he said. He never took his eyes off Davy.

"Thanks," I said. "He's seen the business plan and Joely went over the financial projections with him. I think our next step should be coming up with a maintenance list."

"Agreed," said Stewie. "We'll bring the requisition in to you as soon as we know what we're dealing with."

I thanked him and headed back to my office to start my real workday.

Chapter 36
Rosie Meets Rafe

Except when I arrived at my office, Rafe Cummings was sitting in one of the visitors' chairs. He'd turned it around to face the wall instead of the desk, the better to admire the massive, framed print hanging there. It was an enlargement of the shot I'd taken of Rafe and the hammerhead, floating eye-to-eye.

It had arrived from the framers yesterday, and Eugene and Stanley had hung it overnight. This was the first time I'd had a chance to sit and admire it myself, so I flipped the other visitors' chair around and sat next to him.

The detail was exquisite. It was perfectly in focus, and the clear Cayman water did nothing to block the view. I could see the rough texture of the shark's skin and the gleam of his sharp teeth.

Rafe's brilliant blue eyes shone through his mask without a trace of fear, and you could see the faint hint of a smile peeking out from around his regulator. He'd just turned his head, so even his bubbles were behind him.

Everything was sharp and well-defined. It was lucky that I'd given Rafe that silver RIO branded dive skin to wear. He was sleek and shiny—and the RIO logo was clearly visible. Every little bit of marketing helps. I knew this image was an award winner, and I was proud of my work and of Rafe for being so cool when he came face-to-face with the fearsome beast.

We looked at each other and at the time, we said, "Thank you." Then we both laughed.

"We make a good team," he said. His eyes shone, and his smile was mesmerizing.

I nodded, but I jumped up before I lost myself in those eyes and that smile.

He didn't seem to notice my uneasiness with our closeness. He just sat there staring at the photo. "How big do you think that guy was, anyway?"

I shrugged. "I'd guess about 1,000 pounds but there's no way to be sure unless you can get him to hop onto a scale." We laughed again, and then we fell silent. The silence felt charged, and I shuffled my feet nervously.

Rafe cleared his throat. "I've been hearing a lot about your pet octopus. Any chance you can introduce me?"

"Rosie's not a pet. She's an Atlantic pygmy octopus and a stellar research subject...except I guess I do love her like a pet. Either way, I'll be happy to introduce you. Follow me to the research lab, the real heart of RIO. All this other stuff is what we do to earn money to support the research."

"I know. I read the brochure." He grinned at me. "Where to?"

I led the way down the long corridor to the research area. Rosie was in a small tank in the main lab. I directed Rafe to the sink to wash his hands. While he was rinsing, he had a mischievous gleam in his eye. The next thing I knew he'd splashed a giant handful of water toward me.

I squealed and stepped back, then lunged forward, pushing my hands under the stream of water from the faucet. I sent a substantial wave Rafe's way, and it hit him in the face.

He sputtered and splashed me again. By this time, we were laughing like two little kids frolicking under a hose in their backyard on a hot day. We were soaking wet, water dripping from our hair and our eyelashes and making our clothes clingy.

Rafe went still and stared at me, his lips slightly parted and his eyes wide. He leaned in, and I knew he was going to kiss me. Part of me wanted him to, but I stepped back and shook my head. I would never forgive myself for hurting Liam the way I had. I wouldn't do that to him again.

Rafe gave a little half smile. "Sorry. I forgot." He looked around. "Where's Rosie?"

I led the way over to the small aquarium where Rosie made her home. As we approached, the tank looked empty. Nothing but a jumbled pile of multi-colored objects in one corner, and a lovely shell in another corner.

I put a finger in the water, and almost immediately, one of Rosie's tiny tendrils flicked outside the shell. It waved, tasting the water, then Rosie's entire body oozed out and headed over to my finger. She latched on with two tentacles and gazed up at me with her enigmatic eyes.

"Go ahead," I said. "Put your hand in—not too close. Just hold it steady. She'll investigate when she's ready."

Rafe's hand was only an inch or so away from mine, so Rosie sent a free tentacle over to investigate.

Rafe gasped. "It feels so weird."

"Yup. You'll get used to it. Give her a minute to get to know you."

While we were talking, Rosie sent another tentacle over to explore Rafe's hand. Then a third. She gazed up at his face. He didn't move, except to flick his eyes to one side so he wasn't staring straight at her.

I smiled with approval. She wouldn't like knowing he was scrutinizing her until she'd decided whether or not she liked Rafe.

Another tentacle floated toward him. And then another, each one curling around his fingers and his hand, exploring the textures and flavors of his skin and nails. Suddenly, she gave what could only be described as a hop, and all her tentacles were now exploring Rafe.

"I think she likes you," I said laughing at his awed expression. "Do you want to see how smart she is?"

He nodded. "I've read your research paper, but I'd love to see her do her stuff in real life."

I removed a small deck of cards from the shelf under Rosie's tank. "Pick a card. Any card—although I suggest starting with one of the simpler ones."

With his free hand, Rafe selected a card with an image of a blue ball.

"Good. Now hold it where she can see it." I told him.

He placed the card against the tank glass, directly in Rosie's sightline.

Rosie took off like an eight-legged bullet and made a beeline for the pile of objects in the far corner. Without hesitation, she picked up a small blue ball and brought it back to our side of the tank. She placed it carefully on the gravel that lined the bottom of her tank and waited expectantly.

Rafe was beaming like a proud father. "She's so smart," he said.

"Yup. Smart enough to know she deserves a treat for that performance." I opened the small tin of minced clams we kept for training Rosie and held it out to Rafe.

He took a piece and dropped it in the tank near her. She snatched the morsel before it touched bottom, then she passed it along her tentacles to her mouth. Once she'd ingested the clam, she flashed her thank you by changing her skin to a lovely pink color.

Rafe looked delighted. "Will she do it again?"

"Probably. But don't overdo it. She'll get fat gorging on clams."

Rafe laughed. "Okay. Just one more."

When Rosie had finished her second clam, I turned to Rafe. "She has a new behavior she just mastered. Would you like to see it?"

"Sure would," he said. "I'm honored."

I took a small Lucite box from the shelf and placed it on the table. Inside the box were a series of panels that I could arrange and rearrange to make different maze layouts. The endpoint of every maze was always a small chamber with a clam in it as a reward for Rosie for successfully navigating the labyrinth.

After I set up the panels in a new pattern, I dropped a chunk of clam in the reward chamber. Then I closed the door to the box, and flipped a sliding latch closed before slipping a small piece of plastic twine tied in a loose knot through the hoop where you might normally hang a padlock.

I placed the box in the center of Rosie's tank while she watched me solemnly from inside her shell home. She waited a few seconds after I withdrew my hand before she came out to investigate. She floated over to the box and sent out several tentacles to examine it from multiple sides. She very quickly recognized that the piece of twine was holding the box shut, so she untied it, lifted it out of the latch, and put it aside.

In the blink of an eye, she had the door open.

Rafe gasped.

I smiled at him. "She's done that part before, so she can complete it pretty fast. But the maze is always different."

We watched as Rosie floated down each miniature hallway, pausing at intersections to decide which way to go. Although the Lucite panels were solid and nearly invisible to humans underwater, they didn't seem to slow Rosie down at all. Almost unerringly, she chose the correct path on her first try every time. She completed the maze, picked up the clam, and scooted out of the box and back to her shell in record time.

Rafe was floating on air from his time with Rosie. She had that effect on people. Her entire body, with tentacles fully extended, was smaller than my palm, yet her brain and personality were giant size. It was hard not to adore her.

Chapter 37
A New House

RAFE and I walked back to my office together, but we took the long way around to stop by the café for a lemonade for me and a cup of mineral water for Rafe.

He might be a world famous movie star, but he didn't take his success for granted. He understood the requirements of his job, and he put in the necessary effort to maintain his famous physique. I knew he worked out hard every day, and he showed extraordinary discipline in his eating habits. I admired his self-restraint.

I'd seen the results of that discipline on display when we were diving. With minimal body fat, his muscles were clearly visible rippling beneath his skin whenever he moved. He was incredibly fit.

For him, the downside of all that self-restraint was that while I'd picked up a sugary lemonade and two of RIO's famous chocolate chip cookies, Rafe made do with just ice water. We sat at the round table, Rafe sipping morosely at his mineral water.

Taking pity on him, I broke off a small piece of one of my cookies, barely a nibble, but about the size I'd seen him eat before. I figured it was small enough that he'd think it would be okay for him to have it. I put the pitifully small chunk of deliciousness on a napkin and slid it across the table toward him "Enjoy," I said when his eyes lit up.

"Bless you, my dear," he said after his first mini bite.

I munched my cookies and Rafe picked at his crumbs in companionable silence, each of us lost in our own thoughts until the sound of his phone ringing shattered our peace.

He grabbed it and walked into the hall before answering.

I shrugged. We were friends, but he had a right to privacy. I moved over to my desk and opened my photo portfolio to work on the *Ecosphere* spread that would feature Rafe and the movie—and my by-lined photos.

I worked on my files until Rafe came back in, a happy smile on his face. "I just bought a house. It's the first house I've ever owned!"

I stood up to shake his hand, but he swept me into a hug and started dancing me around in circles, laughing with joy. I couldn't help but laugh along with him until he kissed me. Then I broke out of his embrace and took a step back.

He looked contrite. "I'm sorry. I know I shouldn't have done that. It won't happen again. I promise." Then his face lit up. "I'm just so happy."

"I can imagine. Owning your own home is a great feeling." I remembered how overjoyed I'd been when the deed to my home appeared in my twenty-first birthday card from Newton. At that point, I didn't know Newton at all, but that didn't keep me from loving the house. It took me a while to learn to love the man though.

I smiled, remembering the joy of finally getting to know my long-lost father.

Rafe grinned at me. "Makes me happy already. I can't wait to tell my brother."

"You have a brother? How wonderful for you. Where is he?"

"I'm not really sure where he's gone to right now," Rafe said. "We used to be very close. My family was homeless for several years when I was a kid. My dad was pretty abusive. He used to beat Dougie and me with a broomstick. Mom tried to stop him, but one day my mother just disappeared. We only stuck around a few weeks after that."

"I was in the fifth grade then, but Dougie was a few years older than me, so he dropped out of school to get a job to support us. Even so, we lived on the street or in his car most of the time. It wasn't easy for him, but even when I was old enough, he wouldn't hear of letting me quit school so I could help out too." I saw mist in his eyes. "Then one day, he disappeared. I had no way to get in touch with him, and I never saw him again. Broke my heart."

"T-8 and I were friends from school. He was homeless too, and we'd always kind of had each other's backs. A few months after Dougie disappeared without a word, we decided to hitchhike to Hollywood. We thought we were going to make it big in the movies. We lived on the street or shared a room in flop houses for years before we even earned enough for a security deposit on a low-rent apartment. But then T-8 got a few roles, and I started out as his stunt double and personal assistant."

"After a while, he decided he didn't like acting, so he got into producing and directing. I slid into the acting arena by auditioning for the roles T-8 turned down, and he helped me get some of them. Eventually, we both hit it big, but I never stopped looking for my brother. I've had a PI looking for him ever since I could afford to hire one. I have a feeling we're getting close to finding him."

His eyes held a faraway look as he sighed. "So, after all that, owning a house of my own means a lot to me."

I felt renewed respect for this man who'd had such a tough life. He'd worked hard to get to where he was, and he deserved his success. "Congratulations. Your history makes owning your own place even more wonderful. Where is your new home? Somewhere in Hollywood, I expect. Do you have pictures?"

"I do. And the best part is, it's here in Grand Cayman. See how great it is? It's right on the water..." He stood close to me and held his phone so we could both see the pictures on the screen.

I almost choked. The house he was showing me was the one that used to belong to my ex-husband, Alec Stone. In Hell. Where

Oliver's sister Lily had stayed. Where terrible things had happened.

His smile faded when he saw my face. "Don't you like it?"

I pasted on a smile. "I do like it. Very much. I know the person that used to own it, that's all. It's a great house, and I'm happy for you. But won't it be a tough commute to Hollywood?"

He shook his head. "Most of my movies are shot on location, so as long as there's an international airport nearby, I can live anywhere between films."

"That's perfect. I'm really happy for you. It will be great to have you around when you're between movies."

His smile regained its glow. "You'll have to come see it some time. As soon as I get it fixed up the way I want it."

"I'd like that," I said. "But right now, I have work to do."

Chapter 38
Enviroman

I GATHERED UP MY MAC, my iPad and a few notecards and walked out the back door. I knew if I stayed in my office, there'd be a constant stream of people wanting to ask a question or chat with me. I needed to get my work done quickly so I could get back to what I love, which is diving.

Liam's new boat the *Enviroman* wasn't in its slip across from mine. It was a great boat, and it was easy to see how happy owning it had made him. Obviously, we'd be splitting our boat time between *Enviroman* and *Tranquility* in the future, at least whenever Liam was in town.

I felt a little pang. I loved *Tranquility* and being aboard my boat always made me feel closer to Ray, my late stepfather, whom I'd adored. But I could give up a little of that to make Liam happy. Ray wouldn't have minded.

I worked diligently for several hours, putting together the latest projections for when RIO would become self-sustaining. When Maddy had started RIO, it was wholly dependent on donations and the fees we received from the network for our annual documentaries. This year, because they'd slanted the terms so heavily in their own favor, I'd declined to sign our contract at all.

But over time, the fees had dwindled, leaving RIO continuously on the verge of bankruptcy. Two years ago, I'd gone to Newton and Maddy with a plan to make the institute self-sustaining by adding peripheral businesses that would contribute all their profits to funding the research.

Maddy had agreed to the plan, although she had some misgivings. I negotiated the deal with T-8's production company to pay us for the use of our facilities for their next movie and to give us a few percentage points of the film's profits.

But Maddy's concerns made me anxious, so I frequently went back over RIO's financials to make sure we'd be okay. I hate numbers, so it was a very draining task, and I had to concentrate hard. Because it was so difficult for me to focus, I was wearing noise cancelling headphones. Not to listen to music, but to block out any noise around me that might break my train of thought.

I started by listing the current and planned businesses. Ray's Place, our on-site restaurant, had been the first of these endeavors, and it was now well-established as one of the most popular restaurants and bars on Grand Cayman.

Christophe Poisson's freediving school had been the second business to launch. It was just about breaking even now, but as its reputation grew, it would begin making a larger contribution.

We'd also stepped up our scuba training and dive shop sales, under Stewie's management. That business was also doing well. The soon to open submarine ride attraction would contribute more.

When I'd once again reached the conclusion that RIO would squeak by the next two years and then become self-sustaining, I breathed a sigh of relief and stood up to stretch. Through the window across from the galley table where I'd been sitting, I noticed that Liam's boat was still gone.

I was surprised he'd taken the boat out without letting me know, but maybe he'd seen how hard I'd been working and decided not to disturb me. I assumed he, Oliver, Newton, and Gus had taken a cooler of beers and gone fishing. Good for them if they had. They all worked hard and deserved a break.

And so did I. I leaned back, supporting myself with my hands until I felt my stiff muscles relax. As I'd taken on more of the administration of RIO, I'd had less and less time for the things I loved—diving, swimming, photography. I needed to find a way to put more balance in my life.

Wearily, I gathered up my things and stepped off the *Tranquility*. When I looked over to Liam's slip, I saw that something had torn apart the narrow decking that marked the boundary between slips. A few broken boards floated on the water, marred by scrapes of white paint. A ragged rope dangled from the cleats.

This was not a normal occurrence even in a storm, but it was downright weird on a beautiful windless day like this. It would have taken a lot of force to create this destruction, and Liam was a superb boat handler. I couldn't believe that he would have done such a poor job of taking his new boat out. Something was obviously wrong.

I stood on the far edge of the dock and saw *Enviroman* bobbing around over deep water. It looked like it was unanchored, floating free, and it was running in circles at high speed. I didn't see anyone aboard, so I pulled out my cellphone to call Liam. He didn't answer.

That scared me. I ran up the ladder to the *Tranquility*'s flying bridge and started the engines. After quickly backing out of my slip, I headed straight for *Enviroman*. I called out as I drew near the boat but received no answer. From this distance, I could tell that the boat was definitely on its own.

"Liam," I shouted. "Are you there?"

Silence.

I tried his cellphone again. The faint sound of his ringtone reached me over the roar of the engines, but he didn't pick up. Fear clutched my heart.

I dropped *Tranquility*'s anchor until I felt it snag in the sand below. I slipped on my fins. Carrying a line, I dove off the gunwales and swam as fast as I could to *Enviroman*. The engines were running hard, and the swim platform was still upright. That would make it tricky to get aboard.

I dove under the water to check out the engine configuration. Just like with my boat, two 350 horsepower Yamaha engines frothed the water. It was hard to see anything and very dangerous to get too close. I could stay nearby and wait for the boat to run out of gas. But Liam could be aboard and need my help. My only hope of getting on the boat was to attach a line to one of the cleats on the gunwales. I tied one end of the line around my left wrist and made a wide loop like a lasso with the other.

I was treading water, watching the boat's movements until I felt comfortable with the pattern of its movement. I swam in close to where I calculated the *Enviroman* would next pass broadside to my position. If my calculations were wrong, it would be difficult to get out of the boat's way and dangerous for me if I couldn't.

Well, I'm Fin Fleming. My parents joked that Foolhardy should have been my middle name, but I could always count on my luck. Although Newton and Maddy frequently reminded me that luck can be fickle, so far my luck had never let me down. Plus, water is my natural element, and difficult and dangerous are exactly what I like. And what I do best.

As Liam's boat swung past me, I tossed the rope like a lariat, hoping to get the loop to fall over one of the cleats.

I missed.

Undaunted, I dropped back a few feet and watched the boat as it circled. Once I was sure I knew its path and speed well enough to predict its travel pattern again, I moved in closer. At what I hoped was just the right moment, I tossed the loop up.

This time, my luck held. The loop landed over one of the cleats. I tugged gently, once, twice. Again. At last, the loop was tight around the cleat.

Holding on to the rope, I surface swam back to the *Tranquility*, letting the line spool out behind me as I swam. I removed my fins and flung them onto the deck before I climbed up the ladder to the dive platform. Still holding my end of the line, I rushed across the *Tranquility*'s deck and removed the loop from around my wrist. I dropped it over one of my boat's cleats and pulled it tight. Then I hauled back on the rope, pulling Liam's boat a few feet nearer. I wrapped the loose line around the cleat and hauled again.

And again.

Again. Over and over.

I kept pulling the boat nearer and tying off the slack line so it couldn't drift away. As the boat drew closer to me, I could see it was in disarray. Scuba gear was lying out on the deck, and tanks rolled back and forth with the rhythm of the waves. Charts and maps were splayed on the floor, melting in the sea water that had been splashed aboard. Piles of clothes and a few books littered the stern. It was obvious from the mess that something terrible had happened. But I couldn't think about that now. I only knew I had to get aboard that boat.

At last, it was close enough that I felt sure I could jump across from the *Tranquility* to land on *Enviroman*'s deck. If I failed, I'd fall in the water, which was good. Unless *Enviroman* made an unexpected turn and crushed me or pointed her lethal engines my way. Which would be very bad.

I stood on *Tranquility*'s gunwales with a hand on the transom to steady me until the perfect moment to jump. I breathed slowly and deeply, waiting for my moment.

I waited.

And waited.

Suddenly, *Enviroman* slewed in, reducing the gap between the boats. Without a moment's hesitation I sprang across the open water between the boats. I caught my left foot on the *Enviroman*'s gunwales and fell to her deck.

My toes hurt like crazy, but at least I was on board. I ran below.

Liam. Where was Liam?

He was lying on the deck under the bridge, a pool of blood spreading slowly around him. His face was badly bruised, and his mouth was swollen. A sickening bite mark defaced his cheek, and a honking big gash marred the rest of his face, from his once perfect cheekbones to the crown of his head. Blood matted his blond hair, turning it a nasty shade of brown. One hand looked broken, and the fingers on the other were twisted and deformed.

I knelt beside him to feel for a pulse. It was there, thready, and weak, but thank God, it was there. Tears sprang to my eyes.

I grabbed the radio and called Stewie at RIO's dive shop.

"Fin, what got into Liam?" he said when he answered. "The dock's a mess. I've never seen…"

"Never mind all that. Get Doc and bring her out here in one of the Zodiacs. Liam's been attacked. I don't know if we have much time."

"Got it," he said. He dropped the radio. I wanted to hold Liam's hand, brush back his hair, tell him I loved him. He was breathing and no longer bleeding, so there wasn't anything I could do to help him until Doc arrived. He was so bent and broken I couldn't see any place I could touch him without causing him pain, so I stretched out beside him as close as I could get and whispered in his ear. "You'll be alright. I'll find whoever did this. Doc is coming. I love you."

I continued the litany until I heard the roar of the Zodiac's arrival. Doc and Stewie tied up to *Enviroman* and came aboard. Stewie went right to the bridge and shut off the engines while Doc knelt beside Liam and opened her medical bag.

"It's alright. I've got him now," she said.

I sobbed with relief and put my hands over my face to hide my tears. I gave a start when Stewie touched my shoulder.

"Where's the other kayak?" he asked.

Chapter 39
Hospital Redux

Doc rose and whispered in Stewie's ear. He nodded and walked to the bridge where he radioed the rest of Doc's team to rush out to the *Tranquility* with a body board. I started shaking, but Doc put her arm around my shoulder. "The board is just a precaution. I don't want to cause him any pain while we move him to the hospital. I've checked him out as well as I can here, but I need more equipment to understand the full extent of his injuries. I promise to keep you posted, and right now, nothing looks life threatening."

I knew Doc would never lie to me, but I also knew she wasn't above keeping certain scary facts to herself. I wouldn't be okay until Liam opened his eyes and told me himself that he was fine.

We weren't that far away from RIO, so it didn't take long for the water ambulance to arrive. The EMTs hopped aboard and very quickly had Liam strapped to a gurney and transferred to their boat.

"I'll take care of the boats," Stewie said. "Don't worry about a thing."

Then he handed Doc a long flat piece of metal that looked the one used to keep the door to the engine compartment closed. He'd wrapped it in a plastic bag. "For Dane," he said.

197

"Thanks," she said, giving it a look filled with anger. She tightened her lips. "Coming?" she asked me.

I nodded and hopped aboard the water ambulance for the short journey to Georgetown where they would transfer Liam to Cayman Islands Hospital.

Dane met us at the dock. He and I stood together while the EMTs transferred Liam to the ambulance, which took off with a roar as soon as Doc and her patient were aboard.

He put an arm over my shoulder. "Come with me. I'll take you to the hospital. Maybe I'll be able to get a little more information than you would on your own."

I looked at him through zombie eyes but followed him slowly to his unmarked police car. He flipped on the siren and headed to the hospital.

We didn't speak during the short ride. Dane walked me into the emergency room and led me to a seat. Then he talked to the person at the desk to find out where Liam was. I was barely aware of anything until he sat beside me and pressed a cup of hot black coffee into my hand.

"Drink this. You'll feel better," he said.

I took a sip. It tasted like dirt, but I swallowed it anyway. By the time I'd finished half the cup, I realized Dane was right. I did feel more like myself. Except terror still had me frozen inside.

He patted my hand. "The ER doctor will be out in a few minutes. Don't worry. Doc's in there with him too, and she'll make sure he gets the best possible care."

I just sat, huddled in misery. I'd been only a few hundred feet away while Liam was fighting for his life on the cold, hard deck of his boat.

I don't know how long Dane and I sat there without speaking. He slipped out without a word to start the investigation when Newton joined us, bringing fresh coffee and lemonade, and with his leather Prada briefcase slung over his shoulder. He put the cups on the table and sat beside me. He gathered me to him, and I put my head on his shoulder and sobbed.

"Shh, shh, honey. It will be okay. The doctors are doing everything they can to make sure Liam comes through this as good as new. You have to think positive thoughts. I promise he'll feel them, and those good thoughts will help him find his way back to us."

But despite Newton's assurances, I was still sniffling and sobbing softly when Doc and the much despised Dr. Henry came out to talk to us.

He stood ramrod straight in front of us and focused his eyes over our heads. "Mr. Lawton is still unconscious, and we are admitting him. He sustained several heavy blows to the head, and to quite a few other parts of his body. Despite the severity of his injuries, we have every hope he'll recover."

Dr. Henry's bedside manner had not improved since he had cared for Mimi. He still spoke like a robot while standing stiffly in front of us.

"When?" I asked. "When will he wake up?"

"That I don't know. It's in the hands of mother nature and Mr. Lawton himself. Doctor Warren has requested to take over his care, if that's ok with his next of kin." He looked at each of us in turn.

"He doesn't have one. I'm his fiancée though, and I'm fine with Doc caring for him. She's the best."

He nodded. "She is the best, but unfortunately, a fiancée doesn't have legal standing to make those decisions. Do you have a power of attorney?"

I shook my head. "No, but..."

Newton stood. "She doesn't have it yet, but I do. I'm Mr. Lawton's personal attorney, Newton Fleming." He turned to the briefcase he'd placed on the floor near his feet. After opening the flap, he handed Dr. Henry some papers. "They're all in order. You can keep those copies for your records. Please transfer the patient's care to Doc Warren as soon as possible."

Dr. Henry took a moment to scan the papers, then he turned to Doc. "He's now your patient. I'll make the arrangements." He walked away without a word.

Doc sat in the chair Newton had vacated. "I want to keep Liam here at least overnight. They have some equipment here I don't have at RIO's infirmary, and I don't want to take any chances with him. Are you okay with that?"

I nodded. I'd trust Doc with my life. In fact, I frequently did.

"Would you like to see him now? You can only stay for a few minutes, but I think it will help you both." She took my hand and pulled me to my feet. "Ready?"

She led me to Liam's room, and I tiptoed inside. The nurse had drawn the shades, and the room was dim, but I could see him lying under a light blanket. They'd wrapped a huge white bandage around his head above his battered and bruised face. A plaster cast encased one of his hands. His fingers on his other hand were swollen, the nails broken. He'd obviously fought back as hard as he could, but as strong as he is, the head injuries must have been too much even for him.

He was so still he didn't even seem to be breathing, and I cried out and put my hand to my mouth. "Is he...?" I couldn't finish the thought.

Doc put her arm across my shoulders and drew me close to her. "He's unconscious, but we have no reason to believe he won't wake up when he's ready. And if you're ever worried, you can always just look at the patient monitor and see that he's okay." She led me over to the rack of machines near his bed and showed me where to look to check that his breathing, heart rate, and blood pressure were all still functioning normally.

I already knew all that. I was so scared that I hadn't been thinking clearly, so I took a deep breath and tried to settle down. The important point was that Liam was alive. I sat in the chair beside the bed and put a hand on his shoulder. I murmured in his ear, telling him how much I loved him and begging him to come back to me. He never moved.

After a while, Doc came over to tell me she was leaving to pack some things. She planned to spend the night here with him. I nodded, and she slipped out while I was fluffing his pillow.

Eventually, the room grew even darker, and the nurse came in to tell me visiting hours had ended.

"I can't leave him," I said.

"He needs his rest. He'll heal faster if he sleeps undisturbed, and I promise to call you if he wakes up."

"You mean *when* he wakes up, don't you?" I said.

"Yes, that's exactly what I meant. And you don't need to worry about him. He's in good hands. Doc just called. She's on her way back, so he won't be alone for long. In fact, if you like, I'll stay here with him until she arrives."

I nodded, grateful for her kindness.

She smiled with sympathy. "Good. Then it's settled. Now say goodnight. Your brother is here to take you home."

I nodded and kissed Liam's forehead. "I'll be back in the morning. Oliver's waiting to take me home so you can rest." The nurse started fussing with the tubes connecting Liam to his monitors, so I walked out alone, expecting to see Oliver.

But it was Rafe waiting for me near the nurse's station, wearing dark glasses and a baseball cap pulled low over his forehead. He wore fake teeth that made his lips bulge out like he'd ODed on Botox. His face was lined, his skin sagged, and his chin was covered with stubble. Despite my worry over Liam, I smiled at the disguise. He always looked like a movie star no matter what he did.

"How is he?" he said when I reached him.

"Same," I said. "They say we'll know more in the morning."

"Did you have dinner?" he asked. "We can stop to get you something on the way."

I shook my head. "That's okay. I'll raid the café fridge. Marianna won't mind, and my car's at RIO anyway."

"Where will you sleep?" he asked.

"On the *Tranquility*, of course. I spend about half my nights on the boat anyway." I thought with longing of my beloved boat. It was better than being alone at home.

"Well, eat your dinner and then you go right to bed. You need plenty of sleep if you're going to take care of Liam and do everything else on your plate. Remember, filming starts tomorrow."

"Thanks for the reminder," I said. "I'll see you then." I'd completely forgotten about the first day of filming. I knew I couldn't be in two places at once, and I wasn't about to leave Liam lying in a hospital bed alone all day. I'd have to beg T-8 for a delay. Or if it came to that, I'd resign.

I sent a text to Benjamin and Chaun, who lived near me, and asked them to drop by my house to feed Henrietta and Chico. We had a pet sitter who fed them when Liam was out of town, but the sitter wouldn't know that Liam was incapacitated. I got a thumbs up emoji from my friends as a response, so I was good for the night.

Rafe pulled up at RIO's main entrance. "You sure you'll be okay?"

I nodded. "I'll be fine." Then I walked to the door and used my keycard to get in and hurried to the shuttered café. I went into the kitchen and made myself a sandwich and filled a mug with lemonade. I put the sandwich in my tote bag and left through the pool house door that led to the back where the movie company parked their trailers. I wanted to talk to T-8 about Liam's condition and explain that it would affect my availability for filming until I was sure he was out of the woods. It was late, but I hoped T-8 would still be up.

Chapter 40
Eavesdropping

T-8's TRAILER WAS the closest one to the locker room entries to the pool house. Dim light was spilling through the trailer's windows, barely lighting my path for the few steps it took to reach it. I'd just raised my hand to knock on the door when I heard raised voices from inside.

"All I'm asking for is a different name tag. One with my real name on it. He doesn't...Family is all a bunch of crap. He didn't even...garbled, garbled...recognize...."

The voice was angry but sounded vaguely familiar.

"Or maybe he just didn't want to recognize me. He's such a big star now." There was a sound like a fist slamming into a wall, and the trailer shook. "And you! After all I did for you."

T-8's voice, "C'mon, Doug. I did the best I could for you. I gave you a job, didn't I?"

"But not a good job. Couldn't you have found something else?" said the unknown voice. "Something better? Or just...I don't know...maybe a part in the movie, Mr. Big Shot Director?" There was a pause. "Or at least let me use my own name. It's just a name tag."

T-8 shouted. "No, throw that thing away. I need to protect Rafe. He can't afford to have his name linked with..."

There was a loud crash, like something hard breaking against something even more solid. I heard a scuffle, so I stepped back into a nearby pergola shrouded in flowers and vines as the trailer door banged open. A figure raced out across the lawn toward the pool house, but it was too dark for me to see who it was.

T-8 stood in the door of his trailer, shaking his fist. "Don't come back unless you're ready to play this my way," he yelled. "And I'm warning you. Stay away from Rafe. He's been through enough. He doesn't need your aggravation."

He slammed the door and pulled down the shades in all the windows. A few minutes later, the lights went out, one by one, so I knew he'd gone to bed. I'd have to wait until morning to talk to him.

I stayed in the shadowy pergola for a long time before I walked away. It was late, but the bar at Ray's Place was still open. I didn't want anyone to see me, so I skirted around behind the dive shop. I didn't have the strength to make small talk tonight, and I couldn't bear it if Theresa or one of my other friends felt like they had to stick around to comfort me.

I didn't need comfort. I only needed Liam to be okay.

I stepped onto the *Tranquility* and walked along the gunwales to the bow. I stared at the moon while I ate a few bites of my sandwich. I wasn't really hungry, but I knew I had to eat. When I'd drained the last of the lemonade, I went below to the daybed, where I fell into a troubled sleep.

When I awoke just before sunrise, there was a steaming hot mug of coffee and a warm blueberry muffin on the galley table. Still half asleep, I said "Liam?"

He brought me coffee and a muffin almost every morning, so it took me a second to realize he couldn't have brought it. I bit back a sob.

Since I hadn't heard from the hospital overnight, I figured that was a good sign. But if it hadn't been Liam, who would have brought me the food? From the deck, I didn't see a soul around, although the lights were on in the dive shop. Must have been Stewie, I thought.

I went back to the galley and ate the muffin and drained the coffee. Then I rinsed out the mug to return it to Stewie when I walked past the dive shop on my way to the locker room. I gathered up the clothes I'd need for my day and stuffed them into my tote bag. When I had dawdled as long as I could, I headed down the pier.

Chapter 41
Arrested

THE TOP HALF of the dive shop's Dutch door was open, and I could hear Stewie belting out an old Neil Young song as I approached. I called out "Good morning," and Stewie abruptly stopped singing. I giggled.

His face turned beet red when he saw me in the doorway. "I don't usually sing in public," he said, obviously embarrassed.

"And the public thanks you for that courtesy," I said, and we both burst out laughing.

I placed the mug on the small shelf on the bottom half of the door. "Thank you for breakfast. I brought your mug back. Or should I bring it back to the café?"

Stewie stared at me. "I'll return the mug for you," he said, "but I didn't bring you any breakfast."

I was puzzled. "Then who did?" I asked.

Stewie looked at the ceiling before he spoke. "I don't know for sure, but maybe it wasn't meant for you at all. That movie star was hanging around the dock when I got here this morning. Maybe it was his breakfast."

"Rafe? Where is he now?"

Stewie seemed startled. "I'm surprised all the hubbub didn't wake you up. Dane and Morey arrested him earlier. They thought you might be next on his hit list, although he said he was guarding you. Happened about an hour ago. I expect he's at the police station by now."

"What? Why?" I couldn't believe I had slept through all that. I guess Rafe had been right last night when he said I needed sleep.

Stewie shrugged. "Dunno. I thought you'd know. You two have been spending a lot of time together. What do you suppose he's gotten into?"

"Nothing that I'm aware of. Although we're not together ALL the time," I said, giving him a pointed look. I was steaming at Stewie's implication and the unfair arrest of a man I knew it my heart hadn't done anything wrong, but I didn't want to waste time on a pointless argument, especially when I was sure Dane would let Rafe go later today.

"As soon as he arrived, bad things started happening. First someone murders that photographer fellow, then attacks your poor sweet grandmother. Someone steals a valuable artifact, and then poor Liam—Liam!—gets attacked and left for dead. Makes me wonder what the connection is."

I glared at him. "You don't think I had anything to do with all the bad stuff, do you?"

He looked startled. "Of course not. I've known you your whole life, and I know you're straight as an arrow. Just…just, things are changing here."

"I'll admit a lot of bad things happened lately. But good things happened too. And when the movie comes out, we'll be in a much more stable position financially. Meanwhile, the cast and crew are spending a lot of money at the dive shop, the café, and at Ray's Place, and that will help keep us going. We've got a couple of new businesses about to open up, and that will help the finances too. Liam and Mimi will recover, and we'll get to the bottom of this, I promise."

"Sure," he said. "I didn't mean to be unfairly critical. Overall, you're doing a great job. Everybody thinks so."

I snorted. "No, they don't. But they will, I promise. And you can always tell me what you think, Stewie. You've earned that right."

I looked at the dive watch on my wrist. "I'm going to stop in to check on Liam at the hospital first, but after that my next stop will be police headquarters to talk to Dane. I trust him, but he jumped the gun on the arrest. I know Rafe's innocent. Call me if anything comes up."

Hoping that spending a few minutes with the man I love might help calm me down for the confrontation with Dane and his team, I went to see Liam first. It was too early for visiting hours, so I thought I'd have to sneak into his room. Luckily, I bumped into Doc in the hall, and she and I walked in together like I belonged there. Which in my opinion, I did.

The room was dim, but Doc immediately went to the windows and opened the blackout drapes. "Research has shown that exposure to sunlight might help in certain health issues. And it can't hurt him."

"Good idea," I said. "I want him to have every possible advantage."

She smiled. "Of course you do."

Doc busied herself checking Liam's vitals and looking at his wounds to make sure there was no incipient infection, while I sat with one hand on his arm and using the other to brush his hair back from his forehead. He looked so frail it broke my heart.

After a while, I asked Doc. "What's your schedule look like for today?"

She thought for a moment. "I have to check in at the infirmary later. If there's anyone waiting to see me, I'll head over there for a while. But I have a lot of friends at this hospital, so I'll make sure someone is in here with Liam anytime I have to go."

"Should I get him private nurses? Mimi has them, and I feel better knowing she's never alone." I worried about both of them, but the thought of Liam being unconscious, alone, and at the mercy of whoever had hurt him made me feel awful.

Doc thought out loud. "Mimi's been in the coma for a while, and because of her age and the nature of her injury, each day makes it a little more unlikely that she'll wake up. She needs a private duty nurse. But Liam's in a completely different situation. He's young and strong, and he has you to come back to. Let's wait a few days before we decide. In the meantime, he'll have plenty of company. I'll make sure of it."

Not only did Doc's words make sense, but they also made me feel a lot better. "Thank you. And since you'll be here for a while, do you mind if I head out for a little bit? Stewie told me they arrested Rafe this morning, and I'd like to know why."

She bit her lip but didn't say what I could see she was thinking about my concern for Rafe. "Sure. I'll call you if anything changes here."

"Thanks." I kissed Liam's wrist and tucked it under the blanket. "Come back safely, my love. And soon." Then I left the room.

The police station isn't far from the hospital, and there weren't any cruise ships in town, so I walked over. Five minutes later, I was standing in the lobby requesting to see Dane Scott.

I didn't know the staff person at the desk, and he obviously didn't know me either. In a snooty voice, he said, "DS Scott is very busy right now. Would you care to make an appointment? You can come back later when he'll have time to see you."

I smiled politely. "Thank you, but it's important that I see him now. Would you let him know that I'm here?" I reached into my tote bag and pulled out a crumpled and dirty business card. It didn't look very professional, but at least my name and title were clear.

The desk person read it out loud. "Dr. Finola Fleming, COO, The Madelyn Anderson Russo Institute of Oceanography." He handed it back to me. "And this is supposed to be you?"

I nodded, suddenly aware I was wearing yesterday's clothes and hadn't even taken the time to comb my hair this morning because I'd been in such a hurry. "He knows me. Please just tell him I'm here."

Luckily Morey happened to walk through the lobby just then. "Hey, Fin. Here to see the boss?"

I took a deep breath. "Yes, please. Can you take me back there?"

He turned to the staffer at the desk. "Please give Dr. Fleming a visitor's pass. I'll take her back to see Dane."

210

I thought the guy at the desk was going to swallow his tongue, but he pulled himself together long enough to scribble my name on a visitor's pass. "Here you go, Dr. Fleming," he said grudgingly.

Morey held the door to the back office area open for me, and I headed straight to Dane's office. He looked tired and stressed out. "I'm surprised it took you so long to get here," he said. "I expected you hours ago. As soon as we made the arrest, in fact."

"I was asleep. I didn't even know you'd arrested Rafe. What made you do that?"

"We found Liam's missing kayak tied up at Rafe's place, and that stupid hat he was always wearing was in it."

"Because of the common methodology, we were pretty sure the person that attacked Liam was the same one that killed Jeffrie West and struck your grandmother, but we couldn't figure out who would have it out for those two plus Liam. We knew there had to be a connection to the movie because everything happened at RIO at pivotal times in the movie process. Then Maddy got a call from Newton, and he told her Liam had taken over the investment in the movie that Mimi had promised but never gotten around to processing. He wanted her to know so she could stop worrying about RIO's finances."

He sighed. "That's when we knew for sure the connection was through the movie. Rafe's the star, and we knew he'd been wearing a hat like the one we found at the scene. I got a warrant, and we went to pick him up. Lucky we found him when we did. I think you were next on his hit list because when we found him, he was sitting on the dock next to the *Tranquility*. I shudder to think what might have happened if we'd arrived any later."

I was stunned. "Rafe wouldn't do something like this. He's very sweet and gentle."

Dane shrugged. "Some of the worst killers in the world seem sweet and gentle—until they're not."

The idea that Rafe would hurt anyone didn't make any sense to me. I'd spent so much time with him that I'd gotten a chance to know him well. Then I realized that I had spent a lot of time with him yesterday, and that time probably overlapped with the time of the attack on Liam.

"Rafe and I were together for hours yesterday. He couldn't have attacked Liam if he was with me."

Dane didn't look happy when I said this. "Fin, don't try to interfere in the investigation because you have feelings for Rafe…"

When Dane spoke, I realized that what he said wasn't true. The only feelings I had for Rafe were respect and friendship. Sure, I admit the attentions of a genuine "movie star" had dazzled me for a time, but I loved Liam with all my heart.

"That's not true. Liam and I came to work together, so we know it was after that, and his boat wasn't in his slip when I went out to the *Tranquility* to work, so we know it happened before that. I was with Rafe for a good chunk of the time in between. I don't know exactly what time the attack on Liam occurred, but I bet by now you do. I'm going to make a list of all the times and places Rafe and I were together yesterday, and when I show you, you'll see it couldn't have been him who attacked Liam."

Dane opened his mouth to speak, but I held up my hand to stop him. "No, let me make the list for you before you tell me what time it occurred. That way you'll know I'm not just covering for Rafe."

Dane sighed, but he handed me his notebook and a pen. I started writing down all the times and locations Rafe and I had been together since the last time I saw Liam yesterday.

Rafe had joined me in my office after my meeting with Davy, so around lunch time. Then we'd spent a couple of hours in the lab, looking at research and playing with Rosie. Back in my office, we'd had cookies and lemonade while he told me about the house he'd bought.

Along with the approximate times and locations I'd been with Rafe, I included the names of anyone who might have seen us together, like the café staff. I noted that the security cameras would have seen us approaching and leaving the lab. There's only one entrance to the lab, so the video would verify the time we'd been in there together.

I tore the page from the notebook and handed it to Dane. He

scowled when he read it. "Can you have someone send the security tapes to me right away? I'll need to verify this information."

I pulled out my phone and called Eugene at RIO. I asked him to email yesterday's security footage from the lab corridor to Dane right away.

"Oh, no," he groaned. "Did something happen to the lab again? I'll get right on the cleanup..."

"No, no. It's nothing like that. I just need Dane to see the footage. As quickly as you can, please," I said.

"On it." He disconnected the call.

Dane drummed his fingers on his desk while we waited for the video to arrive. When his email dinged, he motioned to Roland and Morey to join him as he watched it. It didn't take them long to verify the times Rafe and I had entered and left the lab.

"Cut him loose," he said when they finished watching. He groaned. "I can see the lawsuit now."

"There won't be a lawsuit. I promise you Rafe isn't like that," I said.

"I hope you're right," he replied.

Chapter 42
Another Kiss

IT TOOK a while to process the paperwork for Rafe's release, and I didn't want to waste too much time hanging around. An hour later I was still cooling my heels in the lobby when he finally walked out. He looked dazed and shaken.

"Thank you," he said. "I know you had a hand in my release, so whatever you said, thank you for saying it."

I smiled at him. "I didn't have to say very much. I just gave Dane the security video that showed the times we entered and left the research lab. Dane knows there's only one exit from there, so there's no way you could have been the person who attacked Liam."

He shuffled his feet. "I'm sorry about what happened to Liam. He's a good guy. Will he be alright?"

"They don't know for sure yet. The doctors seem to think he'll be fine, although he was still unconscious when I saw him this morning just before I came to get you." I blinked back tears and pulled my keys out of my tote. "Where should I take you?"

"I had planned to head to my new house this morning, once I was sure you were safe. That was before DS Scott arrested me, but if it's not too far out of the way, would you drop me off at home?"

"Sure, I can do that, as long as you don't mind if I go by RIO to drop off the faux sea stars." His house was totally out of the way, but I was curious about the interior. I was hoping he'd invite me in to see it since I'd never been inside when Alec Stone owned it. Come to think of it, I wasn't sure Alec had ever been inside it either, since Lily, his girlfriend, had moved in right after he bought it and then immediately dumped him. Served him right.

I called Stewie and asked him to meet me in front of RIO to take charge of the sea stars and to ensure that Genevra knew he had them so she and Chaun could get them set up in the new display case under enhanced security.

I'd only seen the house from the water side before, so after Stewie took the heavy rolling trunk out of the back of my car, I used my GPS to find the route to the exact address of Rafe's new house. After a few twists and turns, we pulled into the driveway.

The house was magnificent. Not in the same sense as any of the multitude of mansions on the island, but purely because of its elegant lines. Although it was by no means small, it looked smaller from the street side than it did from the water. It was dark red, an unusual color for the island, where the most common house colors were soft pastels, whites, or sandy hues. Rafe's house had black window shutters, and to be honest, the whole effect was kind of spooky.

This was the same color scheme the house had when Alec owned it. I wondered if Rafe planned to paint it to be more in keeping with the island esthetic. Just as I completed this thought, Rafe spoke.

"What color do you think I should paint it? I love the color of your house, but I don't want you to think I'm copying you."

I laughed. "Our houses are miles apart, so I wouldn't be concerned about annoying me. And I love the color of my house too." My house—and Liam's house next door to mine—were both painted a soft watery blue with crisp white shutters and trim. "I'll see if I can track down the exact color for you."

"Thanks. Do you want to see the inside? I haven't been in it myself yet, so who knows what we'll find. We can explore it together." Rafe looked at me with hope shining from his eyes.

"I thought you'd never ask," I said with a laugh. "But I can't believe you bought a house without even going inside."

He shrugged and pulled a key out of the pocket of his cargo shorts. We walked along the untidy crushed shell path to the front door. As we neared the house, I noticed the paint was peeling and the shutters were hanging loose and missing some slats, adding to the spooky vibe. I had the uneasy feeling the lack of upkeep would continue on the inside. Both Alec and Lily had left the island about a year ago, and neither of them was much for home maintenance— or even house cleaning.

When we walked inside, I was simultaneously shocked and delighted. The door opened up into a huge central area that included space for relaxation, cooking, and dining. The entire back wall was glass and offered an expansive view of the ocean. A grand staircase graced one side of the room, leading to an open loft area framed by floor to ceiling windows that looked out to sea. An empty outlet in the vaulted ceiling where a chandelier had once hung had several bare wires hanging out of its dark interior. Two hallways branched off from the main room, one on each side, and I assumed they led to the bedrooms.

As I'd expected, the house had beautiful lines, but it was a total wreck. Dirt and grass littered the floors. The windows were grimy. Broken furniture lay in a heap in one corner, and the other held a pile of books and personal belongings. The walls were a dark, drab, mustardy color, and the paint was peeling. All the appliances were missing from the kitchen, and half the cabinet doors were falling off, most held up by just one hinge.

But Rafe didn't seem to notice any of the house's drawbacks. His eyes shone when he turned to me. "A little paint, some elbow grease and new appliances, and it will be fabulous. A dream come true."

I'd thought the house's condition would appall Rafe, but he seemed delighted by everything. I let out my breath and smiled at him. "It will be lovely when you get it fixed up the way you want."

He beamed at me. "But it'll never be as lovely as you." Before I knew it, he'd taken me in his arms and kissed me again.

It would be so easy to just let him. I liked him a lot. He was gorgeous. Funny. Smart, Sweet. All good things. Except he wasn't Liam, and nearly losing the man I adored had reinforced the depths of my love for him.

I stepped back. "Rafe, you have to stop doing that. I'm engaged to Liam, and even more important than the engagement is the fact that I truly love him. He trusts me. I'll never leave him, and you and I can never be together. If this happens again, I'll have to end our friendship, and that would be a shame because I like you very much as a friend."

He dropped his arms to his sides and stared down at his feet. "I'm sorry," he said. "I won't let it happen again. It's just I've never met someone who just likes me for me, you know? Most people I meet only see a movie star."

I took another step back. "I'm sure that makes things difficult for you, but if you keep looking, you'll find someone who loves the real you. And she'll make you very happy. You just have to relax and be open to letting it happen."

He nodded. "I'll try. If I promise to keep my hands and my lips to myself, can we still be friends in the meantime?"

"I hope so, but that's up to you." I turned toward the door. "I have to go now. Maybe I can see the rest of your house another time."

I walked out the door to my car, feeling Rafe watching me leave. A very small part of me was wishing I didn't have to hurt him by leaving, but in my heart, I knew leaving was the right thing for me.

Chapter 43
Scrapped

I DROVE SLOWLY BACK to RIO, feeling guilty that I'd hurt Rafe and feeling even worse that I'd hurt Liam, even if he didn't know the full extent of it. I planned to finally take that shower, change my clothes, grab something to eat, and then spend the rest of the day at Liam's bedside.

When I arrived at RIO, the line for the exhibition snaked all the way out the door, even though we'd replaced the most famous exhibit, the Silas Anderson Sea Stars, with a set of copies. Rather than fight the crowds, I hiked around to the back of the pool house and went in through the locker room doors. I took a shower, and when I finished, I felt better than I had all day.

I rummaged through the stacks of clothes I keep in my locker and finally found a clean pair of cargo shorts and a mostly clean blue RIO t-shirt. I'd have to swap this lot of clothes out and replace it with fresh clothing from home very soon. I made a mental note to do that. Then I traded my flip-flops for another pair that were identical to the ones I'd been wearing except they were blue instead of red, so they matched my shirt. I had tons of flip-flops in a bevy of colors. They were all alike except for the color because that simplified my daily choices.

After I'd combed my hair, I went out the back door of the pool house to walk around the building to RIO's back entrance. There was another line at the dive shop waiting to pick up tanks, and Ray's Place looked full.

Good. Business was doing well.

I rummaged through my canvas tote until I found my ID badge. The back door opened with a click, and I scurried past Joely's office and around the corner to my own. I wanted to check a few things before I left to go to the hospital, and I needed to let T-8 know I wouldn't be working on the film until Liam woke up. If he needed to replace me, so be it. Liam was far more important to me than this film and my career. More important than anything, for that matter.

I sent Gary Graydon the text and images file for this month's column and then looked at the revised budgets Joely had sent me. Budgets make my head spin, so I sent her an email asking her to have Newton approve them because right now, I was just too distracted to focus on numbers, my well-known nemesis.

I signed off on a bunch of requests from department heads, and then I started working on the email to T-8. I knew it was going to be hard, so I'd put it off till last.

But I needn't have worried. I'd no sooner opened my email program when T-8 walked in. He wore his usual jeans and rock star t-shirt, with sandals on his feet. Once again, he'd gathered his long hair into a man bun with the silly looking mini-pony tail sticking out of it, although several straggly locks had escaped and hung down to the middle of his back. The front of his hair flopped over his right eye. He wore a blue ball cap and had an expensive watch on his wrist.

"I need to talk to you," I said.

At the same time, he said "We need to talk."

"I'll go first," he said. "It may make whatever you have to say irrelevant."

I gulped. "Yikes. What's up?"

"I've decided to shut down the production. For good this time. This movie is cursed. The finances are a mess. My star is mooning over another man's girlfriend…"

"Fiancée," I broke in.

He glared. "Another man's fiancée. The exhibition that was supposed to build word-of-mouth is a shambles."

"We've got the faux sea stars on display. People don't seem to mind the substitution."

T-8 shook his head. "Don't care. It's time to cut our losses."

"What losses?" I asked. "Didn't Liam agree to completely fund the production?"

"Yes, but he's unconscious."

"Newton has his power of attorney. He can initiate the funds transfer."

T-8 scowled. "Liam already transferred the money. But still, I've decided to shut down."

"But why?" I asked. "You've got a great script, a bankable star, a built-in marketing hook, an entire issue of *Ecosphere* dedicated to the movie's launch. What's the problem?"

"It's my movie and my decision," he said.

"Maybe so, but why would you do that to all the people who are depending on you for a paycheck?" I couldn't understand his logic.

"That's their problem," he said in a voice like ice. "Now what did you want to talk to me about?"

"My original topic is a moot point now. But I do want to make sure you refund Liam's investment since you've decided not to move forward."

His response was a single word.

"No."

"No? What do you mean? Surely you don't intend to keep the money and not make the film. That has to be a violation of the agreement."

"Nope. It's not. There's nothing in the agreement that says I actually have to make a movie. It just calls the money an investment in the production company which I founded. I own it outright —one hundred percent. There's no clause requiring a return of funds for any reason, so there's no way for him to claw back the money. It's mine to do with what I please. And what I please to do is spend the next few years living the good life. We'll be out of your hair by the end of the day."

He turned and walked out, his long brown hair straggling behind him.

I sat at my desk, seething over T-8's duplicity. I couldn't believe Liam and Newton had signed an agreement as one sided as T-8 claimed it to be. They were both extremely astute businessmen, and Newton was a lawyer to boot.

I put in a call to Newton, but it went straight to voicemail. I left him a message about what T-8 had said, and suggested he get over to RIO immediately before T-8 had a chance to leave the island as he'd threatened. Then I left a voice mail for Dane with essentially the same message, asking him to detain T-8 if he could until we had this mess straightened out.

I'd always heard that the movie business has its own set of rules, and contracts can often be one-sided. Could that be what had happened here? Had my father and my fiancé fallen prey to sharp business practices? Given their reputations in business, it was hard to believe that either one—never mind both of them—would have agreed to what T-8 said they had. T-8's interpretation must be wrong. I hoped Newton could fix this.

I had no idea how much Liam had agreed to invest, but it had to be millions. That was a drop in the bucket compared to his net worth, but still, it would sting when he woke up. And now I was back in trouble with no way to finance RIO's operations for the next two years. The loss of the income I'd anticipated from our share of the movie's profits practically doomed us to failure. We'd have to shut down soon.

I put my head in my hands and gave in to a moment of despair. I let myself wallow for a minute, then I squared my shoulders. I would find a way to fix this no matter what.

Chapter 44
Wake Up

My plan was to spend the rest of the day at the hospital with Liam. I loaded up my tote bag with work, and grabbed my trusty tablet so I could keep busy while I was sitting with him. When I entered his room, Doc was in the chair in the corner, her face drawn and gray. My steps faltered.

"Oh, no! No, no, no," I moaned. She looked so beaten that I knew the worst had happened. All the air left my lungs, and it felt like my heart stopped.

She looked up when she heard my frightened moans, and she rushed across the room to put her arms around me. "It's all right, Fin. He's fine. I didn't mean to scare you. I'm just worn out. I've been here since you left. All I need is a nap."

I gasped in a breath. "I'm so sorry. I shouldn't have left you here all alone. I should have hired private duty nurses. I took advantage of your good nature, and I am so, so, sorry…"

She smiled and interrupted me. "Hush. You didn't take advantage of me. I volunteered, remember? And I could have asked one of the nurses to help me keep an eye on him, but I wanted to be here myself."

I was still shaking from the aftermath of the terror I'd felt, but I patted her shoulder. "I'm sorry. I should have been here earlier to give you a break. Why don't you go home now? I'll stay with him overnight."

But Doc was fiercely protective of all her patients, especially the ones she knew and loved. She'd never leave a patient alone if she could help it.

She gave me a hug. "I'll tell you what. I'll go home and take a quick nap. Shower, maybe spend some time with Stewie. But I'll be back before lights out, so you can go home and get some rest. We need you to keep RIO running smoothly. We all depend on you."

I smiled at her. "You're the one we all depend on, Doc. Let me be the one to stay."

She shook her head. "I'm used to these long hours from medical school. I'll be fine."

I didn't mention that medical school had been a long time ago. I'd bet if she put her head down and closed her eyes, she'd sleep through the night and then some. "Okay," I said, "but don't hurry back, and it's no problem if you change your mind and decide you want to spend the night in your own bed."

"Deal," she said. She grabbed her medical bag, gave me a hug, and left.

I settled in the chair next to Liam's bed with my hand on his arm. For a while, I chattered away about all the happenings around RIO, and T-8's plan to shut down the movie production. Liam slept on, his battered face serene and reposed.

So still. So very still.

I ran out of things to talk about. That never happened when Liam was awake. Sometimes, we would talk all night, sharing tidbits of our day-to-day lives, or telling each other our hopes and dreams.

And laughing. Liam always made me laugh.

His stillness was unnerving, and it was making me crazy. It would be better for my mental health to try to get some work done rather than to just sit here worrying. I pulled out my tablet and connected to the hospital's Wi-Fi, but I couldn't focus on work. Then I remembered Rafe saying T-8 had been in several movies back when they first arrived in Hollywood. Maybe one of those would be entertaining.

I did a search under the name T-8 but didn't find anything. Rafe had said he'd been T-8's stunt double in the early days, so I looked up Rafe on the internet. I scrolled through all his movies until I found the very oldest ones, where the credits listed him as "assistant to Tate Crusoe."

Tate Crusoe. That must be T-8's real name.

I tried to find one of T-8's movies on the major streaming services, but none had any of his films available except the more recent ones where he was the director. Nine pages into the search results, I finally stumbled across a link to an old movie and clicked on it.

The hospital's Wi-Fi gave me a warning message. "Standards violation. No X-rated or pornographic content allowed on this network."

Oh.

That might explain why T-8 was so secretive about his real name and his early film work.

Now I thought I understood what was going on. T-8 had turned to directing to escape his X-rated past, and now he was going to run off with Liam's money to escape his failed director efforts.

Except, not on my watch. I would never allow anyone to hurt the man I love.

I started to pack up my things when I heard a sound from the bed. I turned around. Liam's eyes were open, and he was watching me. I dropped everything and threw myself onto the bed, although I was careful not to touch any of his injuries.

Slowly, carefully, he put his arms around me. "What happened?" he rasped.

"Someone attacked you on the *Enviroman*. You've been unconscious for a few days, but everything will be just fine now that you're awake."

He tried to smile, but it turned into a grimace. "Head hurts."

"I can imagine. You took quite a wallop. But it'll get better. I promise."

225

He bobbed his head, and I realized he was trying to nod.

"Where going?" he said.

"I had some business to take care of, but it can wait. I want to get Doc in here to check you out before I go anywhere. And I'll stay with you until you fall asleep."

He yawned, wincing as his jaw went wide. "Won't be long."

"Let me call Doc. She'll want to check you out herself." I stood up and pulled my phone out of my tote bag. I'd thought she'd be sleeping, but she answered on the first ring. By the time I'd finished talking to her, Liam was asleep. As I'd promised, I stayed with him.

Doc breezed through the doorway twenty minutes later." Thank God," she said. She pulled out her stethoscope and listened to his heart and lungs. "Good," she said. "I'll take him down for a brain scan when he wakes up, but everything looks good."

I started to cry, and she pulled me into a hug. "Let it out," she said. "You've been very brave."

I put my head on her shoulder and sobbed until I had no more tears. When I backed away from her, she smiled.

"Go home. Get some rest. I'll stay with him, and you can see him again in the morning when you'll both be feeling better."

Chapter 45
Return

But I didn't go home. Finding out that T-8 intended to steal Liam's money and abandon producing the film had me upset. I wanted to talk to Rafe about it, to see if he could offer any insight into why T-8 would act that way. They'd been friends a long time, and if anyone would know what made T-8 tick, it would be Rafe.

Although at this point I felt like I'd been awake for days, in the real world it was just coming onto dinnertime. I stopped at a convenience store and picked up a couple of salads and some soft drinks in case Rafe hadn't eaten yet either.

All the lights in his house were on, but when I rang the bell, there was no answer. I banged on the door with the same result. Nothing.

I walked around to the ocean side of the house in case Rafe was out there enjoying his first evening as a homeowner. He'd unearthed a couple of rickety chairs and placed them on the stone patio, but he wasn't there either.

A slight breeze caused the tattered curtains on the open sliding doors to blow around, startling me. But since the door was open, I thought I might as well go inside and make sure Rafe was okay. I put the food on the counter in the kitchen and walked through to the open living area.

In a corner of the floor there was an enormous pile of cloth and some cleaning tools that hadn't been there when Rafe and I had been exploring the house earlier. I assumed Rafe was making a bundle of things to put in the trash, so I ignored it. I walked through the rest of the house, marveling at how beautiful—and how derelict—the house was. I didn't find Rafe anywhere, so I'd have to leave him a note to let him know I'd come by.

While I was rummaging through my tote bag looking for a pen, I heard a noise. It was soft, barely perceptible. I didn't hear it again for a few seconds, so I went back to my note.

There it was again. It sounded like a soft groan. I went back into the living area and looked around. The only thing there was the bundle of rags on the floor.

Then the rags moved, and I heard the sound again. I raced to the corner and flipped the bundle over. It was Rafe. Someone had beaten him. The bloody broomstick lying on the floor next to him must have been the weapon.

I reached over and touched his neck to check for a pulse, and his heart was steady but slow. He didn't even move when I touched his neck. I pulled my cellphone out of the pocket of my cargo shorts and called Dane.

"Not another one," he said when I told him where I was and what had happened. "Go back to your car and lock the doors. Don't get out until we get there."

"Okay," I said, although I had no intention of leaving Rafe alone on the floor. I sat down next to him with my back against the wall.

He twitched and moaned, and over the sound of the moan I heard a clink. Another twitch; another clink.

I got on my knees and carefully looked under the voluminous white terrycloth robe Rafe was wearing over his sweatpants. The folds of the robe partially hid a black leather satchel. Careful not to move his neck or his back, in case he had spinal injuries, I slowly eased the heavy bag away from his body.

When the bag was fully free, I unzipped the top, wrapping my fingers in the hem of my t-shirt so I wouldn't mess up any fingerprints. Inside the bag, nestled in the folds of a couple of rockstar t-shirts, lay the Silas Anderson Sea Stars, glowing softly in the fading sunlight.

Chapter 46
Fin Confronts the Killer

DANE and his team arrived a few minutes later, along with several ambulances filled with EMTs. I'd bet that Dane had mentioned who the victim was, and everybody wanted to go out on the call. It made me sad for Rafe that he was always such an object of curiosity, but in this instance, I was glad because it meant he'd be getting excellent care.

Dane and I were sitting on the back patio. He was questioning me while Roland and Morey searched the house. It was hard for them to tell what might be a clue and what was just junk left over from prior residents, so we could hear them grumbling through the open sliding door as they bagged and labeled all sorts of debris.

The only thing I was certain was a clue was the rockstar t-shirts that had been in the bag with the Sea Stars. To me, that pointed to T-8 as the thief, and I felt sad for Rafe that the friend he'd always counted on might have turned out to be one of the bad guys.

The head EMT stepped out on to the patio. "He's stable. We're about to take him to Cayman Islands Hospital."

I stood up. "May I ride in the ambulance with him please? He doesn't have any friends or family."

The EMT shrugged. "Okay but try to stay out of the way if we need to work on him."

231

I nodded and followed the gurney out the front door, across the yard, and to the ambulance. The EMTs raised it up, and once they'd secured it, they offered me a hand to hoist me aboard for the ride.

One of them drove, and the other stayed in back with Rafe and me. I sat beside the medic, leaning forward to hold Rafe's hand. He'd curled his fingers into a tight fist, and I stroked the back of his hand, hoping it would help him relax.

After a few minutes, the patting motion seemed to soothe him, because his hand dropped open. I felt something small leave his grip and settle in my palm. I didn't say anything to the technician, but I knew that even though he was unconscious, Rafe had just handed me a powerful clue. Surreptitiously, I slid it into my pocket and buttoned the pocket closed so I wouldn't lose whatever it was.

The ambulance came to a screeching halt outside the emergency room, and the techs rushed Rafe's gurney inside. I followed a little more slowly, wondering what I should do next.

I didn't want to call Doc and pull her away from caring for Liam to stay with Rafe. I was too restless to go home, and I knew staying at the hospital was a waste of time because the doctors would have Rafe tied up for hours with tests and medical procedures. I called Newton and Oliver, but both their phones went to voicemail. I put my phone down on the table beside me and thought about what to do.

I couldn't sit by and do nothing. I was afraid T-8 would leave town and be out of the jurisdiction by the time Dane and his team recognized the t-shirts in the leather sack as an important clue and not just random packing material. I would have to confront T-8 on my own.

I took a cab from the hospital back to RIO, but I didn't go inside. I race walked around the building to the open land beyond the pool house where we'd allowed the movie company to set up trailers for the cast and crew.

Most of the trailers were shared dressing rooms or used for things like makeup or wardrobe, but both Rafe and T-8 had private trailers, close to the pool house entrance and with direct views to the water. Just like the last time, I could see light spilling out onto the grass from inside. Loud music filled the air, so I knew he hadn't left the island yet. I rapped on the door and waited.

And waited some more.

By the third time I knocked, I was annoyed. T-8 must be inside. If he hoped I'd give up and go away, he was never going to get his wish. I don't ever give up, and I don't like it when people disrespect me like this. Taking matters into my own hands, I opened the unlocked door and stepped inside.

I was shocked. Someone had nearly destroyed the inside of the trailer. They'd ripped all the built-in furnishings off the walls and overturned everything. They'd pulled out the contents of the cabinets and thrown it all on the floor and sliced open all the cushions and tossed the stuffing everywhere. The place was a wreck, to say the least.

"T-8," I said. "Are you here?" I picked my way through the rubble on the floor and shut off the loud music. The blessed silence was deafening. When my ears finally stopped ringing, I heard a faint moan from the bedroom at the far end of the once luxurious trailer.

I waded through the litter on the floor to the bedroom. If anything, the destruction here was even worse. But the saddest sight was T-8, lying on the floor in a pool of blood. His hands and bare feet showed signs of a beating, and several of his twisted fingers looked broken. His assailant had pulled out some of T-8's hair, and large welts rose across the top of his head. His torso was bare and still darkening with deep purple bruises. A police baton lay on the floor next to him, covered with blood.

I bit back my horror and unbuttoned my pocket to get out my phone to call Dane. When all I found in my pocket was the scrap of fabric that I'd found in Rafe's hand, I realized I'd left my phone on the table at the hospital.

I looked at the scrap in my hand. It was a small piece of cloth, dark blue with gold trim, like the uniforms the movie company's security team wore. It was a piece of a patch the guards stuck to their shirts above their breast pockets with a hook and loop fastener. Each guard had a badge embroidered with their name.

The scrap of cloth I held was only a small part of one of these removable tags, but it had one letter initial. It was a letter D, as in Douglas.

The light dawned. Rafe's brother's name was Doug. Sammy Douglas—the grumpy guard—must be Rafe's missing brother, and also the man I'd heard arguing with T-8 last night.

I had to get to a phone. I ran to the entrance to the pool house and let myself in. I raced through the locker room to the pool area. All the lights were on, and the massive space was brightly lit.

I loped a few steps toward the house phone on the wall when all the overhead lights went out. The only illumination came from the dim safety lights high up in the corners of the massive room. I stopped running, waiting to give my eyes a chance to become accustomed to the dimness.

Suddenly, a voice came over the PA system. "Open the pool."

I shook my head. "No."

The voice came again. "Retract the cover and open the pool. Now. Or the same thing will happen to you as the others."

Slowly, I turned around. Sammy—who I now knew was Rafe's brother Douglas—was standing there, just a few feet away and holding a long wooden dowel like a bat. I recognized it as a piece of the emergency opener for the retractable pool cover. I knew the dowel was strong because it had to withstand pulling against the heavy weight of the pool cover in an emergency.

I took a deep breath, hoping it would steady my voice. "Douglas, thank goodness you're here. I'm going to go to my office to call emergency services and tell them there's been an accident. T-8 needs medical assistance as quickly as possible. Will you please go to his trailer and stay with him until they arrive?"

He looked at me like I was crazy. "Do I look stupid to you?"

I thought it was better to say nothing.

"You're not going anywhere until I figure out what I want to do with you. And with that traitorous scum Tate Crusoe. One thing you can be sure of though—nobody's calling the cops. Got it?"

I nodded. "Sure. Take your time. The only thing is, someone will be coming to look for me soon."

234

"That right? Who's coming?" he sneered.

I knew I couldn't say it would be either Rafe or Liam, because he knew they were both in the hospital. The dive shop wasn't open this late, so it was unlikely that Stewie would be around. Theresa was working at Ray's Place, but I couldn't drag her into this.

"It wasn't that hard of a question. I guess you must be lying. C'mon. Get over there." He gestured toward the pool with the heavy wooden dowel.

I didn't want to get too close to him. He'd proven to be dangerous—even lethal—with his sticks. "Why? Where are we going?"

"Better you don't ask questions," he said. "Now move it."

I started to run. I hadn't gotten more than a couple of strides away when I felt an excruciating pain across my back. I tumbled to the ground, rolling over as I landed and putting my hands and feet in the air to protect my head from the blows of his dowel.

Douglas rolled his eyes. "I told you not to be stupid." He swung the rod at my shin, and it connected with a loud thwacking sound.

My leg hurt like mad, but I didn't think he'd broken it. Shakily, I stood up.

He smiled. "I took it easy on you, but next time you won't be so lucky. Now get over there and open the pool cover."

He poked my back again. "Move it." He guided me toward the edge of the pool using his stick as a prod to keep me moving in the right direction. When I neared the edge of the deep end, he said "Lift off one of the flooring segments so the water is visible."

"Why?" I asked. But I already knew why.

"Because this way no one will find you until the exhibition is over. I'll be long gone by then. Now do it."

"I can't. The segments don't lift off individually. They're all connected and controlled electronically."

"I don't care if they're controlled by magic. Get it open. Now!"

We'd concealed the motor that controlled the deployment of the floor in one of the exhibit's display cabinets. I walked over to the right one and knelt down to fumble with the controls. The manufacturer had engineered the temporary floor to look like hardwood, although it was a high-strength flexible plastic capable of supporting thousands of pounds. A stainless steel framework underneath offered additional support and held the floor a few inches above the pool water.

The controls were pretty simple. One button's label read Retract. The other said Extend. You had to hold down a button to make it work. As soon as you removed your finger, the mechanism stopped the cover from moving any further.

I pushed the retraction button and held it. The floor began to slide back.

When a ten foot wide sliver of water showed, he said, "Stop there. That's enough. I don't want to open it so far that it wrecks any of the exhibits. I'm going to need to close it right back up in a minute." He peered over my shoulder at the controller mechanism. "Tell me how it works."

When I finished explaining it to him, he nodded. "I got it. Okay, now go get in the pool."

I stood up and faced him. "No."

He poked my belly hard with his dratted staff. "Get in."

I winced when he poked me, but I wasn't going to show any fear. "I said no."

He drew himself up to his full height and puffed out his shoulders and chest the way men do when they want to look intimidating to a woman and leaned into me. "If you don't get in on your own, I'll push you in. Either way, you're going in."

Although he was much heavier and more muscled than me, we were almost the same height. I stood up tall and stared a challenge into his eyes. He might be able to push me in, but he'd have to fight for it.

He raised his arms, and I knew then that he was getting ready to push me. I grabbed his arms and twisted, using his momentum so we both fell over, plunging heavily into the pool. Doug managed to grab one of the steel supports when I let go of him, but I sank all the way to the floor of the deep end. I swam underwater toward the edge of the pool before surfacing. I put my arms on the ledge and kicked hard to get high enough that I could climb out.

Doug lifted his legs through the water and gave a mighty kick, striking me in the middle of my back and knocking the wind out of me.

I clung to one of the steel bars, trying hard to regain control of my breathing. I had barely recovered when he lifted his foot and kicked me again. I sucked in a breath and sank to the bottom.

He raised the heavy stick and positioned it for a mighty blow to my head, but he didn't reckon with the difficulty of applying force underwater.

The stick headed my way, but I had plenty of time to dart away. I sat on the bottom, just out of his reach for close to a minute.

When I surfaced, Doug had taken my place at the edge of the pool, and he was trying vainly to hoist himself out. He was only using one hand to push himself up, and he had less leg strength than I do, so he didn't have a prayer of succeeding. His pants were drooping, practically falling off him, and I started to laugh.

He turned around and glared at me. "What's so funny, you miserable…"

"Not only do you have a heavy weight in your pocket that's threatening to send your pants to the bottom—I'm guessing it's one of the Sea Stars—but you can't even swim, can you, Dougie. Never spent much time in pools, I guess. And the Sea Star in your pocket is going to be the death of you. You'll never be able to lift yourself out of the water with only one hand, and if you let go of the steel bar you'll sink like a stone. Those Sea Stars weigh about thirty pounds each."

He snarled. "Get over here and give me a boost."

I was floating vertically, out of his arms' reach. "No." I gave a little kick backward to make sure I was far enough away to be safe from him.

"Where's the ladder?" he asked. "Tell me or I'll kill you right now."

I knew we'd removed all the ladders before we installed the temporary floor, so he'd soon realize he was out of luck. I smiled at him. "You'd have to catch me first, and you can't do that. You're stuck there unless you drop the Sea Star, and even then, you'll never catch me."

"Do you have any idea what these things are worth?" he said. "I'd have to be a fool to leave it behind."

"I guess you'd rather drown," I said.

He started trying to get closer to me by moving his free hand along the steel beam. Each time he let go to move a little way, he sank from the weight of the sea star in his pocket, and he had to struggle hard to regain the surface and grab the bar the few inches further along. He'd exhaust himself quickly at this rate.

"Help me," he said again, still holding onto the scaffolding. His voice sounded scared.

I started laughing. "You can't swim at all, can you? You don't even know how to float."

He didn't say anything, so I had my answer. Meanwhile, I just bobbed, easily treading water with just an occasional flick of my toes or a wiggle of my fingers.

Water is my element. As long as I stayed out of his reach, I could safely stay in the pool all night. And maybe all day tomorrow.

Douglas, on the other hand, was starting to panic. His terrified breathing turned into a pant, and he was flailing one of his arms and both legs.

"Getting tired?" I smiled at him. "Or maybe you're cold?"

He made an angry lunge toward me, and I swam away with a few backstrokes while he panicked and tried to catch me. As he sank, I reached over and grabbed his hand. I pulled his arm up so he could grasp the steel rail and swam away again before he'd even caught his breath.

I'd been angling myself a little closer to the edge of the pool each time he moved, while he'd been getting further away. Right now, we were in twenty-five foot deep water, but in just a little way, the depth changed abruptly to a maximum of five feet. I had to get out of the pool before he figured that out. When I knew he was far enough away that he couldn't get to me before I could get out of the pool, I started to swim toward the edge furthest away from him.

238

I lurched forward to cover the last few feet to the coping, draped my arms on the tile, spread my hands, and pushed down with my arms as I kicked with all my might. I was up on the pool deck before he even knew what I was doing.

"Nice trick, that," he said. "Now give me a hand, will you?"

"No," I said. I knelt next to the control panel and pushed the Extend button. The floor started moving, reducing the size of the open water. I held the button down while Douglas screamed in a panic.

I wasn't as heartless as I seemed. I knew there was an air pocket between the surface of the water and the underside of the floor where the scaffolding was. If he hung on to the steel reinforcement bars and tilted his head back, he'd be able to breathe easily, probably for hours. He was actually in no danger, but I could hear him screaming and pleading as I raced over to the house phone to call the police.

"Dane," I said when he answered. "I caught the killer."

Chapter 47
Another Arrest

A FEW MINUTES later the sound of sirens announced that Dane had arrived. He walked into the pool house alone and looked around. I was sitting on the bleachers by myself, and the pool house looked empty. He looked dejected when he saw me. "Don't tell me he got away," he said. "And with no cameras in here it'll be your word against his."

"Don't worry. He's here. I've got him securely confined." I walked across the pool covering to the cabinet that housed the controls and held the retract button until the floor slid back enough to reveal Douglas still clinging to the stainless steel framework.

His lips were blue from cold, and he was panting from fear, not air starvation. He looked me straight in the eye when he saw me near the controls. "I'm sorry. Help me out of here and I promise I'll leave you and everyone else around here alone." He obviously hadn't seen Dane yet.

I shot Dane a glance. He read my mind and stayed where he was. He was out of sight when he pulled out his cellphone and started the record function. When he nodded, I knelt near the edge of the pool, just out of Douglas's reach. "Tell me what you did so I know what you're promising not to do any more of."

He scowled. "You know what I did."

I shrugged. "Maybe. Maybe not. I might not know the whole story. Why don't you tell me, or else be prepared to spend the night in the pool. Maybe all day tomorrow too, depending on my mood. You never know…"

"All right. I'll tell you. Jeffrie West and I planned to steal the Silas Anderson Sea Stars before the exhibition opened, but Jeffrie got greedy and stole them by himself. Luckily, I caught him before he got too far. I'd picked up that old lady's cane earlier because I thought it might be valuable." He sounded highly affronted. "Can you believe that fancy dolphin on the end of the cane was nothing but plated metal? It wasn't even real gold. On a rich old broad like that! Imagine."

"Imagine," I said. "Go on."

"When I caught Jeffrie trying to sneak the loot out of here, I gave him a whack with the business end of that cane. I guess I hit him harder than I meant to because when I checked, he was dead. I heard someone coming so I pushed him into the pool and ran out through the gym. By the way, pretty fancy place you got here. It has everything."

He seemed to be having trouble sticking with the facts. I was worried about the battery in Dane's phone's dying before Doug got to the details we needed. "Granted. RIO is a very nice place. Please continue."

"I ran out the back door and threw that cane as far as I could into the ocean. I had no idea you'd find it and pick it up so soon, but it still worked out okay for me because the police suspected that old lady."

"Glad it worked out for you," I said. "And by the way, that old lady is my grandmother."

"No kidding? Well, sorry about that because after the cops let her go, she started poking her nose in where it doesn't belong. She offered to fund that stupid movie after Jeffrie's father pulled out. That meant she had to go because I needed Tate to fail so I could approach my brother without him interfering."

"Then your boyfriend, that Lawton guy, decided he'd give Tate the money…"

242

"And the Tate you're referring to is Tate Crusoe, also known as T-8?" I said.

"Yeah. Tate. Known him forever. He always was an idiot. And he's even dumber now, but he's swaggering around like he's a big deal. He and Rafe. Thick as thieves. Always were."

He took a deep breath. "Sorry about your boyfriend. I didn't want to do him. I always really liked playing that game he wrote. Got me through my last stretch in the pen."

"Okay. You whacked Liam too? Is that what you're saying?"

"Yup. But he was stupid. He fought back. If he'd just laid down quietly, I wouldn't have had to rough him up. It's his own fault he's hurt so bad." He took a deep breath. "Help me out now?" he asked hopefully.

"Not quite yet." I said. "Explain how you stole the Anderson Sea Stars without anyone noticing."

He snorted. "So easy. I'm in security. I knew there were no cameras, and I have all the keys. I just opened the case, put them in their chest and wheeled them out to my car. Once they were safe, I went back in and broke the glass. Then it was just a matter of some-body noticing so I could act like it must have just happened."

I nodded. "Yep, easy. What about Rafe and T-8? I mean Tate. Why them?"

"I had to. I took the Anderson Sea Stars from the exhibit, and I was gonna leave the island. But I wanted to say goodbye to my baby brother..."

"You mean Rafe Cummings? He's your brother? You're Dougie Cummings? Is that right?"

"Nope. Douglas Samuel. Rafe changed his name."

There was a nostalgic gleam in his eye. "Nobody's called me Dougie since the last time I saw Rafe, a lotta years ago. You know I gave up my life for that kid. I got picked up for shoplifting some food to bring back to the alley where the three of us were living. Not my fault the shop guy died. He shoulda just let me take the food and go. Anyway, they sent me up for it. Ten years of my life, down the tubes. With Rafe living on the streets, I had no way to communicate with him. No phone number for him. No address. We lost touch. Imagine my surprise when they finally release me, and I find out my kid brother is a big deal movie star. I send him a couple of letters, but I get no replies. Ungrateful kid. Then I hear he's making a movie and there's lots of valuable stuff that goes along with the movie."

"I come here, and I talk to T-8. Tell him I need a job in his movie. But what does he do? Does he put me in his stupid movie? No. He makes me a freakin' security guard, and tells me not to let Rafe know who I am. Even makes me wear a stupid badge with a fake name on it. He looked at me, real pain in his eyes. "Rafe —my own brother—didn't freakin' recognize me. I know I look different now, older and a lot more beaten up, but I used to look just like him. He should have been able to see that, right? When he didn't recognize me, I knew that he forgot all about me because he's so busy being a movie star. Ungrateful, that's what he is, especially after all I did for him back when we were kids."

"I go to him, at this fancy new house he bought, and I tell him I've got the Sea Stars. They're worth millions. We can go home, live like kings. Be brothers again. But you know what? He don't want no part of that. He says I have to give the Sea Stars back. That he doesn't want to hurt you or your grandmother." He scoffed. "Like either of you are hurting."

"So anyway, one thing leads to another, and we say stuff we don't mean. I get mad, and I see a broom in the corner. He's been cleaning house, but all I see is our dad, whaling on us with a sawed off broomstick. And the next thing I know, Rafe is down. I leave most of the Sea Stars, figuring the cops'll think he took 'em, and I'll be home free. I don't have to be greedy. They're worth a mint. I have two of them stars in my pocket right now."

"I come back to see Tate. I can't sell the Sea Stars here—they're too hot right now. I need enough money to get off the island. He has the nerve to say no. He tells me to stay away from Rafe and to stay away from him. I can see he thinks he's too good for me now, so I whack him too. Honest to God, I didn't know I still had that guard stick with me until I saw him lying there. I took off, but then

244

I see you heading toward his trailer, so I hid behind one of those fancy benches with all the flowers."

I nodded. "And then you came into the pool house behind me and whacked me too. And tried to drown me in the pool by closing the cover on me so I couldn't get out. Is that right?"

He nodded sadly. "Except you pulled me in with you and you wouldn't help me out. Lucky there's an air pocket under there. I could have drowned when you left me for dead."

"Except I didn't leave you for dead because, unlike you, I knew the air pocket was there. And I called the police as soon as I got out. Would you have done that for me?"

He grinned, and his grin was like the evil stepbrother of Rafe's open and engaging smile. "Nope," he said. "Honestly, I was hoping you'd drown in there."

I looked across the pool house to Dane. "Got enough?"

He nodded. "Yup. All set. You can pull him out now."

I helped Dougie out of the pool, and Dane snapped his wrists into cuffs while I found him a dry shirt from Liam's locker. By the time he'd put it on, Roland and Morey had arrived, and the three cops and their prisoner left me alone in the pool house.

Chapter 48
Reunion

MY CAR WAS STILL at Rafe's, so I called a cab to take me to the hospital. I had an entire crew I needed to visit, and I was already exhausted. But first things first. I needed to see Liam, and make sure he knew how much I loved him. On my way in, I stopped at the front desk to find out where Rafe and T-8 were, so I could see them after I saw Liam. And Mimi.

I poked my head around the edge of the door to Liam's room. He was out of bed, playing cards with Doc at the table in the corner. I rushed to him and threw my arms around his shoulders. "I love you," I whispered into his ear.

He laughed. "I know."

That was my favorite line from my favorite movie, and because he'd said it, I knew we'd be okay.

Doc stood up. "The patient has made a remarkable—although not entirely unexpected—recovery. I believe my work here is done, at least for tonight. I'll be back in the morning to process your discharge, Liam."

She kissed my cheek and gave me a hug. "Remember, he's still healing. Don't overdo anything."

I felt a blush spreading over my cheeks, but I grinned at her. "I promise to be careful with him."

She laughed and ducked out the door.

Liam and I sat on his bed talking for at least an hour. I filled him in on everything that had been happening while he'd been stuck in the hospital.

"Why do you always take so many risks? You could have been killed," he said when I'd finished.

"But I wasn't," I said.

Then I winked at him. "Wanna go visiting?"

"It's after visiting hours, Dr. Fleming. I don't believe it's allowed."

"It is for us." I shrugged into the white coat Doc had left hanging in the closet and released the wheels on Liam's chair. I backed the chair through the door and headed toward the room Rafe and T-8 shared.

We knocked on the door and heard a muffled, "Come in."

Rafe was awake, sitting up in bed reading. T-8 was in the other bed, either asleep or still unconscious.

Rafe saw me look questioningly at T-8. "He'll be okay. He's just sleeping."

He threw his book aside. "Thank you for coming. To the house, I mean. Here too, but if you hadn't come to the house, who knows what would have happened." He looked at Liam. "Your fiancée is an amazing woman."

"And don't I know it." He smiled at me. "I realized how amazing she is the first minute I met her. And she proves it to me over and over, every single day. I'm a lucky guy."

Rafe bit his lip and looked away before speaking. "So now you know Tate's secret. He has a lot of trouble reading. When we were teens, he dropped out of school because it was hard for him to keep up, but he can't continue to go through life like this. Once he got out of the porn biz, I helped him learn his lines by reading his scripts to him. I was always on set with him in case of changes, but it got harder and harder to cover for him. We finally agreed he'd do better as a producer and director so he wouldn't have to learn his lines. Then we realized that made the problem worse. Production notes, scripts, contracts…there's a lot to the job. I don't know how to help him anymore."

"He just needs some specialized teaching. You can help him there. Coach him through it like he helped you when you two were younger," I said.

He nodded. "He doesn't like to talk about it, but I can try."

"You heard about Dougie?" I asked.

He nodded. "I can't believe I didn't recognize my own brother. And I've always been grateful for everything he did for Tate and me back then. I wish I'd known he was in jail. Maybe I could have done something."

"Like what?" said Liam. "You were just a kid back then. On your own. Homeless. There's nothing you could have done."

Rafe looked pensive. "You're right. I couldn't do anything then. But in the years since, I could have done more. The truth is, I thought for sure he was dead. He was always getting into fights. Like our dad. I knew someday it would catch up to him, and it did." His voice cracked on the last word.

He continued. "But I can help him now. Dane played the recording of his confession for me. It's clear he'll be going back to prison. I've already asked Newton to get him the best lawyer on the island. I'm paying for his medical care and his legal bills. He's so morally confused I don't think he'll ever be able to live on his own, so I'll pay for whatever he needs when that time comes too. I owe him that after he gave up so much for me."

I patted his hand. "You're a good brother." I glanced at Liam, and he nodded. "Do you need anything? We have to get going so we can see Mimi sometime tonight. Hopefully before the nurses figure out that I stole the lab coat and this patient."

Rafe smiled. "I don't need anything. And don't worry. I'll explain the contract to Tate so he knows the money's not his to spend." He sighed. "I don't think he understood the contract terms, if he even bothered to read it. He'll go ape when he realizes that you guys are now partners, and that unless he finishes making the movie, you become the sole owner of his production company, but I'll handle telling him that."

249

Liam said, "Good. And thank you for offering to be the middle-man. I wasn't looking forward to having to explain it to my new business partner." He paused a moment. "And when you two are ready, we'll discuss what to do about the movie. I'm still in if you are."

Rafe smiled. "Thanks, Mate."

Chapter 49
Departure

IT WAS A NIGHT FOR MIRACLES. When Liam and I entered Mimi's room, she was awake, sitting up in bed and grousing at her nurse because the poor guy wouldn't give her a cup of tea until a doctor had okayed it.

Maddy, her face shining with happiness, was standing by Mimi's bed, holding her hand, and trying to keep her from completely alienating her nurse. She looked up when I entered and smiled.

"Oh, here's the doctor now." She stared hard at my lab coat, hoping I'd get the hint to play along. The name on the pocket of the lab coat I wore read "Doctor Warren," and Doc's ID badge dangled below the embroidered script, with the picture side turned inward.

I shrugged. "What's the issue here?"

Mimi tried to look pitiful, but she was such a powerful personality that it really didn't work for her. "I just want a cup of tea. All they'll give me is water."

I picked up her chart and looked at the medications listed. None of them was on the list of drugs affected by green tea which I'd memorized during Maddy's recent illness. "Let her have a cup of tea." I glared at Mimi. "But just one tonight. And no more until morning. Understood?"

Mimi smiled at me. "Yes, Doctor. I understand."

The nurse left to get the tea, and I walked over to kiss my grandmother. "This is a surprise. I'm glad you're awake. We were so worried."

"It takes more than a thunk on the noggin to keep this old lady down. I was just resting my eyes to give you a chance to figure everything out."

While I knew this wasn't true—her injuries had been severe—I let it go. "Nonetheless, I'm glad you're awake. How are you feeling?"

Mimi yawned. "Better now that you're here. I assume you've figured the whole thing out now and taken care of all the bad guys."

I nodded, just as the nurse bustled in with Mimi's tea. He put it on the table and turned to Maddy. "Okay if I take my dinner break now? Since you're all here to watch out for her?"

Maddy smiled. "Of course. Take your time."

We watched him leave, then Mimi patted the bed beside her. "Sit here and tell me the whole story. I can't wait to hear all the details."

I parked Liam's wheelchair and sat beside Mimi. For the second time tonight, I told the entire story while my audience listened attentively.

Mimi nodded along as I spoke, and it was late by the time I finished. Liam and I were just about to slip out when Doc came in. "I thought I'd find you here," she said. "And I figured wherever you were, my lab coat was probably with you. May I have it back now?"

I shrugged out of the coat and handed it to her. "Sorry," I said.

"No harm done. I assume you just borrowed it because of the chill, right? You weren't impersonating a doctor or anything, were you?"

"No, Ma'am," I said. "I'd never do anything like that." I winked at her.

She winked back at me. "Good," she said. "Okay, Mrs. Anderson. As you requested, I've arranged for the medical flight you wanted. You'll be leaving in the morning, and you should be in Philadelphia in time for lunch. I'll take the flight to Philly with you and fly back commercial once I've transitioned your care to your regular doctor. Sound good?"

"Excellent," Mimi said. "Thank you."

"What?" I said. "You can't leave so soon. I didn't have enough time to get to know you."

Mimi sniffed. "I don't like this island. Never did."

She looked meaningfully at Maddy. "But the good news is, now that we've broken the ice, you can come visit me whenever you want. And if you can't make it to Philly, I suppose I can come back here occasionally if it's okay with the rest of the family." She smiled at Maddy, and Maddy smiled back.

I was sad that my grandmother was leaving so soon, but as she said, I could always go to Philadelphia to see her.

"And make sure that when you come to visit your poor old grandmother that you bring that fiancé of yours," she said. "He's quite the looker."

Liam blushed scarlet.

I'd never tell him that she'd originally been convinced I'd throw him over for Rafe. I was just glad she was back and that I hadn't lost her before I had a chance to really get to know her.

Chapter 50
Final Dive

It was two weeks later, and Liam and I were aboard the *Tranquility*, hooking up to the mooring at Starfish Reef.

His bruises had mostly faded by now, but he had a waterproof cast on his hand, and his two broken fingers were still splinted and taped together. Because of the concussion he'd received when Dougie whacked him with his lethal broom, Doc hadn't given Liam the okay to scuba dive yet.

But she knew she didn't have a prayer of keeping us out of the water altogether, so she'd grudgingly given the okay for him to snorkel, as long as he took it easy, stayed on the surface, and didn't dive down to get a close look at anything.

He was annoyed by the restrictions, but as I told him, "Being in the water, even on the surface, is always better than not being in the water. And I'm not taking any chances on losing you, so I'll make sure you follow Doc's orders. Got it?"

He laughed. "By now I know better than to mess with you. I'll be good. I promise."

So here we were, hoping to see some red cushion sea stars. Actually, they were so abundant at this site on Grand Cayman's North Sound that seeing them was a foregone conclusion.

We donned lightweight dive skins for sun protection and

slipped on our snorkeling vests and fins. Then we pushed off from a seated position on the *Tranquility*'s dive platform so we wouldn't go under—although we had anchored in water that was only about five feet deep. I didn't want to take any chance with Liam's health.

We kicked along the surface, marveling at the hundreds of sea stars on the bottom. Some were as small as Rosie, while others measured nearly two feet across. Almost all of them appeared to be stationary, but faint trails in the sand beside some of them said that sea star had moved after a recent feeding.

Liam and I held hands and kicked out a little deeper, hovering over the nearest patch of sea grass, where we saw a southern stingray, several parrotfish, and a few razorfish. We stayed over the vegetation, looking down and letting the waves move us wherever they wanted.

It was peaceful.

Relaxing.

And sort of dull.

I couldn't wait for my next adventure to begin, and if I didn't make some changes, my life would become unbearable. I knew what I had to do.

Chapter 51

Reorg

I CALLED a meeting the next morning, inviting Joely, Genevra, Stewie, Benjamin, Maddy, and Theresa.

"It's time we reorganized RIO's executive team," I said when we were all gathered around the conference room table. "You all know I hate this administrative stuff I've been doing, and to be perfectly honest, we all know I'm not very good at it."

They started to protest, but I held up a hand to stop them. "I'm good at creating strategy, as long as there's someone around to take notes and execute on the plan. But that person can't be me. It's killing me."

I flipped on my computer and projected the new organization chart I'd come up with the night before while Liam was sleeping. Maddy and I had reviewed it before the meeting, and she'd agreed with the changes I wanted to make.

"As you can see, Maddy will obviously continue in her role as CEO. Joely, you're still the CFO, but with more autonomy. No more checking with me on your decisions. Genevra, I'm promoting you to COO, which is only fair because you've already been doing the hard stuff. Benjamin, you're in charge of new business development, and Theresa, with Mariana's retirement next month, you'll be the new VP of Food Services. I hope you'll see fit to make Noah the manager of Ray's Place, but that's up to you since you'll be in charge of your own show."

Everybody stared at the screen. What about you?" Genevra asked. "What are you planning to do?"

I'd deliberately left my name off this version of the org chart, but now I flipped to the next slide. There was a new box off to the right. It read "Fin Fleming, Chief Underwater Photographer and VP of Marketing."

My dream job.

Everybody looked at Maddy. She was smiling brightly through her tears. "You've done an amazing job, but I admit I've missed running this place. I'm happy to take back the reins, and I love your new organization structure. I'm in."

The room burst into cheers, laughter, and congratulations all around. I sat back and breathed a sigh of relief. I was back where I belonged.

Links to my Books

Shop my online store

Shop the Series Page on Amazon

Afterword

Just so you know, the movie production stuff in the book is pretty much not the way movies are made, so don't expect realism. The movie is just a framework for introducing the characters I wanted you to meet.

There's a lot of food in this book, especially coffee and chocolate chip cookies, so I guess I must have been hungry the entire time I was writing it. I tried hard to remove at least a few of the cookies, but they refused to go, so maybe it was really Fin that was hungry.

Rosie is still immortal, and it looks like Suzie Q might be too. I got so much flak when Harry the stingray died, I'm not about to kill off Rosie or another stingray.

And in case you noticed, Fin is still twenty-eight. She aged a year or two in each of the first few books, but I think she may stay twenty-eight for a good long while. Neither you nor I want her sitting in a rocking chair reminiscing about her days as an action heroine.

Hey—maybe that solves my animal immortality problem. If Fin never ages, just like Sue Grafton's Kinsey Milhone, then everyone around her can stay the same age too.

And luckily this time I don't have to warn you scuba divers not to try any of the foolhardy things Fin does, because she didn't do any. She wanted to though.

Acknowledgments

Many, many thanks to all the people who help me with the Fin Fleming novels.

Andrea Clark, you are the best at putting your finger on the weak spots. I love you. Thank you for your help.

Kate Hohl, my writing soul mate. Thanks for all you do.

So happy to have met you both at that magical Yale Writers workshop. Seems like forever ago.

Mary Beth Gale, my most long-standing writing buddy. Thanks for putting up with me.

Stephanie Scott, you are the most cheerful person I know, even in hard times. I'm so glad we met at Hallie Ephron's Tuscany workshop. Say 'hi' to James for me.

Michele Dorsey, my friend. So glad we took the self-publishing journey together.

And Hallie Ephron, a continuing example of class, charm and great writing. Best writing teacher ever. Thank you for everything.

Teri Hoitt, you get your own line this time. 😎

And always:

Erin, Scott, Cam, Taylor, and Milan Lambrinos.

Erin, Pat, Colin, and Anthony Rogers.

Josh, Jenn, Parker, and Isaac Ward.

Ed, Bob, and Dave Hoitt. Good brothers all. With great wives, Patti, Teri, and Trish.

About the Author

Sharon Ward is the author of the Fin Fleming Scuba Diving Mystery Series, which includes *In Deep, Sunken Death, Dark Tide, Killer Storm, Hidden Depths*, and *Sea Stars*. The seventh book in the series, *Sea Monsters* is coming in December 2023.

Sharon was a marketing executive at prominent software companies Oracle and Microsoft before becoming a writer. She was a PADI certified divemaster who has hundreds of dives under her weight belt. Sharon is a member of Sisters in Crime, MWA, ITW, Grub Street, the Authors Guild, and the Cape Cod Writers Center. She lives in Massachusetts with her husband Jack and their miniature long-haired dachshund Molly, who is the actual head of the Ward household.

Also by Sharon Ward

In Deep

Sunken Death

Dark Tide

Killer Storm

Sea Stars

Rip Current

Or see the entire series Fin Fleming series by following the link or use the QR code on the previous page.

If you enjoyed Sea Stars, you can continue reading about the adventures of Fin and the gang by following the links above.

Also, nothing (except actually buying the book) helps an author more than a positive review, so please give Hidden Depths (and me!) a boost by leaving a review. Here's the link:

Sea Stars or use the QR code

Link to the Sea Stars Review sitr

And if you'd like to subscribe to my totally random and very rarely published newsletter, you can sign up here. or use the QR code

Link to SharonWard.com

Made in the USA
Las Vegas, NV
28 June 2024

91610226R00163